PART ONE

THE PLAN

The terrible grumble, and rumble, and roar,
Telling the battle was on once more.
Thomas Buchanan Read

THE KILLING GROUND

The Killing Ground

Alan Savage

This first world edition published in Great Britain 2003 by
SEVERN HOUSE PUBLISHERS LTD of
9–15 High Street, Sutton, Surrey SM1 1DF.
This first world edition published in the USA 2003 by
SEVERN HOUSE PUBLISHERS INC of
595 Madison Avenue, New York, N.Y. 10022.

British Library Cataloguing in Publication Data

Savage, Alan
    The killing ground
    1. Davis, Tony (Fictitious character) - Fiction
    2. Soldiers - Great Britain - Fiction
    3. World War, 1939-1945 - Campaigns - Yugoslavia - Fiction
    4. Yugoslavia - History - Axis occupation, 1941-1945 - Fiction
    5. Adventure stories
    I. Title
    823.9'14 [F]

    ISBN 0-7278-5889-0

Except where actual historical events and characters are being
described for the storyline of this novel, all situations in this
publication are fictitious and any resemblance to living persons
is purely coincidental.

Typeset by Palimpsest Book Production Ltd.,
Polmont, Stirlingshire, Scotland.
Printed and bound in Great Britain by
MPG Books Ltd., Bodmin, Cornwall.

Press where you see my white plume shine, amidst the ranks of war.

Thomas Babington Macaulay

One

The Command

'They are coming!' The young woman manning the radio set panted, breath misting in front of her nostrils in the chill air, dark hair drifting out from beneath her sidecap, pretty features distorted by a mixture of apprehension and exhilaration.

Tony Davis looked at his watch. 'Bang on time.'

'It is a national characteristic,' Sandrine Fouquet agreed.

'What is the distance, Anja?'

'He says he can see them, and that they will be abreast of his position in ten minutes.'

'Say ten miles from here,' Tony mused, mentally envisaging the outpost's position – he had placed it himself the previous day. 'Good girl, Anja. You have been on duty for three hours. Go and have something to drink and eat.'

Anja Britic looked from the general to the colonel, sitting so comfortably in their little hollow overlooking the road. They were a legendary pair, Brigadier-General Davis, the Englishman, tall and dark and saturnine, a man with a fearsome reputation as a killer of the enemy, and Colonel Fouquet, the Frenchwoman, a tiny five feet four in height, possessing exquisite features framed in long yellow hair, confined in a plait as she was about to go into action. Davis and Fouquet were together the victors, and more important, the survivors, of more than a dozen desperate encounters with the Nazi forces occupying Yugoslavia. That they were also

3

known to be lovers only increased the romantic aura that hung about them. But to be so relaxed at such a time . . .

'He says there are at least a hundred trucks,' Anja said. 'All full of men. Each with a machine gun. And there is a squadron of tanks in front.'

'That sounds about right,' Tony agreed. 'When you get to the camp, ask Colonel Astzalos and Major Janitz if they would be good enough to join me.'

'Will we attack them?'

'That's why we're here.'

'But . . .' She looked down at the road as if expecting to see the military convoy already in sight.

'There's time,' Tony said. 'Off you go.'

Anja glanced at Sandrine, who nodded. She saluted and hurried down the hillside.

'She is nervous,' Sandrine remarked, changing from Serbo-Croat to French, the language they always spoke when alone.

'New recruits always are.'

Sandrine stood up and jumped up and down a few times to restore her circulation; like all the Partisan women she wore blouse and pants and canvas boots, to which she had added a threadbare coat. But it was very cold in March in this year of 1943, although their position was in the relatively low-lying foothills of central Serbia, overlooking the main road that led from the Hungarian border, through Belgrade, to the Greek frontier. 'I was nervous, in the beginning,' she admitted. 'When we were escaping from Belgrade, in April 1941, I was terrified. I would never have made it, without you.'

'I've been rewarded,' Tony said. 'Just by having you around.'

'Ha! Do you know that in a month's time I will be twenty-nine?'

'I did know that.'

'So I will be older than you. Again.'

'But only for a few months. Again.'

She considered this for several seconds, then she asked, 'Do you ever think of Elena?'

'I try not to think about the past, at all. Or the future. Just the here and now.'

'She was your fiancée. Did you not love her?'

'Not as I love you.' He knew she could have no doubt of that, but it was her nature to constantly seek reassurance. Because she *was* nervous, even after two years of campaigning: where once she had expected to die at any moment, now she had become used to surviving, and wished to go on doing so.

'But if the war had not happened, you would have married her and taken her back to England.'

'I didn't see that happening. Elena wasn't really the sort of girl the British army expects their officers to marry. It was her idea that we should consider ourselves engaged.'

'And you went along with it because it got you into her bed.'

'Guilty as charged,' he admitted. 'Two years. God, what a child I was then.'

'She was my friend,' Sandrine said thoughtfully. 'Am I the sort of woman you would be allowed to marry?'

Tony blew her a kiss. He had never really understood – and he had never wished to inquire – how a smart, well-educated French journalist, in every way the height of chic, as Sandrine had been before the war, could have become so friendly with the daughter of a Croatian boarding-house keeper. Elena had been a handsome girl, certainly, but she had also been coarse and earthy. She had been the ideal sexual companion for a disillusioned young British officer, fed up with being seconded from his regiment to the supposed backwater of Belgrade as a military attaché following the serious wound he had suffered during the retreat to Dunkirk.

A backwater, certainly, in which British, German, French, Italian and all the various nationalities that had made up the

Yugoslav federation had mingled in neutral bonhomie until they had been thrown violently apart by the Nazi invasion of April 1941. For him, perhaps, the explosion had been the most violent of all, as, separated from the British embassy when it had been ordered to close down and get out, he had found himself fighting with the Yugoslav resistance which had immediately sprung into being.

He knew he wouldn't have had it any other way, now. The life of a bandit appealed to him, whatever the odds against his surviving the conflict. And where the British army regarded any man who had been wounded – once, much less four times – and who walked with a limp as good only to sit behind a desk, the guerillas welcomed and respected anyone who was prepared to fight for their cause. Besides, had he been evacuated with the embassy staff, he would not now be looking at the most gorgeous woman in the world, and know that she was all his.

'Do you ever think of Bernhard?' he asked.

'Only that I had a lucky escape. But for the invasion I would have been a *Hausfrau*.'

Bernhard Klostermann, her boyfriend in those days, had been an officer in the German army, like Tony serving as a military attaché, at the German embassy in Belgrade.

'Now they are both dead,' she said, again thoughtfully. 'And we . . .'

'Have a battle to fight.' Tony stood up himself as the two other officers approached him. 'Time,' he said. 'Are your people ready?'

Sasha Janitz rubbed her hands. A tall, handsome woman, long dark hair tucked inside the collar of her blouse, whose reputation almost equalled that of her superiors, bubbling with passion, she lived only for destroying the invaders, her no less bubbling sexuality submerged in the tragedies of the men, and the women, she had loved and watched die. 'My girls are always ready.'

'As are my men,' Astzalos growled. A short, dark man,

he seldom smiled and was inclined to look on the black side of life.

'Then take your positions. Sandrine, the women on the far side. Get them across now. We have only a few minutes. Remember, no firing until you see my rocket. Then let them have everything you've got. But maintain your position until I fire my second rocket, then close in.'

'What about prisoners?'

'We will kill them all,' Sasha declared. Having come too close to the methods used by the various SS and irregular detachments employed by the Nazi invaders, her feelings for the enemy were shrouded in hatred.

'Let's destroy the column first, and worry about prisoners afterwards,' Tony suggested.

Sandrine nodded and hurried off, Sasha beside her.

'Make sure your people are ready to envelop the rear,' Tony told Astzalos. 'Then rejoin me here.'

'With my mortars?'

'Yes, your mortars. Go, go, go!'

Astzalos went down the hill.

Alone for the moment, Tony took his binoculars from their case and made sure both his Verey pistol and his revolver were loaded, then checked his tommy gun. Then he listened. There was a very faint rumble of sound in the distance, cutting across the quiet of the afternoon. About half an hour, he reckoned.

He surveyed the position he had chosen for the ambush. It was close – some might have said perilously close – to Belgrade, but he had selected it for that very reason. With a break in their long journey almost in sight, the enemy would be in a steadily relaxing mood – not that they would in any event be expecting guerilla activity in this apparently pacified part of the country. Equally important, this brigade was on its way back to the fatherland for rest and recuperation; resisting an attack would be the last thing on their minds.

But he had also selected this position for tactical reasons. Here the highway narrowed as it passed between the hill on which he stood and a dense little wood on the other side. This not only would restrict the mobility of the tanks, but it afforded his people maximum cover. He looked down at the women streaming across the road, carrying their machine guns, every one armed with a tommy gun and string of grenades. They made an evocative sight: their hair fluttered as they moved, and through his glasses he could see them chattering to each other. Their tendency to prattle, even in action, was, he thought, their only weakness as a fighting force.

He regarded them with pride, as they were largely his own creation. Unlike General Draza Mihailovic, who commanded the Cetniks, the other main guerilla force, and whose attitudes and movements, and indeed, loyalties, were governed by strict adherence to military procedure and to the concept of Serbia as the principal force in the federation, his rival, General Josip Broz, who called himself Tito, had recruited wherever volunteers were to be found, be they Serbs, Croats, Slovenes, Bosnians, Macedonians, Albanians, and whether they were Christian or Muslim. Thus he had accepted women almost from the beginning, although without any high expectation of their value as a fighting force, and indeed without any intention of so using them, other than in a strictly defensive capacity. But Tony, placed in command and aided by Sandrine, had shown just how eager and how effective they could be.

He gave a grim smile as he watched them disperse and hide themselves amidst the rocks and trees on the far side of the road. Only six months ago there had been hardly five hundred of them, fighting for their very existence. But that had been before the capture of Bihac last autumn, the Partisans' greatest victory so far. Not only had there been a vast store of arms and ammunition in the town, enough to enable them to resume an active rather than a purely defensive campaign, but also recruits had come flooding in. Instead of the few thousand men and women Tito had led in the desperate retreat from Foca into the mountains of western Bosnia, he now commanded over twenty thousand effectives, and with much of the Wehrmacht, and more importantly, the Luftwaffe, having been called to Russia in a vain attempt to rescue the Sixth Army at Stalingrad, the Partisans were seizing their opportunities.

Thus instead of a single regiment, Tony now commanded a brigade of three battalions, close to a thousand women in each. Two of his battalions were now deployed. And around him were gathering Astzalos' command, a further three battalions. These were men, who perhaps looked more scruffy and unkempt than the women, most of whom took pride in their appearannce, but were nonetheless confident and battle-hardened warriors. Tony watched them setting up their mortars with practised expertise.

Now the noise was very close, and rumbling across the hills and valleys. 'How many?' Astzalos asked, face tense.

'The scouts reckoned a hundred trucks. Say forty men to a truck . . .'

'Four thousand. And they will have tanks.'

'Six. But we have the advantage of surprise. They have no idea we would risk coming this far into Serbia. Stand by.'

Astzalos pulled his nose, but crept away to make sure his battery of mortars was ready. Tony checked his Verey pistol again. Now the lead tank came into view, followed by the rest of the squadron. They certainly were not anticipating an assault: their hatches were open and their commanders were enjoying the crisp afternoon air; most even had their helmets off as they no doubt reflected that they would be enjoying the fleshpots of Belgrade tomorrow.

If they're lucky, Tony thought as they rumbled past beneath him. This was always the trickiest part of any ambush. Discipline in the Partisan army was harsh, but could not be relied on with people to whom indiscipline was a way of life, and who had had very little barrack-square training. Thus although he had hammered the point that they had to obey orders, there was always the chance of some over-excited young woman firing before the signal was given. But he knew the tanks would turn back at the sound of firing. It was the column he did not wish either to escape or to have the time to deploy.

The first trucks came into view. Tony let them too rumble by, counted another twenty, and then fired his Verey pistol.

The rocket arced over the road and the column, and the afternoon exploded. The women, as Tony had instructed, fired everything they possessed, machine guns clattering, tommy guns chattering, interspersed with the deeper reports of side arms. Immediately to his left the mortars opened up, dropping their shells on to the road – which meant into the midst of the convoy – backed up by the rapid fire of their infantry support.

Within seconds several of the trucks were in flames, their occupants screaming as they leapt in search of safety, only to be cut down by the hail of bullets. Behind them, men were also disembarking from the so far undamaged vehicles, unslinging their rifles, some even fixing bayonets in anticipation of hand-to-hand combat, while others feverishly unlimbered the heavy machine guns. Whistles blew and officers ran to and fro. And all the while men fell.

Tony was more interested in the tanks. As he had anticipated, these had stopped and were now turning, a slow business on the narrow road. He glanced at Astzalos, and the colonel nodded, directing his mortars to be re-aimed. A few moments later, as the first tank began to return to the battle, the long muzzle of its cannon moving to and fro with consummate menace as it sought a target, a shell landed on the road immediately before it, throwing up a huge plume of dirt. This was followed by another, which blew off a truck. The tank slewed sideways, completely blocking the road. Immediately it was rammed by the vehicle behind it, the one flying the pennant of the squadron commander, and pushed down the parapet into the ditch beside the road. The next shell landed immediately behind the command tank, but appeared to do no damage, although presumably it gave the men inside a headache. And then it came up to the lead trucks. These had already been evacuated by their occupants, who were returning fire at their unseen enemy. They were now also pushed aside as the tank rolled back to the first of the burning vehicles, its cannon exploding again and again as it poured shot into the hillside, seeking the mortars rather than · the still invisible women.

'Keep hitting them,' Tony told Astzalos. And then added, 'Shit!'

A woman had left the shelter of the trees and run forward. She had lost her cap, and her hair was streaming behind her. Presumably this apparition confounded the already panicking infantry. Thus they did not immediately shoot and she was able to reach the command tank before she was fired at. She staggered, but recovered and scrambled up the side of the now halted machine. As she reached the cupola she was fired at again, and nearly tumbled off. But she clung on and threw up the hatch. She had already drawn a grenade from her belt and pulled the pin. Now she dropped it through, and disappeared along with the tank in the following explosion. But the tank ceased firing as it blazed.

'Brave,' Astzalos said. 'Brave.'

'Bloody brave,' Tony muttered, and fitted another cartridge into his Verey pistol; with the remaining tanks both leaderless and cut off from the battle by their burning commander, and the infantry clearly in a state of disarray, now was the time to finish the job, before the enemy could rally. A moment later the rocket burst over their heads.

'Go!' Tony told Astzalos, and himself got to his feet, unslinging his tommy gun as he did so. He scrambled down the slope, followed by the cheering Partisans, while from the far side of the road Sandrine led her women out of the trees, now hurling their grenades. There was a flurry of shots and some of the guerillas went down. But more of the German force fell, and the rest had lost their stomach for further resistance. Rifles were thrown to the ground and hands were raised, while the jubilant Partisans whooped and cheered as they surrounded their victims. The surviving tanks – another had been put out of action by a mortar shell – realizing that the battle was lost and that they could only hit their own people if they kept on firing, were turning around to make their escape. The trucks at the rear of the column were trying to do the same, in the opposite direction. But turning the large vehicles on the narrow road took too long, and before any of them could manage it they were also surrounded by the Partisans.

Sandrine saluted. Her cheeks were pink and her chest heaving, but to Tony's great relief she was unhurt. 'A victory. A great victory.'

'Thanks to your heroine. Who was she?'

'Anita Hagar. She acted without orders.'

'She will be remembered.'

'What are we to do with those?' Sasha asked.

Tony followed her pointing finger with consternation. One of the trucks had apparently contained nothing but women; several of these had been hit, and at least two were very obviously dead. The rest were gathered in a group, mostly sitting on the road, weeping and wailing. 'What nationality?'

'I think they are Greek. But does it matter? They are German whores.'

'My men can use them.' Astzalos had joined them.

'Your men have wives back at headquarters,' Tony reminded him. 'Let's try to be civilized.' He led them to the women, who were becoming aware that they were in the presence of officers and that their fate was about to be decided. They huddled closer together. 'Does anyone here speak German?' Tony inquired, in that language.

There was a brief hesitation. Then one of the women said in a low voice, 'We *are* German. These are our husbands you have killed.'

The woman was well-spoken, and well-dressed too, although her dress was crushed and bloodstained. Of average height, aged perhaps in her early thirties, she had a good figure and strong features, surrounded by neat shoulder-length brown hair. Tony reckoned she was the natural leader of these unfortunates. 'What is your name?' he asked.

'My name is Mathilde Geisner,' she said.

'And your husband is?'

'Major Wilhelm Geisner. He commands our tank escort. He seems to have got away.'

Sasha snorted. 'Not your husband. My girls blew him up.'

Mathilde Geisner's face twisted. 'Bitch!' she said. Her gaze swept Sandrine. 'You are all bitches.'

Sasha swung her tommy gun and struck her across the face. She gave a little scream and fell to the ground. Sasha would have struck her again, but Tony caught her arm. 'Leave it.'

Mathilde Geisner sat up, hand pressed to her cheek; blood seeped through her fingers.

'Can you stand?' Tony asked.

Mathilde Geisner slowly got to her feet. Her cheek was split and would undoubtedly be scarred. She stared at Sasha with a frightening intensity.

'The fortunes of war, Frau Geisner,' Tony said. 'I am sorry. Have you any medication?'

Mathilde Geisner turned her gaze on him. 'I am not the only one wounded.'

'Well, any medication you have you may keep, and use.'

'What's that?' Sandrine started forward to stand above one of the women lying on the ground; in her arms there was a baby.

'She got hit,' said Mathilde Geisner. 'She is dead.'

'But the child.' Sandrine dropped to her knees beside the

corpse, lifted the babe, who gave a little murmur and began to wail. Sandrine hugged it.

'What will happen to us now?' Mathilde Geisner asked.

'You will have to walk,' Tony said.

'There are three of us wounded. Apart from me.'

Tony inspected the woman. 'I have said you may tend their wounds. None of you are hit in the legs. Again, I am sorry, but we must destroy these trucks. Belgrade is only forty miles away. It should take you about two days. You may take whatever food you can retrieve.'

'And our men?'

'The enlisted men and junior officers will go with you.'

'You are going to let them all go?' Sasha was appalled. 'There are more than two thousand of them.'

'I am certainly not going to shoot two thousand men in cold blood,' Tony said. 'That would be to lower ourselves to the level of the SS. Of Wassermann.' He was remembering how the erstwhile SS commander in Yugoslavia had executed five thousand men and boys at the town of Kragujevac during the early days of the campaign. 'We have gained a victory. We need people to tell the command in Belgrade what happened. Do not worry, their morale will be destroyed.'

'But you will murder the senior officers,' Mathilde Geisner said.

'The senior officers are prisoners of war, Frau Geisner. Their fate will be decided by General Tito. Colonel Astzalos, accumulate all of these weapons and ammunition, and distribute it amongst our people. Then strip the soldiers of their uniforms and set them on their way. We need the uniforms of the dead as well. And their boots.' Shortage of boots was one of the Partisans' biggest problems. 'Bring their senior officers to me. Start moving, ladies. You may not care for the company you are about to keep.'

The women stirred. 'Am I allowed to see my husband?' Mathilde Geisner asked.

'I'm afraid there is nothing of him to see.'

Again her face twisted, but as yet there were no tears. She gazed at Tony for several seconds, memorizing his face, he thought, then turned away.

'What about this baby?' Sandrine asked.

Mathilde turned back. 'His mother is dead.'

'You cannot abandon him.'

Mathilde shrugged. 'Would you not say, Fräulein, the fortunes of war?'

'You *are* a bitch.'

'I am a widow, Fräulein.'

'Let me have her,' Sasha said.

'Get out of here, Frau Geisner,' Tony said. 'As for the child—'

'I will look after the child,' Sandrine said.

'Eh?'

'You are crazy,' Sasha declared. 'That is a German child.'

'A babe in arms has no nationality.' She looked at Tony. 'I will look after this child, Tony.'

Tony hesitated. He was not interested in the nationality of the babe, but he knew they would have enough trouble taking care of themselves, much less a helpless infant, as they made their way back over the mountains to the guerilla headquarters. On the other hand, if they could get there, there were quite a few small children, and indeed babes at the breast back in Bihac, and he knew that Sandrine, as ruthless as any man in battle, had a very soft centre when the shooting stopped.

He also knew how much she dreamed of a normal life, with him, as wife and mother. She was too intelligent to risk pregnancy while she was a serving soldier, but becoming a surrogate mother, whatever the problems in their circumstances, might go some way towards alleviating the angst which from time to time afflicted her, and which so distressed him. So he said, 'You can have her, sweetheart. I'll take my turn at changing nappies.'

Sasha snorted.

*   *   *

15

'This is an outrage, sir,' said the German brigadier as he surveyed the naked white bodies of his men being assembled. 'It is against the Geneva Convention.'

'I do apologize,' Tony said. 'I had no idea any of you gentlemen had ever read the Geneva Convention. What would you have done had we been your prisoners? Of course, you would have had us all shot.'

The brigadier gulped. 'But to have my men stripped, before your women . . . They are laughing at them.'

'At least they are not raping them,' Tony pointed out. 'Now, gentlemen, we have a long walk ahead of us. A matter of a month. So let's get started. But General, I am placing you in command of your officers. I must warn you that my men, and my women, have orders to shoot anyone attempting to escape.'

'You are barbarians,' said one of the other officers, who wore the insignia of a major.

Tony frowned at him; his face was vaguely familiar. But the only German officers he had ever come face to face with before today had been the Gestapo Major Hermann Ulrich, only briefly, and Sandrine's erstwhile fiancé, Bernhard Klostermann. 'Then we are in good company,' he agreed, and beckoned the captain he had placed in command of the prisoners.

'General?' The captain joined him out of earshot.

'Keep those men away from the women.'

The captain raised his eyebrows. 'You don't suppose they'd try—'

'No I don't. But I do not wish the women near them. Any of the women, even the officers. Understood?'

The captain saluted.

'This is outrageous.' Heinrich Himmler spoke quietly, as usual, but the pale blue eyes behind the rimless glasses flickered with the intensity of his feelings, and the black-uniformed officers seated round the table shifted their feet uneasily. 'A troop convoy of four thousand men, attacked and cut to ribbons, within forty miles of Belgrade. Seven officers ranked captain or superior killed, and three colonels, a major, *and* the commanding general hauled off for execution. The rank and file stripped naked and forced to enter Belgrade in that condition. That is quite unacceptable.'

'The Wehrmacht seems unable to deal with these people,' someone remarked.

'If they were given more men, and perhaps adequate support from the Luftwaffe . . .' a second officer suggested.

'Where are they supposed to find the men, or the aircraft?' interjected someone else. 'They are all needed in Russia, or North Africa.'

'Is Yugoslavia so important, anyway?' asked another officer. 'It is a small, backward country, from which we get very little. And we are told that it is virtually in a state of civil war now, between these Partisans and the Cetniks. Why do we not just let them destroy each other and then step in and pick up the pieces.'

Himmler tapped the table, and the voices fell silent. 'Yugoslavia is important for two reasons, gentlemen. One is obvious. Its valleys provide the quickest and simplest route for the transfer of men and matériel to and from Greece, thus allowing us to maintain our control of the eastern Mediterranean. It is that lifeline which these Partisans have just cut, however momentarily. The second reason is more important. There can be no doubt that the surrender of Paulus at Stalingrad, disgraceful in itself, has created a disturbing situation in Russia. Oh, it will be retrieved. When our new Tiger tanks are in full production, as they will be this summer, the Führer plans a great offensive which will entirely restore our position and may well bring about the final defeat of the Soviet forces. But until this happens, the Wehrmacht does need to concentrate the major part of its resources in the east. However, we must also look to the south. Rommel's defeat at Alamein has thrown our African position into the melting pot.

And now the Americans are pouring men into French North Africa. There can be no doubt that they mean to drive us entirely from the continent. Well, they will find that hard to do: Rommel has some three hundred thousand men. However, we must guard against every eventuality. Just in case there were to be a disaster, we must determine what the Allies are likely to attempt next. It is my belief that they are already contemplating an assault upon Fortress Europe. I may say that I have discussed this with the Führer and he agrees with me. The point is, where would they seek to strike? Obviously it will be in the Mediterranean, as they are concentrating so many resources there. Italy presents a tempting target, but Italy is not only our ally, she is well garrisoned with our troops. But on the other side of the Adriatic we have a virtually undefended coastline, off which there are myriad islands crying out to be occupied by an enemy, while the mainland is largely controlled by these guerillas. My latest information is that they number some twenty-five thousand men. That is virtually two divisions.'

'They must be short of matériel,' one of the generals suggested.

'They have just captured the arms and ammunition of four thousand men, including their machine guns, not to mention their uniforms and equipment. If they are allowed to do that with impunity they are not likely to run out of arms and ammunition very soon. I will not speak of the damage this event has done to morale. The point is that for all the above reasons it is essential that these Partisans are eliminated, once and for all, and as quickly as possible. In view of the overall situation, this is a responsibility I have taken on my shoulders, gentlemen, with the full agreement of the Führer.'

There was another rustle of unease around the table. 'We are being given command of Wehrmacht units?' someone asked. There was no officer present who did not know that the Schutzstaffel were both hated and feared by the regular forces.

'Only a few specialist groups,' Himmler said. 'As I have just said, the Wehrmacht is needed elsewhere.'

'Then where do we find sufficient men? If the Partisans actually do number twenty-five thousand, and if, as is probable, the Cetniks support them—'

'We improvise,' Himmler said. His officers exchanged glances, but he smiled at them. 'There are sufficient forces in the area, if they are properly brought together under one command. We have been promised some Italian divisions.'

'Italians,' someone muttered.

'They wish to see the Partisans destroyed just as much as we do,' Himmler said mildly. 'These people are virtually on their doorstep. Then we have been promised a Hungarian division and also a Bulgarian.' Someone else snorted, but Himmler continued unperturbed. 'Then there are the local forces. The Ustase.'

'Murdering brigands!'

'Absolutely. But as regards the Partisans, they know it is a case of kill or be killed.'

'Weren't the Ustase virtually destroyed as a fighting force trying to defend Bihac?'

'The word is *virtually*. They were, I understand, poorly commanded and suffered a heavy defeat. But there are still a considerable number of them, and as I say, that defeat has only increased their hatred of the Partisans, their desire for revenge. And lastly, gentlemen, we come to the Cetniks.'

'The Cetniks? They are guerillas themselves.'

'True. But Tito and Mihailovic hate each other. They are also ideologically opposed. Mihailovic wants a restoration of the monarchy, and a Serbian-controlled federation. Tito takes his orders from Moscow and dreams of a Communist Balkans. And Mihailovic has cooperated with us before. As the British still apparently trust him more than Tito, and as he is, therefore, the official representative of the Yugoslav government-in-exile, he has to make a pretence of opposing us, even with arms, from time to time, but his heart is in the destruction of the Partisans.'

'If he is that treacherous, can *we* afford to trust him?'

'As long as we remember that he is looking both ways at once while trying to sit astride the fence, yes. But when he has helped us to destroy the Partisans, then we can, shall I say, take a fresh look at the situation.'

'Are we in contact with him?'

'We can be, if we have the right general officer commanding. Which is the real point of this meeting: choosing the right man. It goes without saying that, as we have been given the task of overseeing this campaign, our commander will have to be one of us.' There was more uneasy shuffling. 'What I require,' Himmler said, 'is a man who knows both the country and the people, who speaks Serbo-Croat, and who has contact with the local warlords.'

'I have never been to Yugoslavia,' said the most senior of the generals, with some relief.

'Nor I,' said another. The rest nodded their agreement.

'He must also be a man of proven resolution and ruthlessness.' Himmler looked around the faces, indicating that he was agreeing that none of them fitted the bill. 'I am therefore placing Wassermann in command.'

There was a moment of scandalized silence. Then someone said, '*Wassermann!*'

'The ideal man,' Himmler announced urbanely. 'He has spent most of the past two years in Yugoslavia.'

'As chief of the Gestapo,' someone muttered.

'This is in his favour. He knows the people, and the people know him. They are terrified of him. More importantly, he has contacts with both the Cetniks and the Ustase. He also, while there in his police capacity, established a very useful spy service of his own, which no doubt will prove invaluable in his new task.'

'But, with respect, Herr Reichsführer, did not you yourself

sack Colonel Wassermann only last autumn as a result of his failure at Bihac?'

'*He* did not fail at Bihac. He was not even there.'

'But it was his recommendation that the defence of the town could be left to the Ustase.'

'And they let him down. That can happen to anyone. And I did not sack him. I removed him from active service for a while because I realized that he had not yet fully recovered from that wound he suffered during the pursuit of the Partisans in 1941 – a pursuit in which, I may remind you, his devotion to duty earned him the Iron Cross, first class.'

'But the man is still a cripple. There is some doubt as to his mental stability.'

'He is strong enough for this task. As for his mental state, he hates the Partisans to the point of insanity, certainly. But that may be what we are looking for. I am sure you have heard of an English general, some two hundred years ago, named Wolfe, whose tactical dispositions were so outrageously against the rules of conventional warfare that it was represented to King George III that he was mad. "If he is", the king replied, "then I wish he would bite some of my other generals."'

'But Wassermann is only a colonel,' someone remarked.

'I have already promoted him.'

'OKH won't like it.'

'OKH has nothing to do with it. This is our operation.'

'But you said Wassermann will have the use of regular units.'

'Only a limited number.'

'And Luftwaffe?'

'There too, in limited numbers. This operation cannot be allowed to fail. Are there any other objections?'

'Well, there is that wife of his . . .'

'Please,' Himmler said. 'Backstairs gossip is not a fitting subject for a council of war. I will not deny that Frau Wassermann is, shall I say, a difficult woman, but that is

General Wassermann's problem. And the Yugoslavs', to be sure. So, gentlemen,' he looked around the table, 'we are unanimously agreed that I should propose to the Führer that Colonel Wassermann be confirmed general, and that he be placed in command of all the available forces in Yugoslavia until the destruction of the Partisans has been accomplished.' He waited, and reluctantly each of the officers raised his hand.

Fritz Wassermann opened the front door of the small flat he occupied down a side street off the Unter den Linden. His servant, Manfred, who doubled as a butler, greeted him and took his hat and belts. 'You are home early, Herr Colonel.'

Wassermann regarded him for several seconds, waiting. Forty years old, he was a tall man, but while his somewhat gauntly handsome face continued to indicate the strength and determination of his character, his frame was thin and wasted. The sniper's bullet that had cut him down in October 1941, fired from the hillside above where he had been standing directing his men, had miraculously missed heart and lungs, but had scythed its way through rib and stomach to exit through his genitals. The surgeons had, no less miraculously, been able to sew him up into at least a resemblance of a man. Only he knew different . . . and his wife, of course.

He did not know who had fired that devastating shot, but as he had been engaging the women's regiment in the then tiny Partisan army, he could be fairly sure it had been one of them. And as he knew that that regiment had been commanded by the Englishman, Tony Davis, a vicious outlaw who had tormented him during his period as chief of police in the conquered territory, a man who had slipped through his fingers time and again, it had become his life's ambition to settle that affair. But after the catastrophe of Bihac the previous autumn, and his subsequent removal from office, he had accepted that the chance might be gone forever. Now . . .

'Well?' he demanded.

Manfred realized that he had overlooked something, and studied his employer more closely, then gulped. 'But Herr Colonel – I beg your pardon, sir, Herr General. Oh, my congratulations, sir. My best congratulations.'

'Thank you, Manfred. Now you must pack as rapidly as possible. We leave at dawn tomorrow.'

Manfred gulped. He knew his boss had been relieved of his last command on grounds of ill health; the fact that he had been promoted had to mean that he was again regarded as fit for duty. If *that* meant the Russian front . . .! 'May I ask where we are going, Herr General?'

'Why, back to Belgrade, of course. I am to command there.'

Wassermann followed his tapping stick along the corridor to the master bedroom – he remained unsteady on his feet and was subject to fits of dizziness – and opened the door. His wife sat on the bed, painting her toenails. She was, predictably, naked, and presented an entrancing sight. Still not yet twenty years of age, for all the traumatic events of her brief life – which had included watching her mother, the wife of the then governor-general of Yugoslavia, shot down before her eyes, and spending a fortnight as a prisoner of the Partisans before her exchange had been arranged for the woman Sandrine Fouquet, *his* prisoner – she remained a most attractive girl, her figure slim without being thin, her straight black hair worn just past her shoulders, her features just a trifle too bold for beauty. Only her eyes, cold as a snake's, gave any indication of the seething pit that was her mind, the mixture of hatred and contempt that dominated her every waking moment, and perhaps her nightmares as well. Once, he thought regretfully, only two years ago, they had loved, wildly and desperately. But that had been before he had uncovered her true nature, and before he had become a cripple, at least in bed.

She echoed Manfred, although her voice was low and musical. 'You're home early.'

'We have a lot to do.'

She had not troubled to raise her head to look at him. Instead she said, 'I happen to be going out.'

'You will have to cancel that.'

Now she looked up, and frowned. Her wits were quicker, and her eyes more observant, than Manfred's. 'My God! Has Himmler finally lost his marbles?'

'The Reichsführer realizes that I am the man for the job.'

'What job?'

'I am to command all our forces in Yugoslavia.'

'*You*? After that fuck-up at Bihac? You were *sacked*!'

'That was your interpretation, my dear. I was actually given extended leave, for health reasons. That is what the Reichsführer is giving out, and that is what will be believed. Now I have achieved my greatest ambition, and I intend to make the most of it. So instead of going out with your absurd friends, you will spend this evening packing. We leave at dawn tomorrow.'

'*We*? You expect me to come with you?'

'You are my wife, my dear.'

'Back to Belgrade? You must be out of your mind. I have no intention of setting foot in that ghastly place ever again.'

'I accept that you have some unpleasant memories of it, but this time you will enjoy it. On your first visit you were the daughter of the governor-general. The world, or at least, Yugoslavia, was at your feet. Then, with the death of your mother, it all turned sour. On your second visit, you were merely the wife of the chief of police. You found that important enough for you, until you committed murder. But that is now forgotten.'

'It will not be forgotten by the Serbs,' she said. 'It was one of them I shot.'

'But thanks to the testimony of my faithful Rosa, it was proved that the Bestic woman was a Partisan spy, so you were acquitted. Now you are returning as the wife of the general officer commanding. You will be the most important woman in the country.'

'Fritz,' she said, her voice deceptively low, 'I am not going back to Belgrade.'

'And I say you will. Do you really think I would leave you here, to entertain a different man, or woman, in my bed every night?'

'I can ruin you,' she warned. 'I can tell the world all about your dishonesty, about your crooked dealings with the Ustase, about how you and your Rosa manufactured the evidence, perjured yourselves, to get me acquitted.'

'And talk your way straight on to the executioner's block? Or a dormitory at Ravensbrück? I am told that is even worse than having your head cut off – it lasts longer. Besides, my dear, you cannot harm me now. When I was a colonel, perhaps. But now I am a general, promoted by Himmler personally. He does not like his generals to be ruined. One peep out of you, and you *will* find yourself in Ravensbrück. In the punishment block, for the rest of your life. So you will pack, and you will accompany me to Belgrade. You will enjoy yourself. Because do you know what I am making my foremost priority? Settling with Davis and Fouquet. Are you not looking forward to seeing them hang? Besides' – he smiled – 'think how pleased Ulrich will be to see you. Not to mention Halbstadt. Those swine thought they had got rid of me, forever.'

Two

The General

The male secretary placed the telegram on the desk of his commanding officer, clicked his heels, and withdrew. Major Hermann Ulrich reached for it with some apprehension, and leaned back in his chair to read it.

Short, and somewhat plump, with round features and thinning dark hair, despite his black uniform he looked a most unlikely SS officer. But then he had always known himself that he was in the wrong profession. As a detective inspector in Hamburg before the war, he had earned himself something of a reputation, thus it had seemed obvious to the powers that be that when he was conscripted he should be inducted into the ranks of the Schutzstaffel, who in the occupied but not entirely pacified territories acted as a superior police force and controlled not only the local guardians of the law but also the Gestapo. The Nazi hierarchy held the opinion that there was no man who, with adequate training, could not be turned into a strong and unbending guardian of the Reich.

Ulrich had not been able to fault the training, but it had been a total failure as regards changing either his character or his attitude to his job. He enjoyed police work, and even more, detective work, the challenge of unravelling a twisted skein of clues to unmask a guilty man. But there were few opportunities for that where the Gestapo was concerned. When they wished to discover the truth, or, more importantly, what they wanted to be the truth, they beat or burned their victims with electricity until he, or she, would confess to anything.

At least for the first eighteen months of his posting in Yugoslavia he had been in a subordinate position, as a good soldier, bound to obey the orders of his superior – even when that superior had been such a sadist as Fritz Wassermann, whose atrocious behaviour had more often than not been inspired by his even more atrocious wife. But when Wassermann had been sacked following the fiasco of Bihac last autumn, Ulrich had found himself promoted. He had in fact protested to Himmler that he did not feel he was up to the job, and had been told that as a German officer it was his business to accept whatever task was given to him, and to carry it out successfully.

To his relief, the winter had been quiet. Having fought their way into the relatively safe haven of Bihac at great cost, the Partisans had needed to rest and recuperate, re-arm and recruit. Ulrich had been content to let them get on with it. Out there in the Bosnian mountains, several hundred kilometres from Belgrade, Tito's people were the business of the Wehrmacht, not the Gestapo. His business was the security of the capital and the various other large cities in the country where the Germans had established themselves.

He had always been confident that when the Partisans decided to move again, in the small groups they had always employed in the past, bent on sabotage or assassination, he would learn about it in sufficient time to take effective counter-measures. The event of the previous month had come like a thunderbolt from hell. Instead of small and relatively impotent groups, the guerillas had moved several thousand men and women, if the survivors of the ambush were to be believed, right across Bosnia and into Serbia, without being detected. And the survivors had to be believed, because a force capable of virtually destroying a brigade of German troops had to have been considerable.

Worse yet, if the woman Geisner was to be believed, the

Partisans had been commanded by the two most wanted people in Yugoslavia, after Tito himself: the Englishman Davis and the Frenchwoman Fouquet. Not to mention the almost equally wanted Bosnian terrorist Janitz. And Mathilde Geisner also had to be believed, because she had apparently spoken with all three and had given accurate descriptions of them. Ulrich had only once, very briefly, come face to face with Tony Davis. In view of the Englishman's reputation, he knew he was very lucky to be sitting at this desk now. But he had encountered both of the women. The memory of Sasha Janitz, always linked to her blazing tommy gun, still made him shudder. As for Sandrine Fouquet, he had had her in the cells beneath his office for a fortnight, and he had not laid a finger on her. Partly this had been orders. The Frenchwoman had been far too valuable a prisoner to be carelessly destroyed, and in fact after that fortnight she had been exchanged for the governor-general's daughter, Angela Wassermann, who had managed to get herself captured in turn by the Partisans.

But Ulrich did not think he would ever have been able to flog Sandrine Fouquet, much less force electrodes between her legs. Sandrine possessed a quality of fragile beauty, allied to a calm courage, which he had found as fascinating as it was admirable. In fact, it was that forbearance that had saved his life: it had been Sandrine, in gratitude, who had intervened to stop her lover from shooting him. Yet, as the ambush had proved, she could be as ruthless, and deadly, as her partner.

He had known there would be repercussions, no doubt his own dismissal, for not having discovered the Partisan movement and informed the military in time for them to take the necessary counter-measures; he had expected the axe to fall before now. Thus he scanned the words almost fearfully, and then slowly sat straight, the blood draining from his face. He took a handkerchief from his pocket to wipe his neck and forehead, then picked up his internal phone. 'Ask Captain

Halbstadt to come in, please.' At least, he reflected, his voice wasn't shaking.

Erich Halbstadt arrived in a few minutes. Young, dark-haired, not very tall, fresh-faced and handsome, he made an even less likely SS officer than Ulrich, although he was utterly dedicated to his job. The two men had always worked well together. 'Close the door, and sit down,' Ulrich invited. He had used the few minutes before his subordinate's arrival to regain control of himself. Halbstadt obeyed, frowning. 'I wish to ask you a personal question,' Ulrich said. Halbstadt shifted in his seat uneasily. 'Would I be right,' Ulrich said, 'in assuming that you had an affair with Frau Wassermann when she was here last year?'

Halbstadt's head came up with a jerk. Ulrich raised a finger. 'I know it is not my business to inquire into an officer's private life, except where it may interfere with his duties, or his ability to carry out those duties. Unfortunately, in this instance, your behaviour may involve just those things. So I would like an answer.'

'Well . . .' Halbstadt flushed. 'She was insatiable. And I am sure you know, Herr Major, that her husband, since his wound, can no longer . . . *perform*.'

'I do know that, Captain. Now tell me this: did Colonel Wassermann know of this liaison?'

'Oh, good heavens, no.'

'What makes you so sure?'

'Well, I mean . . . Well . . .'

'He neither had you shot nor sent to the Russian front? I'm afraid that you do not know Wassermann very well. He thinks of himself as a gigantic spider, sitting in the centre of an equally gigantic web, making things happen, sucking people into his orbit so that they can be devoured. That he has been singularly unsuccessful in all his most cherished projects does not bother him at all. He has the patience of a spider as well.'

'But there is no way he could possibly have known about

29

it,' Halbstadt protested. 'The only other person who knew was that girl Jelena Brolic, and she was executed by the Partisans when they captured Bihac.'

'Your naivety frightens me,' Ulrich remarked. 'Why do you think Frau Wassermann shot her housekeeper, the woman Bestic?'

'Well, because she had discovered that Bestic was a Partisan spy. That came out at the trial.'

'That was perjured evidence, given by the woman Rosa Malic, who *was* a Partisan spy.'

Halbstadt's jaw dopped. 'But . . . she was never arrested. She is walking around Belgrade at this moment, absolutely free. She works in this building.'

'That is because, to save her skin, she agreed to work for Wassermann, and since his return to Germany, she has been working for me.'

'Has she?!' Halbstadt's consternation was clearly genuine. 'You mean she is also . . . Well, she is a two-timing little bitch!'

'She is not *my* mistress,' Ulrich snapped. 'I have a wife waiting for me in Hamburg. She is an employee of this office, and a very useful one; her official job in the canteen is a cover. It was Bestic who told Wassermann about his wife's peccadilloes, which is why Angela shot her.'

Halbstadt gulped, and then recovered. 'Well, it is all water under the bridge now. The colonel is retired, and . . .'

Ulrich flicked the telegram on his desk. 'I suggest you read that.'

Slowly Halbstadt picked the paper up, studied it. As had happened with Ulrich himself a few minutes earlier, all the colour drained from his cheeks. 'There must be a mistake.'

'I'm afraid telegrams signed by the Reichsführer are seldom mistakes, Captain. Colonel Wassermann has been promoted to general, and is arriving in Belgrade on this afternoon's train.' He looked at his watch. 'That is, in two hours' time.

You had better organize a guard of honour, with a band, right away,'

'You wish me to meet the train?' Halbstadt's expression was that of a man who had just heard the death sentence passed on him.

'I do not think that would be a very good idea,' Ulrich said. 'Wassermann is returning as GOC of all armed forces in Yugoslavia. How he managed that I shall never understand. But as GOC he will also command us, and as he is an officer in the SS himself, we cannot appeal to a higher authority, no matter what he may require of us. I think your best bet is to put in for a transfer right away. I will do my best to expedite it. But first of all, the guard of honour. I will meet the train. Dismissed.'

Halbstadt stood up, saluted, and left. Ulrich studied the telegram again for several minutes, then picked up his phone. 'Get me the governor-general.'

Ulrich hated the main platform at Belgrade Central; it held too many memories, all of them bad.

He had stood here in October 1941, waiting with Wassermann, then a major himself, to welcome the first governor-general. Anton von Blintoft had been accompanied by his wife and his so handsome, and then so innocent, daughter. And within ten minutes of their arrival Frau von Blintoft had been cut down by a sniper's bullet. That bullet, he knew, had been intended for the general himself, but the catastrophic accident had affected the lives of everyone present, not least the Partisans who had fired the fatal shot. And it had turned Angela von Blintoft into an avenging angel – only 'angel' was never a word to be used in connection with that walking mass of angry vengeance.

He had stood here again only a few weeks later to see her off, back to Berlin with her gravely wounded fiancé, and had hardly got back to the office, where he had been placed in temporary command, when he had learned that the train had been blown up. He had reflected then, as he reflected now, how much better it would have been had both Angela and Wassermann been killed in the explosion, for their own sakes as much as anything. But they had survived, and Angela had been taken prisoner by the Partisans in order to exchange her for Sandrine Fouquet. That experience had left her even more bitter and twisted than before.

And he had stood here to welcome the unholy pair in May of 1942, after Wassermann's amazing recovery, following which Wassermann's efforts to corner the Partisans, and particularly his arch-enemies, Davis and Fouquet, had ended in such a humiliating failure.

Now Wassermann was returning again, with more power than ever before – and undoubtedly more hatred than ever before as well.

He heard the whistle, and signalled both the captain of the honour guard and the bandmaster; the governor-general had decided not to attend the ceremony; he had been as surprised and disapproving as Ulrich himself at the reappearance of such a man with such power. The train pulled to a halt, the bandmaster raised his baton, and as Wassermann appeared on the platform the music blared forth while the guard clicked to attention and presented arms. Wassermann also came to attention and saluted, waited for the anthem to be completed, and then came down the steps, stick tapping. Ulrich hurried forward, and the two men exchanged salutes before shaking hands. 'Herr General!' Ulrich said. 'How very good to see you looking so well. And my most hearty congratulations, sir.' His hypocrisy left him thoroughly ashamed, but a man had to do the best with every situation, however unpleasant.

'Thank you, Ulrich. It is good to be back. We have unfinished business, eh?'

Angela came down the steps, followed by Manfred with the personal luggage. As always she wore a sable fur coat with a matching hat, and again as always she looked at once contemptuous and vaguely apprehensive. That could have been because this station, this city, held even more unpleasant memories for her than it did for him, or it could have been merely a result of being married to a man like Wassermann, but as events had so often thrown them together so intimately – although, he thanked God, she had clearly never found him the least sexually attractive – he suspected that she lived in constant fear of her own secret desires.

He bent over her hand. 'How good it is to see you again, Frau Wassermann.'

'Responsibility suits you, Herr Major,' she remarked, an oblique reference to the fact that he had succeeded her husband as chief of police. 'What dump have you got for me this time?' She had not cared for the house she had been allotted on her last stay in the city.

'General Hartmann hopes that you will stay with him while you are in Belgrade. He knows your father.'

'Everyone seems to know my father,' Angela commented. Among her many resentments was the fact that all of these generals, in themselves junior to Anton von Blintoft, should still be pursuing apparently successful careers while her father lived in disgraced retirement, all for having insisted upon allowing the exchange of Sandrine Fouquet for his own daughter. Would any father not have done the same?

'I am sure you will be very comfortable there,' Wassermann said. 'You may even be given your old room. Now, come along, Ulrich. Let us inspect these fellows and then get down to work. There is a great deal to be done, and it must be done both quickly and secretly. We will use your office. Arrange a car to take Frau Wassermann to the palace.' Ulrich looked at Angela, who shrugged.

Needless to say, Wassermann appropriated the desk, leaving Ulrich to sit in a straight chair beside him. 'Make notes of what I require,' Wassermann told him.

'I'll just summon my secretary . . .'

'You will make the notes personally, Ulrich. I told you,

this is top secret.' Ulrich suppressed a sigh, took a pad of paper and a pencil from the desk, and sat down again. 'Tell me what happened last month. I want the truth, not a propaganda report.'

Ulrich drew a deep breath. 'Somehow the Partisans managed to infiltrate a large force through the mountains.'

'How large a force?'

'I estimate something like five thousand men – and women. You will remember, Herr General, that Tito employs women as well as men.'

'I am not likely to forget that,' Wassermann pointed out. 'It was one of those bitches who shot me.'

'Yes, sir. Well, now there are something like three battalions of them, according to our latest reports.'

'Are they still commanded by Davis?'

'Oh, indeed. He is a general now. Brigadier rank.'

Wassermann snorted. 'And Fouquet?'

'Her too. She is a colonel now. They commanded the raid.'

'You have proof of this?'

Ulrich nodded. 'One of the survivors spoke with them.'

'I wish to interview this man.'

'She is a woman.' Wassermann raised his eyebrows. 'A Frau Geisner. As you may recall, I mentioned in my report that there were several German women returning from Athens with their husbands. Major Geisner commanded the tank squadron which formed the advance guard. He was killed.'

'I remember. And these women are still in Belgrade?'

'Frau Geisner is. She refuses to go. She keeps badgering me to give her some sort of employment. She wishes to avenge her husband.'

'And she supposes she can do so personally? She is suffering a nervous breakdown.'

'She does not give that impression, sir. She appears very level-headed. And very determined.'

'And have you given her a job?'

34

'Well, no, sir. We do not employ women, except as secretaries or canteen waitresses or cleaning staff. Frau Geisner is not the menial sort, and she has no secretarial training.'

Wassermann stroked his chin. 'Is she good-looking?'

Ulrich suppressed another sigh. He knew that his superior's sexual impotence had in no way lessened his desires; rather, it had merely perverted them. 'She is a handsome woman, yes, sir. Unfortunately, she appears to have been beaten by the Partisans.'

'Your report said the women were not interfered with.'

'I said they were not raped, Herr General. But several were wounded in the battle, and this Frau Geisner was, as I say, beaten.'

Wassermann nodded thoughtfully. 'Still, I will interview her, personally. So, you had no information that this raid was about to take place.'

'No, sir.'

'Why not?'

'Well, you see, since the Partisans' success at Bihac' – he gave the general an anxious glance – 'support for them in the country has grown. People are beginning to believe . . . well, that they might be able to win. You know how simple country folk can be,' he hastily added. 'And then, they have all heard of Stalingrad, which leads them to believe that perhaps the Wehrmacht is not invincible after all. The result is that they are less willing to cooperate with us, give us information.'

'Clearly you have not been shooting enough of them. Where is this raiding party now?'

Ulrich coughed. 'I would say they must be just about back in Bihac. They carried out their attack and were back in the hills before we even knew what had happened. Then we, the Wehrmacht I mean, sent out forces to intercept them, but the commanders did not accept our estimate of their strength. Our people were very roughly handled. If only we had even a squadron of aircraft . . .'

Wassermann considered him for several seconds, then he

said, 'What is your estimate of the total forces under Tito's command?'

'A figure of twenty-five thousand has been mentioned. As I said, again since his victory at Bihac, he is receiving more and more support.'

'Can he arm all of these people? Is he receiving any aid? From the British? Or the Soviets?'

'Not to our knowledge. But there was a considerable arsenal in Bihac, and he will have picked up another few thousand rifles and ammunition, as well as some machine guns, from that ambush. Not to mention a good deal of equipment. You know . . .' He hesitated.

'That our men were humiliated, stripped naked and forced to walk into Belgrade? Yes. What of the women? You say they were not raped? But this Geisner woman was beaten. Were any of the others maltreated? Or at least stripped?'

'No, sir. But they also had to walk, forty miles, in the company of more than two thousand naked men.'

'They were violated by our own people?'

'No, sir. I gained the impression that our troops were too shocked by what had happened. But the women's morale was also severely affected.'

'Morale!' Wassermann snorted. 'It is our business to deal in reality. So those thugs got away with some four thousand rifles and a few machine guns. That does not sound as if they have the capability to fight a pitched battle.'

'In the open and offensively, no. But in the mountains, where they hold a strong position and are difficult to get at, well . . .'

'I have been sent here to destroy the Partisans, once and for all,' Wassermann announced. 'What is your estimate of the force that will be required to accomplish that?'

'To attack them in the Bosnian mountains, drive them from their stronghold in Bihac, and at the same time cut off all possible avenues of retreat . . . Four divisions, with panzer and aircraft support.'

'My own estimation entirely.'

'And you have been promised such a force? An army corps?'

'I have been promised a panzer regiment and Luftwaffe support, providing I finish the job quickly enough. Which is what I intend to do. The ground forces I am to create with some technological assistance from the Wehrmacht.' Ulrich gulped. 'But I also have a brigade of the Waffen SS. They will form the core of my army. Now tell me, how many men does Mihailovic command?' Wassermann continued, unperturbed by his lieutenant's dismay.

'Perhaps the same as Tito. He continues to enjoy considerable support here in Serbia, of course, as he is a Serb, and also amongst the more virulent anti-Communist element in the federation as a whole. But for that very reason – the fact that Tito is a Communist – I do not think there is much possibility of the Cetniks linking up with the Partisans. Of course, if they were to do that it would create an impossible situation.'

'The Cetniks are going to form a division of my army, Ulrich.'

'Sir?'

'They have cooperated with us in the past, where it has been to their advantage. I intend to make them an offer they cannot refuse. I assume you have contacts with them?'

'Limited.'

'Arrange a meeting with Mihailovic. Here would be best.'

'He will not come to Belgrade, even with a safe conduct.'

'Well, give him whatever guarantees he requires.'

'Even then.'

'I wish to meet him, Ulrich. Arrange it. Anywhere he wishes. But this week.'

Ulrich swallowed. 'Yes, sir.'

'Next, the Ustase. I assume you are in contact with Pavelic?'

'Yes, sir. But . . .'

'What sort of force does he have now?'

'He still has a few thousand.'

'Very good.'

'You intend to include the Ustase in your army? They are a terrorist group.'

'Who have also worked with us in the past. All they want is an independent Croatia. Well, I am happy to talk about that. I might even be able to get that prince back.' Granted a form of independence following the Nazi conquest, the Croatians had obtained an Italian prince as their king, but the Italian had needed only a few weeks in his turbulent adopted country before packing his bags and hurrying back to Rome.

'They have also proved quite useless at anything more than murdering their opponents,' Ulrich persisted. 'I am sure you remember that it was their failure to defend Bihac that brought about this situation.' And your disgrace for entrusting that task to them, he could have added, but didn't.

'They will fight, if the alternative is their destruction. Tell Pavelic I wish to see him, immediately. Now, we will be joined by a Hungarian division, and one from Bulgaria. With the Cetniks that gives us three divisions in the north, plus my brigade. The Italians are also going to cooperate; they have considerable forces in Albania, and will move two divisions north to cut off any Partisan retreat. That gives us nearly a hundred thousand men, with armour and aircraft support. That is more than sufficient to deal with a rabble, even if it is twenty-five thousand strong. The Italian liaison officers will be arriving in a day or two. At that time I will issue my orders.'

'Hungarians,' Ulrich muttered. 'Italians.'

'*Soldiers*, Ulrich.'

'If you – *we* fail to take Bihac . . .'

'We will not fail to take Bihac, or at least occupy it, because it will be undefended.'

'But that is where the Partisans are centred.'

'But not where they will stay. Think, Ulrich. Remember,

in October 1941 they captured Uzice, just over there' – he pointed to the south-west – 'in Serbia. We attacked them and they evacuated the town and retreated into Bosnia, where they occupied Foca. In the spring of 1942 we prepared to attack them there. They got wind of it, and evacuated again, over the mountains to Bihac. I agree, our attempt to cut them off there failed. But the pattern, the indication of the way Tito's mind works, is plain. Like Mihailovic, he is looking to the end of the war, when he assumes we will evacuate the country. When we do that – supposing we do – he means to establish a Communist government in Yugoslavia. But to do that he needs an army. Therefore his priority is to keep his army in being. Thus when he learns he is to be confronted by overwhelming force, he will withdraw again, and once we get him into the open—'

'With respect, Herr General, we have had him in the open before, and have been unable to finish him off. And that was when he commanded only a few thousand men.'

'Our failure to finish him off was because of a lack of decisive leadership. That will not happen this time. As far as I am concerned, the more people he has with him the bigger our target. In any event, as we now understand his tactical thinking, I intend to lay a trap, into which he will fall when he leaves Bihac. Because we also know that he cannot sustain himself in the open, in those mountains, over the winter.'

'With respect, Herr General, it is just coming up to summer.'

'But it will soon be winter again. Before then he must find another safe haven. Knowing that, we can pin him down before he reaches shelter.'

'But we do not know where he will go, if – *when* he evacuates Bihac. It could be north, into Croatia. That is his personal homeland. Or he could move around in Bosnia. Or he could even come back into Serbia.'

'He will make for Montenegro,' Wassermann said.

'Montenegro? Oh, no, sir. I do not think he will do that. To get from Bihac to Montenegro he will have to pass through some of the most difficult country in Yugoslavia. And Montenegro is adjacent to Albania, where, as you say, the Italians are concentrated in strength. That would be to commit suicide.'

'He will retreat to Montenegro because he will consider it his best, his *only*, option. I intend to see to that.'

'May I ask how, sir?'

Wassermann tapped his nose. 'We'll discuss it later.'

'But, Herr General, if he retreats into those mountains, we will not be able to follow him. If it is difficult country for him, it will be impossible for us, with our motorized infantry. And we will not be able to use the panzers.'

'I have explained, Ulrich, that while he will flee into the mountains, because, as you say, he will calculate that we will be unable to follow him, he cannot remain there, and survive. He will know this, and seek to come out, as quickly as possible. And then . . .' He grinned. 'You worry too much. Now, set up those meetings for me. And tell me, is Rosa still about?'

'She has a job in the Gestapo canteen.'

'Send her to me. Here.'

'Here, Herr General?'

'I do not think it would be a good idea for her to come to the palace. She is not my wife's favourite person.'

'But . . .'

'I know, Ulrich. I am requisitioning your office. But it was my office once, was it not? I feel at home here. And it will only be for a short while. Oh, by the way, is young Halbstadt still here?'

'Ah . . . yes, Herr General. But he will soon be gone. He has applied for a transfer, and I will see that it is put through as rapidly as possible.'

'No, no,' Wassermann said. 'I do not wish him transferred. He is a most promising officer. He will accompany me on the campaign. There will be plenty of work for the Gestapo.'

Ulrich had an unpleasant feeling that his junior had just been condemned to death. But he said, 'As you wish, sir. Am I also to accompany you?'

'You will remain here and hold the fort. You are good at doing that.' And, Ulrich thought, he knows there is no risk of my finding myself in Angela's bed. 'Now send Rosa to me,' Wassermann repeated.

'And Frau Geisner?'

'Oh, yes. Her too.'

Wassermann sat behind the desk, tapping his fingers lightly on the top while he waited. What memories this place brought back. It was in this room that he had first had sex with Angela, when she had sought an outlet for her grief and anger at her mother's death, and he had been virile enough to satisfy even her perverted tastes.

He knew that her tastes were even more perverted now, but he could no longer service them. When he had first recovered from his wound, he had found an outlet for his frustration by beating her, but then he had made the mistake of allowing her to discover too many of his personal and professional secrets. Thus she had been able to dominate him by threatening to expose him.

As a result they had settled into what could be called an armed truce, and if, as he had pointed out to her, his unexpected promotion had placed him once again in a more or less invulnerable position, he had not yet assimilated his new situation sufficiently to take advantage of it. He intended to do so, certainly. But it would be best to wait until he had successfully concluded this campaign, when his position would indeed be invulnerable. Besides, there were so many other fish in the sea; if he could no longer consummate a relationship with a woman, he could still dominate them, hurt them, make them beg . . .

There was a tap on the door. 'Come,' he called.

The door opened, and Rosa Malic sidled into the room. Short and dark, in her mid-twenties, she had pertly attractive features, which were now revealing a mixture of apprehension and disbelief. Like everyone else in Yugoslavia, he supposed, she had not expected ever to see him again. As Angela's personal maid when they had previously lived in Belgrade, Rosa had been well placed to overhear private conversations, which from time to time concerned German plans and even troop movements. This information she had passed on to her father, who had relayed it to Tito. Thus when Wassermann had unearthed her activities, she had anticipated nothing better than torture followed by a public execution. She had collapsed in abject terror. Thus he had recognized that here was the perfect tool, for use as a double agent, and more, as his personal spy, conditioned by the threat that if she ever betrayed him her parents would die, horribly.

She also had a very buxom body, which had been prepared to accept everything he might wish to do to it in order to stay alive. He had even contemplated taking her to Germany with him when he had been sent home, but had decided to leave her in Ulrich's temporary care; he had always hoped he would be coming back. Now he was more than ever pleased at that decision; with her acceptance by the Partisans, she was the ideal weapon for the implementation of his plan.

'Come in, Rosa,' he invited. 'Close the door.'

She obeyed, licked her lips. 'It is good to see you again, Herr Colonel.'

'*General*, Rosa. I have been promoted.' Her mouth made an incredulous O. Like everyone else, she knew that he had been sent home in disgrace only six months ago. 'Come here,' he invited.

Cautiously Rosa advanced to the desk. He beckoned her again, and she stood beside him. She wore a somewhat shapeless calf-length blue dress which buttoned up the front.

He put his arm round her, squeezed her buttocks, then slid his fingers down the back of her legs to find her hem, slip beneath, and come back up her thick stockings until he reached her drawers and could squeeze her again; this time his fingers closed on bare flesh. Rosa shuddered.

'Does Ulrich fuck you?' he asked.

'The major? Oh, no, sir.' Her surprise at the question was clearly genuine.

'I sometimes wonder if he knows how,' Wassermann remarked, continuing to caress her buttocks. 'Then who is your lover?'

'I have no lover, sir.' She gasped when his caress became a very hard squeeze.

'Have you forgotten what I said I would do to you if you ever lied to me?'

Rosa panted as the grip tightened even more; it felt as if his fingers were actually penetrating her flesh. 'Captain Halbstadt . . .'

The fingers relaxed, and she gave another gasp, this time of relief. Wassermann withdrew his hand, let her dress fall back into place. He leaned back in his chair. That smiling, handsome, *virile* bastard. Well, his time was nearly up. But first . . . 'Sit down, Rosa.' Rosa moved round the desk, thankfully, and sat down, cautiously. 'How are things?' he asked kindly.

Rosa's shoulders hunched. 'They hate me.'

'They?'

'All my people. My parents will not receive me in their house. I am hissed at on the street.'

'All for being a faithful servant of the Reich. They are swine. But you still love your parents, and wish to protect them?'

'Oh, yes, sir.'

'Well, I think that you have suffered long enough. I am going to let you leave Belgrade.'

Rosa's head jerked. 'Belgrade is my home.'

'I do not see how you can consider any place your home where you are hissed at on the street.'

'But . . . where can I go?'

'To where you know you will be amongst friends. You can go to Bihac. To the Partisans.'

Rosa's eyes rolled. 'They would execute me.'

'Why should they do that? What do they know about you, apart from the fact that you are Boris Malic's daughter? They trust your father, do they not?' Rosa nodded, slowly. 'Have you ever gone to them before?' Rosa shook her head, clearly trying to think. 'As I remember,' Wassermann said, 'whatever information you obtained, you passed to your father, and he went into the mountains and contacted the Partisans.' Rosa nodded again, still unable to speak. 'But if what you have just told me is true, your father would no longer accept any information you might give him, because he would not believe it to be true. So, if you were to come into the possession of information of vital importance to General Tito, you would have to take it to him yourself. Is that not so?'

'Information?' Rosa muttered. 'I have no information.'

'I am about to give you some.'

Rosa stared at him as a rabbit might have looked at a snake. 'It is known that I work for the Gestapo.'

'Of course it is known. But if you did not work for the Gestapo, how could you obtain the information?'

Rose put up her hand as if she might scratch her head, then lowered it again. 'Everyone thinks I am a traitor. If they think it in Belgrade, they will think it in Bihac.'

'Perhaps they will, superficially. But your situation is actually no different from what it was a year ago. Then you worked for my wife, and listened at keyholes. Now you work for the Gestapo, and continue to listen at keyholes. The reason you are hated is because you gave evidence which exonerated my wife of the charge of murder, that you denounced Madame Bestic as a spy. But when you go to Tito, you will tell him that you had to do this to retain my confidence in order to continue obtaining information. He will believe you, because of what you will tell him about my plans. Now listen. You will leave Belgrade tonight. I will give you a safe conduct, which will prevent your arrest anywhere in Yugoslavia. I will also provide you with the necessary train and bus tickets to get as close to Bihac as possible. You will have to walk the rest of the way, but you must make all possible haste. You will insist on being taken to Tito, where you will give him the information. Once he reacts as I suspect he will, you can do as you wish. You can either remain with the Partisans, although I do not recommend it, or you can desert them and regain our people. You will still have your safe conduct, and you will be returned here. Do you understand?' Rosa nodded.

'Very good. Now, Rosa, I wish you to understand something else. Should the Partisans *not* react as I suspect they will when they hear what you have to tell them, I will be forced to the conclusion that you have betrayed me. In that case I shall, firstly, revoke your safe conduct and issue instructions that when you are captured, you are to be returned here for interrogation and then execution.' Rosa shuddered. 'Secondly, I will arrest, interrogate and execute your mother and father.' Rosa burst into tears. 'And thirdly, I shall publicize the fact that you are one of my agents, so that if we do not arrest you, the Partisans certainly will, and they will hang you. So now, when you leave here, go and collect whatever belongings you feel necessary, and then return here for your pass and final briefing.'

Rosa panted. 'But I still do not know what I am to tell the Partisans.'

'I am about to tell you,' Wassermann reminded her.

She listened with her mouth open. 'But suppose they do not believe me?'

'I will make sure that they do,' Wassermann promised.

Rosa opened the office door, and checked, looking back at Wassermann. 'There is a lady here to see you, Herr General.'

'Oh, yes, ask her to come in.' He watched the door in anticipation, and then slowly stood up. This was definitely a lady, a glimpse of what Angela could be like in ten years' time – if hatred and alcohol did not consume her by then. Dark-haired, handsome rather than pretty, even if her looks were partially spoiled by the jagged scar on her right cheek, this made her somehow even more attractive. She wore a clearly borrowed and ill-fitting white dress around the left arm of which she had stitched a black band, and which for all its shapelessness still indicated a full figure. She exuded dignity from every feature, with every movement. 'Frau Geisner?'

'General Wassermann. It is very good of you to see me.' Her voice was as dignified as the rest of her, soft with well-modulated tones.

'It is an honour.' He limped round his desk to kiss her hand. 'I am so very sorry about your husband.'

'Will you catch the people who did it? I have been told that their commanders were an Englishman named Davis and a Frenchwoman named Fouquet. I have spoken with these people. And with a woman named Janitz.' She touched her scar.

'Which of them did that to you?'

'The woman Janitz.'

'I see. It is my intention, my job, to destroy all of those vermin. Sit down.' He held the chair for her. 'Major Ulrich tells me that you seek employment.' He sat down himself, behind the desk. 'Are you financially embarrassed by your husband's death?'

'My husband was a wealthy man before he joined the army, Herr General. My parents are also wealthy, and I have only one sister. I have remained here because I wish to avenge my husband, or at least, see him avenged, and I have been told that I can only remain in Belgrade in some kind of official capacity.'

'And you also wish to avenge yourself for that scar,

46

Wassermann thought. 'That is true. However, unlike the Partisans, we do not employ women to do our fighting.'

'You employ them as secretaries.'

'Have you secretarial qualifications?'

'I can learn. I . . .' She licked her lips. 'I will do anything I have to in order to see my husband's killers hanged.'

Wassermann felt almost sick with anticipation. This could have been eighteen months ago, and Angela sitting there, begging for vengeance on her mother. But Angela had been a frightened little girl. This was a mature woman, no less desperate, perhaps, but far more in control of herself. But if she could be wooed and won, might she not prove to be a treasure?

If he would admit it to no one, his loneliness sometimes drove him close to suicide. He distrusted all men. On a professional level, he knew that every member of the party, and most certainly of the Schutzstaffel, was interested only in advancement. On a personal level, he equally had no doubt that everyone who knew of his condition – even Ulrich and most certainly that rat Halbstadt – held him in contempt. Not to mention Angela. To find someone with whom he could share, who would neither laugh at him nor hate him . . . And his instincts were telling him that Mathilde Geisner, so obviously experienced, so calm even in her angry despair – and now also so tarnished because of what had happened to her face – could be just what he was looking for. And if she was not, well, he could drop her on the dung heap with the others.

'And do you suppose,' he asked, 'that sitting behind a desk here in Belgrade will in any way contribute to the capture of Davis and Fouquet? Or Janitz?'

'I would at least know what is going on.'

He leaned back in his chair. 'As I have told you, I have been sent here to destroy these vermin. This I intend to do. But as they are presently concentrated in western Bosnia, that is where the campaign is going to be fought. That is where I

47

am going, very soon. Obviously I will be taking with me my staff. I had not previously thought of it, but it does occur to me that a personal private secretary might be very useful.'

She gazed at him. 'Even if I cannot type and have no knowledge of shorthand?'

'I am sure I will be able to think of something for you to do, and you would be there when we catch up with Davis and Fouquet. And Janitz.' Another appraising gaze, then she again touched her scar. 'That is no matter,' Wassermann said. 'I even find it attractive.'

Her nostrils dilated, and he wondered how much she knew of his secrets. But she could know nothing of them yet. Down to this morning no one had known he was returning, therefore there was no reason for his name ever to have been mentioned in her presence. 'You understand, Herr General, that I am in mourning for my husband.'

'I do understand that. And I shall respect your feelings. But surely you cannot mourn Major Geisner for the rest of your life?'

'No,' she agreed. 'Perhaps not.'

'So, will you accept the job?'

She considered a last time. 'Yes.'

'Excellent. I am sure we will get on very well together.' Wassermann pulled a pad of paper towards him and wrote rapidly. 'Here is a requisition for you to receive anything you need. Fit yourself out with some proper clothes. Secretarial dress, black skirt and tie, white blouses, black stockings and shoes.'

'Black underwear?'

He smiled. 'I leave that to your discretion. When you have completed your preparations, return here. But it must not be later than the day after tomorrow. I intend to leave Belgrade for Zagreb before the end of the week.'

Mathilde took the paper and stood up. 'Thank you. What do I call you?'

'Herr General, or sir.'

'And your wife?'

'You do not have to call her anything. She is remaining in Belgrade.'

Tito stood beside Tony Davis to review the victorious brigade as it marched into the town of Bihac, situated in the northern foothills of the Bosnian mountains. In many places the houses and streets still bore the marks of the successful Partisan assault the previous autumn, but the essential perimeter defences had been restored, and the people, happy to have got rid of the dreaded Ustase, lined the street to cheer their new heroes.

The Partisans were a bedraggled, unkempt lot. It had taken them more than a month to get back, not only because they had had to cover a great distance, but because the Germans had hastily, if belatedly, mobilized every available unit in an endeavour to cut them off, and thus they had had to fight several severe little actions while marching through increasingly inclement weather as they toiled over the mountains. But their weapons were clean and bright – and every man, and woman, carried two or three rifles. They were festooned with belts of cartridge pouches and parts of the stripped-down machine guns, as well as items of German uniform, and their step was brisk and confident: they were the victors.

Tito himself was shorter than Tony, but more heavily built. His features were handsome, exuding both strength and charisma. His expression seldom changed, whether faced with a good or a bad situation, but his eyes were dancing. 'A brilliant success, Tony,' he said. 'As always.' The two men had met in the early days of the war and had liked each other on sight, even if Tony had been fighting for king and country and Tito for a world in which kings would not exist. But from the very beginning he had had the highest regard for the Englishman's courage and determination, as well as his military skill. Now Tony was his most trusted aide. 'Casualties?'

'Seven dead, three men and four women, and thirty-six wounded, fifteen men and twenty-one women.'

Tito nodded; both he and Tony had become used to that proportion of casualties between the sexes, simply because, for all their training, the women persisted in rashly exposing themselves in their eagerness to get at the enemy. 'And the other side?'

'We did not hang about to make an exact count, but I know there were at least seven hundred dead, and an equal number wounded. They never had a chance.'

Tito noted the suggestion of remorse. 'It is not our business to give the enemy a chance,' he pointed out gently. 'And the survivors?'

'We stripped them and left them to walk into Belgrade.'

'That is also brilliant. Their equipment?'

'We brought it with us.'

'Boots? I saw that you have some.'

'We have five thousand pairs of boots; there were a thousand spares in the trucks.'

'What of those trucks?'

'We destroyed all of them, and three tanks; the others got away. But I wish to report that the command tank was destroyed in an act of consummate gallantry carried out by Private Anita Hagar of the Uzice Regiment. She did not survive.'

'The price of victory,' Tito observed. 'She will be remembered.'

'We also brought with us five prisoners. Senior officers. Including the brigade commander.'

Tito nodded. 'Have they yielded any information?'

'They had little to offer, coming from the Mediterranean. I thought they may come in handy for exchanges, if it should become necessary.'

'Good thinking.'

'There is one problem, of which I was not aware at the time they were captured.'

Tito raised his eyebrows.

'One of them is a Major Klostermann.'

'Is he important?'

'Only personally. He is the elder brother of Captain Bernhard Klostermann, a German military attaché in Belgrade before the invasion. Bernhard Klostermann was also the fiancé of Sandrine. She shot him when she encountered him again in the attack on Uzice.'

'Ah. You think—'

'As far as I can gather, while this brother knows that Bernhard was killed by a Partisan in that battle, he does not know who fired the fatal shot. But I do not think it would be a good idea for them to meet.'

'Of course. The officers will be segregated under male guards. But . . .' He pointed. 'What is that Sandrine is carrying?'

'Her baby.'

'Her . . .?' Tito turned his head to look at him. 'You took her with you when she was so pregnant? I did not even know she *was* pregnant.'

'She wasn't. There were some women with the convoy, and one of them had this child with her. She was killed, and so . . .'

'You mean it is a German baby?'

'I think it is a French baby now. I couldn't refuse her, Josip. She has been through a great deal these last couple of years. I don't think it's a case of just being broody. I think it's more a case of, having taken so many lives during that time, she wanted to give one back.'

'What happened to the surviving women?'

'I sent them into Belgrade as well.'

'You didn't . . .'

'No, I did not take their clothes. And not one of them was raped. By our people, at any rate.'

Tito nodded. 'That was well done.' He finished saluting the last of the returning people, then led the way to his headquarters office, situated in the old town hall. 'Now we must wait and see how they react.'

'*Can* they react? What have they got to react with, unless they strip every garrison in the country to the bone?'

Tito saluted the sentries and climbed the stairs to his office, Tony following. 'I am sure they will react, somehow. They have to, or they may as well pack up and leave.' He sighed, and sat behind his desk. 'But I agree, if only our masters would provide us with a few offensive weapons while the enemy is stretched so thinly, why, we could even liberate the country. What I would give for a few tanks. But one cannot assault well-fortified positions, manned by disciplined regular troops, with rifles and hand-grenades, at least not without suffering unacceptable casualties.'

'And they can promise nothing?'

'Oh, they *promise* a great deal. Moscow says that as soon as the German summer offensive has been defeated – they apparently know one is coming – they will let us have everything we wish. That cannot be before the autumn. Britain says as soon as the Axis forces have been entirely expelled from North Africa *.* . Now tell me when *that* is going to happen, Tony. But I tell you what the British *are* sending: a new mission.'

'Not another one.'

'Ah. But this one will be different. It is to be commanded by a brigadier. And what is more important, it is coming to us specifically, not as an offshoot of a visit to Mihailovic.'

Tony frowned. 'What do you make of that?'

'I would say that London is at last starting to wonder why they hear nothing of Cetnik operations against the Nazis, and so much of ours. I think it is a step in the right direction. And this latest success should make them even more inclined to put their money on us rather than those Serbian bastards. We must roll out the red carpet for this brigadier, Tony.'

'Absolutely.'

Both men turned their heads when there was a knock on the door. 'Come,' Tito called.

An orderly entered and saluted. 'The Zagreb probe has returned, sir.'

Instantly Tito was alert. 'There are troop movements?'

'No, sir. They report no troop movements. But they have brought in a prisoner. Well, a deserter.'

'A German, deserting to us?'

'No, sir. It is a Serb. A young woman. She wishes to see you.'

'I really have no time for interviewing itinerant Serbs. Have her processed to see if she is genuine.'

'But she claims to have information of the utmost importance, sir. She also says that you know of her. Her name is Rosa Malic.'

Three

The Retreat

'Rosa Malic?' Tito looked at Tony. 'Isn't she . . .?'
'Boris Malic's daughter.'

'The woman who supplied all of that information.'

'Down to about a year ago. We haven't heard from her recently. Or Boris. There was a rumour she's changed sides. It is certain that she gave evidence at Angela Wassermann's trial, claiming that the woman Bestic was one of our spies, and that therefore Angela was justified in shooting her, at least in Nazi eyes.'

'And now she is here.' Tito stroked his chin. 'It can do no harm to hear what she has to say.'

'Has she been searched?' Tony asked the orderly.

'She does not appear to be armed, General.'

Tony looked at Tito.

'You'd better check her out,' Tito said. 'But be careful.'

Tony nodded, and went outside, followed by the orderly. Rosa stood between two Partisan soldiers, looking terrified. But she had a large satchel slung on her shoulder. 'You are Boris Malic's daughter?' he asked. Rosa's head bobbed up and down. 'Where is your father?'

'He could not come. He is ill. He told me to come instead.'

'Because you have information. What is it?'

'Papa said it must be given to the general personally.'

'I see. Let me have that satchel.' Rosa hesitated, then took the bag from her shoulder and held it out. Tony opened it and sifted through its contents: a change of underwear, a few scraps of food, certainly no weapons or grenades, but . . . He held up the sheet of paper. 'How did you get this?'

'General Wassermann gave it to me.'

'*Wassermann*?'

'Did you not know he is back?'

'And you say he is a general now?'

'He has been promoted. He is now in command of all the German forces in Yugoslavia.'

'Good God! And he gave you this safe conduct?'

'I work for him. He gave me the pass to visit my grandmother in Zagreb.' She gave a brief smile. 'He does not know that I do not have a grandmother in Zagreb.'

Tony studied her for several seconds. Then he replaced the contents of the satchel. 'Lift your skirt.' Rosa glanced at the men to either side, then grasped her skirt and raised it to her waist. She wore thick stockings and drawers. It was necessary to feel the material to make sure there was no concealed knife. Rosa shuddered as he touched her, and screwed up her face. But she had no weapon. 'All right,' Tony said. Rosa dropped her skirt, cheeks crimson. Tony opened the inner door. 'Rosa Malic, General. She has come to tell us that Wassermann is back, promoted to general, and in command of all Axis forces in Yugoslavia.'

Tito leaned back in his chair. 'After his defeat last year? That cannot be true.'

Tony gave him the safe conduct. 'Fritz Wassermann, GOC Yugoslavia.'

Tito looked at Rosa. 'He gave you this?'

'I work for him. That is how I obtain information.'

'Tell us about the woman Bestic.'

'I had to do it. My father told me to do it. Wassermann was becoming suspicious. But when I saved his wife from execution, he trusted me absolutely.'

'And Bestic?'

'She was already dead.'

Tito glanced at Tony, who shrugged. Then he looked at Rosa again. 'And you have come all this way to tell us that Wassermann is back.'

'No, sir. I came to tell you *why* he is back.'

'So?'

'His orders, his only orders, are to destroy you.'

'That is hardly classified information.'

'But this time, sir, they, the Germans, are resolved on it. They are massing an army corps north of Zagreb.'

'You are letting your imagination run away with you, young lady. The Germans do not have an army corps to spare to send against us.'

'This will contain only a few Wehrmacht elements. But there is at least one Hungarian division, and a Bulgarian. They have also obtained the full support of the Cetniks.'

'The bastards,' Tito growled. 'I will settle with Mihailovic if it is the last thing I do.'

'Still, it sounds a rather motley collection,' Tony remarked.

'The force will be supported by a brigade of tanks and the Luftwaffe,' Rosa said.

'Wassermann told you this?' Tony asked.

'I overheard him discussing the plans with other officers. But also . . .' She looked suitably embarrassed. 'He makes me sleep with him.'

'I thought he is a sexual cripple.'

'He is. It is terrible. But he talks, mostly of his determination to settle with you, General Tito, and you, Mr Davis, and Mademoiselle Fouquet.'

'Well, I am sure what you have told us will be very useful, Miss Malic.'

'I know something else,' Rosa said. 'There has been a quarrel between General Wassermann and the Italian general commanding in Albania. General Wassermann wished the Italians to take part in the campaign, but they have refused. Their general says that he can spare no troops because of his fear of an Allied invasion once the North African campaign is concluded.'

'That is also very interesting, Rosa,' Tony said. 'Now go with this orderly.' He turned to the orderly. 'Take her to Colonel Fouquet, and tell her that she is to be fed and quartered. I will join her in a little while.'

The orderly saluted, while Rosa looked from face to face. 'Is what I have told you good?'

'I have said, it is very interesting,' Tony assured her.

'May I have my safe conduct back?'

'Are you returning to Belgrade? It might be safer to stay with us.'

Rosa licked her lips. 'You wish me to stay?'

'For a few days, yes.'

Another quick glance, and she followed the orderly from the room.

'What do you think?' Tito asked when they were alone.

'That she is a liar, and thus a plant.'

'Wassermann's signature was on that safe conduct.'

'Oh, I don't doubt that he's back, although Berlin must really be scraping the bottom of the barrel. But this business of uniting the Cetniks with the Germans and the Hungarians and the Bulgarians . . .'

'If she is a plant, why should Wassermann wish us to know this? Or at least make us believe that it is happening?'

'Because he wishes to drive us out of Bihac, and if it can be done by propaganda rather than force, so much the better for him.'

Tito stroked his chin. 'I take your point. But I must also consider the possibility that Malic may be genuine. If Wassermann can launch an assault with overwhelming force, backed up by panzers and aircraft . . . Well, what have we got to put against them? Rifles and a few machine guns and mortars. We could be wiped out, or at least suffer unsustainable casualties. And if the Italians *were* to come in . . .'

'Well, sir, there are three things we can do before coming to a decision. Firstly, we can send another patrol north towards Zagreb, to discover if there are any large troop concentrations forming there.'

'The patrol that brought in Malic said there was nothing.'

'I think we should send out another probe. Two or three in fact. And this time they should get north of Zagreb and have a good look.'

Tito nodded. 'That is sound thinking. And what else?'

'Secondly, we can send patrols south to make sure that there *is* no Italian presence. And thirdly, we can work on Malic, and find out whether she is genuine or not.'

'Very good, Tony. Carry on. But . . .' He pointed. 'You will not accompany any of these patrols yourself. I cannot afford to lose you. And in the meantime, I will make preparations for an evacuation, just in case it becomes necessary.'

Tony saluted.

'I have decided to call him Charles,' Sandrine said. 'That was the name of France's greatest king.'

'You do realize that Charlemagne was actually a German?'

'There were no Germans then.'

'Or there were no French. You surely can't be giving him anything?'

Sandrine had her blouse open and was allowing the baby to suck. 'I like to feel it,' she explained. 'And it will make him feel secure. I have read this. When he has sucked for a while, I give him some milk, so we are both happy.'

Tony scratched his head. 'You mean, I don't do enough for you.'

'You do everything for me, Tony. I am doing something for him.'

There was a knock on the door of the apartment they shared. Tony raised his eyebrows to Sandrine, and she moved the baby's mouth and closed her blouse. But it was Sasha.

'You are sending out patrols,' she announced. 'Why am I not commanding?'

'Because you, like me, like Sandrine, are now regarded as too senior to risk our lives on patrols. Besides, I have a job for you.'

Sasha regarded her friend and the child; Sandrine had re-opened her blouse and replaced the baby's lips. 'Feeding the baby?'

'Another baby. The woman Malic.'

'I do not like her. I do not trust her.'

'Snap. I would like you to prove that we are both wrong.'

Slowly Sasha licked her lips. She made Tony think of a hungry animal. Because in many ways that was what she was. Yet during Sandrine's captivity in a Gestapo cell, when she had been assumed dead, he had more than once shared Sasha's bivouac, an unforgettable experience, a relationship of which Sandrine was fully aware. However, in the exceptional moral situation created by the war situation, the two women remained the best of friends.

'I do not mean that you should roast her on a spit,' Tony said. 'As she is now serving with the army, I think you should take her on a training exercise, and find out what she really is at. You'll need a back-up.'

'I will take Anja,' Sasha said. 'She is good with fires.'

'Just what do you mean by that?'

'A knowledge of fires is always useful,' Sasha said. 'I will leave tonight.'

'Just remember that, even if you find out that she is a spy, I want her back in one piece.'

'So that we can hang her,' Sasha said. 'I understand.' She saluted, rubbed the baby's head, and left the room.

'Have you just sentenced that poor girl to death?' Sandrine asked.

'That's up to her,' Tony said. 'I am hoping I have sentenced her, and all of us, to life.'

*   *   *

59

Rosa collapsed, falling full length on the ground, rifle and equipment thumping beside her. 'I must rest. I can go no further.'

Sasha and Anja Britic stood above her. They had walked all night, and the first rays of the sun were just emerging above the mountains to the east. Both of the Partisans were sweat-stained and untidy, but neither looked the least tired. Now Sasha dug the toe of her boot into Rosa's ribs and turned her over to lie on her back. 'You are soft,' she said. 'Suppose we were being chased by the Germans. Or perhaps you know the Germans would never chase you, eh?'

Rosa blinked at her. 'I would like a drink of water.'

'Time enough for that,' Sasha said, 'when you have answered some questions.'

'I have told the general everything I know.'

'But he did not know as much about you as I do. Tell me about Jelena Brolic.'

'Jelena . . .' Rosa caught her breath. 'She was a traitor.'

'I think you should light a fire, Anja,' Sasha suggested. 'And we will have breakfast.' Anja obediently started gathering twigs. 'Jelena was my lover,' Sasha remarked. Rosa stared at her. 'We experienced much happiness together – before she was captured. Then she turned traitor. It was not in her nature to do that.'

Rosa licked her lips. 'Perhaps she was tortured by the Gestapo.'

'When she came back to us, to betray us, there was not a mark on her body. She was not tortured by the Gestapo. She was suborned, by that bitch Angela Wassermann. Your mistress. You were there in the house with them. You must have seen it happen.' Behind them Anja had the fire going, and now she poured oil into her frying pan, which immediately began to sizzle.

'I knew they had become friends,' Rosa said. 'I did not know anything more than that.'

'They became friends? In a matter of a few days? Such

60

good friends that Jelena was prepared to betray her lover, her friends, her comrades, her countrymen? You are lying, Rosa. Just as you lied to the general.'

'I did not lie,' Rosa snapped. 'I . . .' She bit her lip.

'Strip,' Sasha said.

Rosa sat up. 'What?'

'Take off your clothes.' Rosa looked left and right. 'There is no one here but us. Are you ashamed to take off your clothes before two of your comrades?'

Again Rosa licked her lips. 'What are you going to do to me?'

'That depends on you. Get up.' Slowly Rosa got to her feet. 'Now strip.'

Rosa was wearing Partisan gear. Her sidecap had fallen off when she had thrown herself down. Now she stooped to unlace and step out of her boots, then unbuckled her pants and let them fall about her ankles. 'Do you wish me as your lover?' she asked innocently. 'Like Jelena Brolic?'

'Who knows?' Sasha asked. 'Get on with it.' Rosa took off her blouse, shivering in the dawn chill. 'And the drawers,' Sasha told her. Rosa stood before her, naked. 'You are a pretty little thing,' Sasha commented. 'Do you wish to stay a pretty little thing?'

Rosa closed her hands over her pubes protectively. 'You have no right to hurt me.'

'I can do what I like to you,' Sasha told her. 'Out here, I am the law. You may scream if you like. No one will hear you. But it would be better for you to tell me the truth.'

Rosa panted. 'What truth? I have told the generals every-thing I know.'

'Is that oil hot?' Sasha asked Anja.

'It is boiling.' The spitting could clearly be heard.

'Very good. Lie down, Rosa.'

'You told me to stand up.'

'Now I am telling you to lie down.'

61

Rosa sat, and then lay on the grass. She was shivering more than ever. 'It is so cold.'

'But we are going to warm you up. Hold her arms, Anja.'

Anja knelt behind Rosa's head, grasped her wrists, and extended them above her shoulders. Rosa gave a tentative tug, but Anja was far too strong for her. Sasha went to the fire and picked up the pan of sizzling oil. Then she stood above Rosa. Rosa attempted to kick, but then subsided in despair. 'Please,' she gasped.

'Tell us what you really came here to do.'

'I came to tell you Wassermann's plan,' Rosa wailed.

Sasha laid the pan on the ground, pulled Rosa's legs apart, and then knelt between. 'I am waiting for the truth,' she said, and picked up the pan. Rosa uttered a terrified scream, which became a shriek of agony when Sasha dripped a drop of the oil on to her groin. 'If I empty it,' Sasha said, 'you will never have sex again.' Rosa sucked air into her lungs – and Sasha's head turned when she heard the roar of aircraft overhead.

The patrol commander was flushed and excited. 'There are troops everywhere, General,' he said. 'Tanks, I saw the ensign of a panzer brigade commander. Vehicles, hundreds of vehicles.' He rolled his eyes. 'And here . . .'

'Yes, we were bombed,' Tito said. 'We have been bombed before. Did you manage to identify any of the enemy units?'

'I saw the Hungarian flag, and the Bulgarian, flying over the cantonments.'

'Did you see any Cetniks?' Tony asked.

'There were Cetniks everywhere, General. There are units both to the west and to the east. We even met some.'

'Did you exchange fire?'

'Briefly. Then they ran off.'

'But you were pursued?'

'No, sir. There was no pursuit.'

'Thank you, Captain.' The captain saluted, and left the

office. 'Well,' Tito said, 'it looks as if our little friend is genuine after all. I hope Janitz did not hurt her.'

'I gather she was saved by the bell. Or at least, the Luftwaffe. There was a small accident with boiling oil . . .'

'I do not wish to know of it. I think she should be commended. She may have saved our skins.'

'Do you mean to evacuate Bihac?'

'We have no choice. If the entire Cetnik army is out there, plus a Hungarian and Bulgarian force, almost certainly each of divisional strength, together with a panzer brigade – exactly as Rosa said – and we already know the Luftwaffe are there, we could be looking at, say, seventy-five thousand men. That means we are outnumbered by three to one, not to mention hopelessly out-gunned. We cannot defend ourselves against such a force, certainly not while they have total air superiority. If I had only one battery of anti-aircraft guns . . .'

'We will be more vulnerable in the open.'

'I do not believe we will. Wassermann will find it very difficult to pursue us into those mountains. His technological superiority will be neutralized. Because of the shadows thrown by the peaks and the peaks themselves, even his aircraft will find it difficult to spot us. In any event, it is a risk we must take. At least if we move now, they will not be able to complete the encircling of us. You do not approve?'

'I agree that we have to go, sir, in view of the odds. It's just that it's all too pat. And why was our patrol not pursued, or at least bombed? The Cetniks must have been in radio contact with their headquarters. It is almost as if Wassermann wants us to go, without a fight.'

'Well, undoubtedly he will trumpet it as a great victory: the recapture of Bihac with minimum casualties. But we will still have the army in being.'

'Will we? We have only Malic's word for it that there is not an Italian army waiting for us.'

'Our southern patrol saw no troops. You are being over-suspicious, Tony. It is an excellent characteristic, but you

63

must never let it override your judgement. We must make our decisions on the information we have obtained, and which has so far proved to be correct. Our plans are made. The army will commence its withdrawal tomorrow night. A rearguard will remain to deceive the Germans into thinking we are still here.'

'Will their aircraft not spot us before we reach the mountains?'

'Not if we move by night and conceal ourselves by day. They may see some movement, but they will not be able to ascertain numbers. In any event, not even Wassermann is going to bypass Bihac and leave it in our possession, to be a thorn in his flank and rear.'

'Yes, sir. Our destination?'

Tito spread a map across the desk. 'Montenegro. I have had agents down there for some time, and I am sure we will be welcomed.'

Tony studied the map. 'And this river? The Neretva? It looks pretty wide.'

'It is two hundred feet wide. But there is a bridge. There. It is both a railway and a road bridge. If we can seize some rolling stock . . .'

'One bridge, for twenty-five thousand men?' And their women, their supplies, and their animals, he thought. 'Suppose it is blown?'

'It will not be blown by the Italians. It is the only railway link between Albania and Bosnia. But we must get there well ahead of the Germans. Once we are across it, *we* will blow the bridge.'

'Yes, sir. And the rearguard?'

Tito sighed. 'They will have to be volunteers.'

Tony nodded. 'I will select them personally.'

Tito pointed. 'But you will not command them. They are a forlorn hope. I cannot risk your loss. Besides' – he gave one of his grim smiles – 'I need you to command the actual rearguard. The post of honour, eh?'

'You are asking me to condemn some of my people to death.'

'I am asking you to exercise the judgement and determination of a commanding officer.'

Tony swallowed. 'What size is this force to be?'

'We can spare a thousand. Five hundred men, and the same number of women.'

'Their orders?'

'They must buy us time. Seventy-two hours. If they can hold Bihac for three days, we will be out of Wassermann's reach. After that, well . . . If they can withdraw as a unit, that will be very good. If not, it will have to be every man for himself. And every woman, to be sure.'

'I will command,' Astzalos said.

Tony looked at him. 'The position must be held for three days. There can be no retreat and no surrender until the enemy have been held up for seventy-two hours.'

'I understand. Am I allowed to pick my own officers?'

'Providing they volunteer.'

'Then I will have Major Janitz as my second in command.'

Tony was astonished. 'Sasha? I thought you disliked her.'

'I do. She is a pervert and a bully. But she is also ruthless and as brave as a lion. Her people will follow her anywhere, and fight for as long as she tells them to.'

'That's true. I take off my hat to your judgement, Astzalos. But remember, she must volunteer.'

Astzalos smiled. 'Do you think there is any doubt of that?'

'I had to hold them back,' Sandrine said proudly. 'The entire brigade stepped forward as one woman. Oh, how I wish you would let me stay with them.'

'You have the rest to command in the retreat,' Tony reminded her. 'And besides, who would look after Charles?'

'I am sure there would be no shortage of volunteers for that, either.'

'And do you want to die?'

'Nobody wants to die. But those girls are going to. How can I walk away from them? A woman has as much honour as a man, you know.'

'I do know. But a commanding officer has an even greater duty: his responsibility to his entire command. As I have just had pointed out to me.'

Sandrine made a face, and then turned to the door when there was a knock. 'Come.'

Sasha entered, accompanied by Rosa. 'She insists upon seeing the colonel,' Sasha announced. 'And the general.'

Sandrine looked at Tony; she regarded Rosa as his responsibility. 'Well?' he asked.

'I would like to speak with you in private, sir.'

'Ha!' Sasha commented.

'It is her privilege,' Tony pointed out.

'Ha!' Sasha remarked again, and left the room.

'What is it?' Tony asked.

'I have been told by the major that I must remain with the defenders of Bihac. I do not wish to die.'

'You are doing a great and noble thing,' Sandrine told her.

'I do not wish to die!' Rosa's voice became a wail. 'And with that woman . . . She is a vicious animal.'

'Which is why she, more than anyone else, is capable of holding this position as long as possible, and of bringing you out alive. Anyway, did you not step forward with the rest of the regiment when I called for volunteers?'

'I had to do it. If I had not, they would have beaten me up. They are always beating me up.'

'Well,' Sandrine said, 'if you stay and fight with them, bravely, you can be certain that they will never beat you up again. Now go and do your duty.'

Rosa looked as if she would have protested some more,

then saluted and went out. Sasha promptly came in. 'Sniv-elling little toad,' she commented.

'Do you suppose she will be any good in a fight?' Tony asked.

'She will be where I can keep an eye on her.'

'Do you still not trust her? The information she gave us has been proved accurate.'

'That is your opinion,' Sasha said. 'And General Tito's, to be sure. I still wish to be convinced. When do you move out?'

'Tonight.'

'Then it is time to say goodbye. Astzalos wishes me to deploy my people.' She embraced Sandrine. 'Take care of Little Charlie.'

'Shit!' Sandrine said. 'I'm starting to cry.'

Sasha held her tightly. 'I am not dead yet. I do not see how any German is going to kill me.' She released Sandrine and faced Tony, for the first time uncertainly.

'Come here,' he told her. She went to him and he hugged her and kissed her on the mouth. 'You are one of the two bravest women I have ever known.'

'Well, take care of the other one.' Sasha kissed him again, stepped back, saluted, and left the room.

'Will we ever see her again?' Sandrine asked. Her cheeks were indeed wet.

'No.'

'Does she know that?'

'Yes,' Tony said.

The flight commander saluted. 'They are moving, Herr Gen-eral.'

'Are you certain?' Wassermann asked.

'Oh, indeed, sir. They clearly began to evacuate the town last night, under cover of darkness, and they appear to have gone to ground for the day. But there is sufficient evidence of an army on the move. Do we attack them, sir?'

'Not at this time. Let them get well away. We do not wish them to feel trapped and turn back. But keep them under surveillance. I would like an estimate as to numbers.' The flight commander clicked his heels. Wassermann surveyed his waiting staff. 'Well, gentlemen? They have gone. And all our troops, even our panzers, are not yet in position. They fell for the sight of those flags.'

'I think I, all of us, owe you an apology, Herr General,' said one of the Hungarians. 'We did not think your plan would work.'

Wassermann beamed at them.

'Do we now move forward?' asked one of the Bulgarians.

'Not at this time. General Mihailovic, are your people in position?'

'They are.' The Cetnik commander was a small dark man, who wore a beard and moustache as well as spectacles, and looked anxious.

'Then let them commence their harassing operation. Harassing, remember. You will stay on their flanks, cut off small parties, stragglers, foragers, but you will not get sucked into any pitched battle, and you must not attempt to block their retreat. Mihailovic nodded. 'It goes without saying that you will take no prisoners,' Wassermann reminded him. 'Unless they happen to be Davis, Fouquet, or Tito himself. Now, gentlemen, prepare your troops. Our first task, as soon as the Partisan army is well clear of the town, is to reduce Bihac.'

'But with every day will not the Partisans get further away?'

'It is my intention that they should do so. I wish them to reach a position where they can no longer change their plans, or the direction of their march. Then they will run into a brick wall and we shall clean them up.' He turned to the Italian liaison officer. 'Are your people in position?'

'As far as I know, Herr General.'

'Let us hope they are. Thank you, gentlemen. I shall issue individual orders tomorrow morning.'

'With respect, Herr General,' said the Hungarian. 'May I ask why it is necessary to reduce Bihac if the Partisans have evacuated it?'

'Because I know these people, Colonel. I have spent the past two years fighting them. Which is why I have been given this command. They will have left a rearguard in Bihac, a body of vicious killers who, if not eliminated, will operate against our lines of communication. They have done this before. Besides, I wish to make an example of the town.'

The officers left, and Wassermann rang his bell. Mathilde came in. He thought she made a picture in her uniform, and she was actually proving quite useful as an aide, keeping his military diary up to date and reminding him of appointments. Thus far she had been nothing more than that, but today he was enjoying a sense of euphoria. Although he would never have admitted it, even to himself, he had also doubted that his plan would work so well and so quickly. Now his victory was assured. 'Well?' he asked.

'I understand that you are to be congratulated, Herr General.'

'Is that all you can say?'

She considered. 'Will Davis or Fouquet be in Bihac? Or Janitz?'

'I should think it is very likely they will all be there. They invariably work as a team, and they are usually charged with the most dangerous duties in the Partisan army.'

'Then, when they are captured, I will congratulate you again.'

'And will you then consider your task to be completed, and return to Germany? After you have seen them executed, of course.'

Another brief consideration. 'If you have no more use for me, Herr General.'

'Could any man not have a use for you, Mathilde?' She gazed at him without speaking, and he got up and went to the door which led to his private quarters. This he opened, and waited. After a moment she stepped through. Wassermann closed the door. 'Do you still mourn your husband?'

'I will always mourn my husband, Herr General.'

He went to the sideboard against the wall of the little lounge. 'Life must go on.'

'As you say.'

He poured two glasses of schnapps, gave her one. 'This should be champagne. But perhaps there will be some in Bihac. What shall we drink to?'

'Your continued success, Herr General.'

'In every field?'

She hesitated. She knew where he was leading. But then, she had known where he had been leading from the moment of their first meeting. It was inevitable, and thus had to be accepted. Besides, after all the rumours she had heard, she was curious. 'In every field, Herr General.'

He took the glass from her hand and set it on a table. Then he took her in his arms and kissed her. It was a deep and questing kiss, without being either as passionate or as brutal as she had anticipated. Nor were his hands at all active on her body. Then he released her and took off his belt. 'Do you know about me?'

'Ah . . .'

'Do not lie to me, Mathilde.'

'I know that you have been severely wounded.'

'Did you know that I am a eunuch?'

She caught her breath. 'I . . . I did not know that.'

'But a eunuch who still feels all the desires of a normal man.' Mathilde's tongue came out and circled her lips. 'Are you squeamish in these matters?'

She shook her head. 'But . . . what can we do?'

'A great deal.' He opened the bedroom door. 'You under-stand, I get very passionate. I like to squeeze, and hurt. I would like you to cry out. I would like to hear you.' Mathilde drew a deep breath, and stepped past him.

*   *   *

70

'They are coming,' Astzalos said. 'My patrol has just returned, and the captain says there are tanks moving up the valley below us, followed by truckloads of infantry. So we may expect an aerial bombardment at any moment. Are your people ready?'

'My girls are always ready,' Sasha said. 'But would it not make more sense if, instead of sitting here like a bunch of dummies, I took them up into the hills to strike at the enemy flanks?'

'My orders are to hold Bihac for three days. Well, we have been here for two, untroubled. We need only hold out for one more day, then we can withdraw. That is, we need only repel one attack. But we are not here to counter-attack. We are here to defend. Understand that.'

Sasha shrugged. 'You have no imagination, Lazar. Tell me this: if you are killed or put out of action, who is in command?'

'You are.'

'Ah.'

Astzalos looked from her face to her belt, to the Luger pistol which hung there beside the string of grenades, but thought better of what he had been about to say. 'So join your women and prepare to fight.'

'As you say, Colonel.' Sasha left the headquarters and went out on to the street, thence to the perimeter, where the Partisans crouched behind the walls and barricades. They were heavily armed as regards personal weapons; every man had a rifle with at least two bandoliers, together with grenades, while every hundred yards there was either a machine gun or a mortar. They would give a very good account of themselves against any enemy advancing across the open slopes before them. But they had no weapons capable of bringing down a bomber.

All the men knew Sasha by sight, and gave her a wave or a shout; she felt that, with her record of survival and success, her very presence gave them encouragement, just

71

as the few civilians to be seen – most of those who had not already fled the doomed town were huddled in their cellars – also cheered or clapped her as she strode by so purposefully.

The women held the west and south bastions, away from the direct line of the German advance. They sat or lay beside their weapons, visibly at least far more relaxed than their male counterparts. Several were eating, some were even fast asleep. Those who were awake were, as usual, chattering animatedly. 'When will they come?' Anja asked.

'When they are ready.' Sasha sat beside her and took a drink of water. Then she nudged Rosa, who lay on her other side, head pillowed on her arm.

'Leave me alone,' Rosa muttered.

'It is a beautiful evening,' Sasha said. 'You should enjoy it while you can.' Rosa burst into tears. Sasha leaned against the brick wall, and closed her eyes. It *was* a beautiful evening; she could feel the heat of the setting sun on her face. It was a good time to enjoy being alive, because in a few hours she would probably be dead. She was disappointed about that. She did not want to die. Over the past two years she had enjoyed living too much.

She had been as afraid as anyone when the Germans had invaded in April 1941, had had the same sense of unreality and outrage – and total confusion. It had all happened so quickly, the collapse of the government had been so fast and so absolute, that no one, even in Belgrade, she had heard, much less in the isolated Bosnian village where she had grown up and where her father had been mayor, had known what to do. Papa had determined that life should go on as usual – Belgrade was a long way from Wicz. It had never crossed his mind that the invaders should, or could, be resisted. That had been a business for the army, and if the army had been incapable of doing its job, they had no right to expect anyone else to do it for them.

But Sasha had from the start been obsessed with the desire

to do *something*, and when word had reached them that there were women as well as soldiers gathering in the hills, she had announced her intention of joining them. Her parents had been horrified, and that had caused the first estrangement; in the light of later developments – such as her father's refusal to help her when she had taken her retreating regiment to Wicz two winters ago, seeking food and shelter – she had realized that their concern had been less for her safety than the fact that her presence in the resistance movement, if traced back to them, would land them in trouble.

Her boyfriend had been no less alarmed. They had actually been unofficially engaged, had been waiting until he could have a farm of his own before getting married. As Sasha had never been one for waiting for anything, she had seduced him, against his principles, into having sex with her, and discovered that he was as boringly inept at that as he was at everything else. She had known an immense sense of relief when he had not only refused to leave Wicz with her, but had declared, pompously, that if she went he would consider their engagement at an end.

Then the great adventure had begun. She supposed many young women – she had been twenty-seven years old at the time – would have been horrified at what she had undergone in the beginning. She had been raped twice, and had had to kill a man. At times she had nearly starved, and had been forced to steal to survive. But always two names had dominated her consciousness, the names that were whispered from village to village: Mihailovic and Tito. The first held no interest for her. She knew that the ex-chief of the Yugoslav general staff was not only a Serb, a people she disliked, but also came from the far side of the tracks. Besides, she had been told that women were not welcome in the Cetnik camp, except as wives or mistresses, and she had no intention of becoming either of those aspects of slavery. Tito was a Croat, another people for whom the Bosnians had no great admiration, but he was known to be a Communist; indeed, he had been secretary-general of the Yugoslav Communist party, and had actually been imprisoned by the federal government for his politics. Sasha did not know enough about the various ideologies to form an opinion, but she had had no doubt that such a man would not only be an opponent of a Serb-dominated federation, but would also have come from her side of the tracks.

Most important of all, however, had been the information that Tito was recruiting women as well as men, and not only as bedmates, but to bear arms. She had gone to the Partisan camp, and been welcomed. Moreover, she had met the two people she valued more than any others in the world, including her own family: Tony Davis and Sandrine Fouquet. Tony had immediately recognized her worth, and placed her in command of the first of the women's companies he had been forming.

Then had followed two glorious years of campaigning, hard, bloody and dangerous, but filled with unforgettable experiences, as when she and Tony had led the women's retreat from Uzice, through the snow-covered mountains, enduring great hardship, but also sharing every minute and every emotion as they had shared their bodies. It was during that retreat that she had gained a reputation almost equalling that of her idol, enhanced by her deeds during the last year, which had culminated in her leadership of the forlorn hope that had made the capture of this very town possible.

And now? She had volunteered for this task because it had been expected of her, and because Tony had expected it most of all. Would he have preferred her to decline, and flee with the army? She could not be sure. She knew she could never rank as high in his affection as did Sandrine. She did not resent this. She adored the Frenchwoman only a little less than she adored the Englishman. But, unable to possess either of them as she would have liked, what did she have to live for . . .

She woke up with a start. It was dawn and Anja was tugging her sleeve. 'Listen!'

Sasha sat up. 'Aircraft,' she said, and listened to the sudden screaming noise. 'Stukas.'

Progress was slow, the going hard, especially at night, and as the army could not afford to stick to the roads, such as they were, because the mountain tracks connecting the far-flung villages seldom led in the direction that was required, they tramped across country, up hillsides and down valleys, splashing through streams, driving their mules and forcing their carts out of ruts and water, surrounded by their bleating goats and their barking dogs, accompanied by their wailing children.

When the command came to a halt, most of them collapsed where they stood. Most of them. For it was always the officers' duty, before resting themselves, to round up the stragglers, post sentries, send out patrols, and have food prepared. They were at least fortunate that as summer approached the weather was fine, in pleasant contrast to their experiences of the previous two years, when their withdrawals had been made in the winter.

Commanding the rearguard, Tony found himself thinking of the Hebrew exodus from Egypt, as they picked their way through the detritus of the rest of the army. At least his women were the most disciplined force in the army, but they could not stop themselves from looking over their shoulders, not in fear of pursuit, but thinking of the five hundred of their comrades who were holed up in Bihac, waiting for death.

'Will we hear the assault?' Sandrine asked on the third morning, performing her daily routine of allowing Charles to suck.

'Not any more,' he said. 'We must have covered more than forty miles.'

'But we would have heard them yesterday.'

'Yesterday morning, perhaps.'

'But we didn't. What does that mean?'

'That they hadn't attacked by yesterday morning.'

She hugged the baby. 'Do you think they have decided not to?'

'No.'

'Shit! When I think of those girls . . .'

'Don't.'

'When will they attack us?'

'Not until after they have finished with Bihac, it would appear.' Yet he found it as disturbing as she did. He went to the edge of the wood in which they were sheltering, and looked up at the aircraft circling above them. Those planes might not be able to see all of them, but they certainly knew they were there. Yet they were not bombing them. He had a strange sense of unreality. He turned his head to look back, and saw smoke, many miles away, but forming huge clouds – above Bihac.

PART TWO

THE PURSUIT

As pants the hart for cooling streams,
When heated in the chase.
    Nahum Tate and Nicholas Brady

Four

The Town

'A communiqué from General Wassermann, Your Excellency,' Ulrich said.

'Well?' General Hartmann revealed no great enthusiasm.

'He wishes to inform Your Excellency that everything is going according to plan, and that he hopes to report the recapture of Bihac within forty-eight hours.'

Hartmann snorted. 'According to plan. I do not even know what this plan is. He did not tell me what it is.'

'As I understand it, sir, the plan was to force Tito to evacuate Bihac and move to the south, where he would encounter substantial Italian forces, which would hold him in check until our people came down from the north. I assume this is what has happened.'

'If they have evacuated Bihac, why is he still attacking it?'

Ulrich glanced at the sheet of paper in his hand. 'It would appear that the enemy left a small detachment to hold the town. This is being reduced now.'

'So he has not yet actually gained any success. This is all speculation.'

'He seems very confident, sir.'

'He is always very confident, Major. However, keep me informed. Heil Hitler!'

Ulrich returned the salute and left the office. He was halfway down the stairs – the governor-general maintained his office in the palace itself – when he saw Angela waiting at the foot, as immaculate as ever, although she wore black slacks and a loose white silk blouse. 'You have heard from Fritz?'

'A radio message came in this morning.'

'And?'

'It all seem to be going very well. He is confident of victory.'

'He is enjoying himself. While I am stuck in this dump. I am bored, Hermann. You do not mind if I call you Hermann?'

'Not at all, Frau Wassermann.'

'And you must call me Angela. Tell me, is that Captain Halbstadt still here?'

'Ah . . . he is in Yugoslavia. But he has accompanied your husband on the campaign. At General Wassermann's insistence.'

'Poor Erich. Well, as I have said, I am bored. General Hartmann and his wife are the two most boring people I have ever met. Do you know what they do after dinner, every night?' Ulrich looked uneasy. 'They have two of the officers from the garrison in, and they play contract bridge. Can you imagine?'

'It is a good game,' Ulrich ventured. 'My wife and I played bridge before the war. That was auction, of course, but I believe this contract is an improvement. Perhaps if you were to learn it . . .'

'Hermann, you are a devil. You are teasing me. Listen, I wish a . . . *companion*, someone to take me out, amuse me. I do not care whether it is a man or a woman. But the man must be handsome, and the woman at least pretty. And clean. Find me someone.'

'Me?'

'You are chief of police here in Yugoslavia. You must know everyone who matters, and who can be . . . *procured*.'

'I could not possibly do something like that.'

'My dear Hermann, you will, because I have asked you to.

80

If you refuse, I will have to tell my husband that you have
seduced me.'
   'He would never believe you.'
   Angela smiled, her eyes colder than ever. 'Try me.'

The planes wheeled above the burning town of Bihac, in a
continuous, lazy spiral, dropping their deadly cargoes into
the clouds of flames and smoke and dust beneath them. Only
when the Stukas, having returned to base to refuel and re-arm,
set their sirens wailing and plunged downwards was there any
animation to the scene. In the sky, that is.
   On the ground, there was frantic futile activity and unend-
ing noise, sounds of despair. No attempt was being made to
put out the fires; the water mains had long been severed.
The dead were left lying where they fell; after two days of
bombardment the stomach-churning smell filled the still air.
The wounded sought shelter or succour by their own efforts,
or lay and moaned, crying out for water. The living equally
sought what shelter they could. There was really very little
point in moving about, as no one knew where the next
bomb would fall, but they moved anyway, crawling from
low wall to pile of sandbags to ditch to earthworks, pushing
bodies aside to gain the company, however temporary, of
someone living.
   Sasha, being one of the most experienced members of the
garrison, never moved at all, save during the night to visit
the latrines, which no longer existed anyway. Then she had
resettled herself between Anja and Rosa. This pair followed
her example, Anja because she always followed Sasha's
example, Rosa because she was too terrified to move. The
other women did move, constantly, but Sasha let them get
on with it. The town was hit just as constantly – she was
surrounded by screams and moans as well as dead bodies – but
there was no use in giving orders which would probably not
be obeyed anyway. 'Why don't they come?' Rosa moaned.
   'Are you in that much of a hurry to die?'

'Anything would be better than just lying here, being blown to bits.'

'Well, they had better come soon. I have finished my rations, and my canteen is empty.' Sasha cocked her head. Without warning the noise was dying. 'I don't think you are going to have too long to wait.' But she remained still for a few minutes. The bombing was definitely over, at least for the moment. The sirens had stopped screaming, and there were no more earth-shaking *crumps* as the bombs struck home. There was still a great deal of noise, but this was all home grown, as it were: the continuing screams and shouts accompanying the rumble of still collapsing buildings. The sky remained obscured by the great clouds of choking smoke.

They had been here four days, a whole twenty-four hours longer than required. That they had not evacuated the town this morning was because they had realized that they were entirely surrounded. Had Tito, and therefore Tony, known that that would happen? Known that it was *bound* to happen? Well, she supposed, it didn't matter now. They had at least done their duty. She got up. 'On your feet, Anja. Summon the company commanders here.'

Anja scrambled up and hurried off. Rosa also got up, but Sasha held her shoulder and forced her down again. 'You stay put.'

She watched Astzalos coming towards her, stumbling over the rubble scattered across the street. The colonel's uniform was torn and dust-stained; he had lost his hat and his face and moustache were also layered with dust. 'What are your casualties?'

'I have no idea. But they are considerable.'

'You must rally your people. They will come now.'

'My people will be ready for them.'

'This is terrible. Terrible.'

'I agree. It is terrible that we should have lain here like dummies waiting to be killed.'

He glared at her. 'My orders were to hold the town. Hold

up the enemy. I have done this. I have gained four days for the army.'

'You have gained nothing. The Germans have not attacked us because they did not wish to attack us. Don't you realize that if they were in a hurry they would have overrun us two days ago? Whatever they are planning, we are a part of it.'

Astzalos snorted, but decided against further argument. 'You will hold this position for as long as possible.'

'Yes, *sir*.'

Astzalos gave her another glare, and then hurried off. 'Do we have to?' Rosa asked. 'If we have really held them up for four days, can we not now run away?'

'We have to,' Sasha told her, 'because there is nowhere for us to run; the town is surrounded.' Rosa wept. Sasha ignored her, and waited while her company commanders assembled. There were only three left; the other two were dead. 'They will come now,' she said. 'Concentrate your mortar fire on the tanks. Make sure that your machine guns are placed to enfilade the enemy attack, but hold your fire until it will be most effective. How are your ammunition supplies?'

'We have enough for several hours,' someone said.

'We haven't fired any yet,' said another.

'Well, now is your chance.'

'And after?' asked the third woman.

'After what?'

'Well . . .' She flushed.

'There is no after,' Sasha told her. 'There is only now. Make it last as long as you can.'

'And our dead?'

'You can do nothing for them. You can only join them.' She saluted. 'There will be no further orders. I will see you in hell.' She smiled. 'Make sure that you take some Germans with you.'

'How can you say things like that?' Rosa asked.

'Because they are true. There comes a time in life, everyone's life, when they know they are soon to die, when nice words and platitudes and meaningless optimism is an insult to the intelligence. Check your weapon.'

Rosa picked up her rifle. 'It is covered in dust.'

'So clean it up and make sure that it will fire.' Sasha checked her own weapons. Unlike Rosa, she had a tommy gun as well as a rifle, as well as the Luger automatic pistol hanging from her belt. She took a cloth from her haversack to clean them all with the greatest of care. As she did so she heard the grind of engines.

Anja was back, kneeling beside her and peering through the barricade. 'I hear them, but I do not see them.'

'That is because they are attacking the other side.'

There was an explosion of sound, the cracking of rifles being overshadowed by the heavier explosions of the tank cannon. 'Should we not go to help them?' Anja asked.

'No, because that is what they want us to do. That would allow them to come into the town from this direction.' As she spoke there were shots from in front of them. The enemy infantry were moving forward, seeking as much cover as they could find. Rosa levelled her rifle. 'Wait for a target,' Sasha warned.

There was a brief whine and an explosion from behind them. 'Mortars,' Anja said. 'We must fire back.'

'We have no target,' Sasha pointed out.

'Neither have they.'

'They have the whole town, stupid. They do not care who they hit.'

The firing from behind them increased in intensity, and now they could even hear the shouts and screams of the combatants. 'They are in the town!' Anja said.

Sasha chewed her lip. Her orders, and her instincts now that they were surrounded, were to stand fast. But if Astzalos' men, in whom she had little confidence, were to be routed, the enemy could come at *them* from behind. 'Right,' she said.

'Go to B Company and tell Captain Zaitsev to withdraw and take up a position in rear of the men.'

'Yes, ma'am.' Anja stood up, and went down again, without a sound, blood exploding from her shattered head.

Rosa screamed, and Sasha swung round to see the thick line of men emerging from the uneven ground behind the town and advancing at a run, firing as they did so. From their uniforms she recognized them as Bulgarians. 'Fire!' she shouted, levelling her rifle and squeezing the trigger. From all around her the women opened up, mortars exploding, machine guns chattering, rifles cracking, tommy guns rippling, even pistols booming. Many of the attackers fell, but they had got too close under cover, and were at the barricades in a few seconds. They had fixed bayonets, and the steel glittered in the afternoon sunlight. Sasha dropped her rifle and levelled her tommy gun, cutting down three men in her first burst. Rosa also dropped her rifle, but it was to run away. 'Bitch!' Sasha snapped, and turned to shoot her in turn, but was struck a paralysing blow on the back which threw her to the ground beside Anja.

Only half-conscious she heard Rosa shouting, 'No, no, I work for General Wassermann! Take me to General Wassermann!' Then Sasha felt hands tearing at her clothes. That she could feel them and know what they were doing meant that she was not dead, or even badly wounded. In fact she was not wounded at all; she had been struck in the back by a rifle butt. But she wanted to be dead, urgently. She tried to roll and her arms were grasped and pulled above her head, while other men, shrieking and snarling, tore off her pants and then her drawers. Then one of them, having dropped his own pants, came down on her. She uttered a scream of angry outrage, and looked past him at an officer. But he did not seem interested in her, and she had to submit to the eager surges of the man's groin against hers while he seemed to be splitting her in two.

Dimly she heard Rosa's voice, chattering, explaining, and then her rapist was dragged off her and pushed to one side, and the officer stood above her. 'Bastard!' Sasha snarled.

'Is your name Sasha Janitz?' he asked in uncertain Serbo-Croat. Sasha spat at him. 'This woman says that you are her commanding officer,' he said. 'She says you are the commander of all these maenads.'

Sasha strained against the hands holding her wrists, tried to kick against the other hands grasping her ankles. 'She is a major,' Rosa said. She appeared to be unhurt, and had lost none of her clothing. 'There is also a reward for her. You must take her to General Wassermann.'

'One day . . .' Sasha said. The Bulgarian officer gave orders to his men, who lifted Sasha to her feet, but retained their grasp on her arms. Then they forced her forward. 'I need my pants,' she said.

'You are more amusing without them.'

Rosa was also marched forward. The battle had now ended, although there was still the occasional shot. Those of the women who had survived – there were only about fifty of them – were being herded together by the exultant troops. Most looked totally dazed, and from the dishevelled state of their clothing – some, like Sasha, were half-naked – all the attractive ones had been raped. 'What will happen to them?' Rosa asked.

'That is up to General Wassermann. I understand it is his custom to drive tanks over his prisoners.'

Rosa gasped.

Wassermann's car stopped on the outskirts of Bihac; it was surrounded by motorcycle outriders; he did not believe in taking chances with lunatics who might refuse to accept surrender. Mathilde sat beside him, and Halbstadt was in front beside the driver. Mathilde was as calm as ever, but Halbstadt was in a highly nervous state. He had been in that state since the campaign had commenced, simply by his proximity to Wassermann. But thus far he had actually had very little to do. Now his work was about to commence, and it would have to be to Wassermann's satisfaction.

The town was still shrouded in smoke and dust; there was hardly a building left standing. An orderly opened the door, and the general stepped down. Waiting for him were several officers, and these saluted. 'I have to report, Herr General,' said Brigadier-General Weismann, his chief of staff, 'that all resistance has ceased.'

'Excellent. Have the photographers and the movie cameramen move in immediately. I want the record made before there is any cleaning up. In fact, there need be no cleaning up by us. Let the surviving townspeople do it. I assume there are surviving townspeople?'

'Oh, yes, sir. We have seen several.'

'Well, let them get on with it.' He held up his finger. '*After* the record has been made. The Führer will wish to see the film. Now, casualties?'

'We lost seventy-one killed, and one hundred and forty-three wounded.'

Wassermann raised his eyebrows.

'The resistance was very fierce,' Weismann explained.

'And the enemy have been liquidated?'

'Well, sir, we have some prisoners.'

'I said no prisoners were to be taken.'

'Yes, sir. But you see, when we got into the town, well . . . Quite a few of the defenders were women. Some of them quite attractive. So . . .'

'Our people got out of hand. And having raped them could not kill them. And they call themselves soldiers? How many of these women are there?'

'Fifty-seven, sir.'

'Very good. Halbstadt, you will take command of the prisoners.'

'Me, sir?'

'Yes, you. That is why you are here. Use our Waffen people.' He had carefully kept the elite troops of the Fighting

SS out of the battle as a reserve. 'Have them shot in batches of ten. See that it is filmed.'

'Ah . . .' Halbstadt had gone quite white in the face. 'Yes, sir.' He looked desperately at Weismann, who gave a gentle cough.

But if Halbstadt was hoping for help he was mistaken. 'There are two of the women who I am told may be of interest to you, Herr General,' Weismann said.

'I have no interest in any Partisan prisoners save for General Tito, Brigadier-General Davis, and Colonel Fouquet.'

'And the woman Janitz,' Mathilde said in a low voice.

'That is exactly it, sir.'

'You have them?' Wassermann was suddenly alert.

'I have a woman who has been identified to us as a Major Janitz, the commander of the woman's contingent.'

'Janitz,' Mathilde breathed.

'You are sure it is her?'

'She will not admit to it herself, sir. But one of the other women has done so. This woman claims to be in your employ. A Rosa Malic.'

'Rosa?' Wassermann gave a shout of laughter. 'You mean she has survived? She was their prisoner, and survived?'

'I do not think she was their prisoner, sir. She was captured with Janitz and had been taking part in the battle. But she claims she was forced to fight.'

'She would say that. She is a treacherous little bitch. But you are quite right, Weismann. I do wish to see these two women. Have them brought to me. Off you go, Halbstadt. I will deal with this pair personally.' Halbstadt looked as if he wished to say something, then saluted and hurried away. 'Yes?' Wassermann turned his head as an orderly saluted beside him.

'A radio message from General Frasciatti, Herr General. He hopes to have completed the crossing of the Neretva River in three days.'

'Three days?! He should have been across by now.'

'The message continues, sir. It reads, he will complete his concentration within a week after that, and will then seek to make contact with the enemy.'

'Complete his concentration?! In the name of God, is he not concentrated already?' He looked at Weismann. 'Those shitting lumps of spaghetti. All they had to do was maintain themselves in front of the river. How long will it take the Partisans to get there?'

'Not less than a fortnight, sir.'

'A fortnight from when?'

'Well . . . from when they began their march.'

'Which is five days ago! So they are within nine days of the river, and Frasciatti isn't even across yet, and wants another week to concentrate. With allies like that, who needs enemies?'

'I will radio the general and ask for haste as well as his dispositions,' Weismann offered.

'That will do no fucking good if he has let them slip through his fingers. Prepare the men to march.'

'We cannot possibly catch them up, sir. Having given the Partisans such a start, we cannot get there before they engage the Italians. Or escape them.' Wassermann glared at him. 'I do not think you can be held to blame, Herr General. Your dispositions were sound. It is the Italians who have let us down. Not for the first time. However, Frasciatti still has, or should have, two divisions. That is, a considerable numerical superiority. Even if the Partisans do manage to slip through, once he has completed his concentration, he can close on their rear.'

'But they will be going in the direction they want,' Wassermann said. 'Once they cross the river—'

'But there is only one bridge, sir.'

Wassermann frowned at him. 'Frasciatti specifically required that that bridge be left undamaged.'

'For him to get his people across, sir. One assumes that he will hold the bridge in strength.'

'I very much doubt that we can count on that. However . . .'
Wassermann snapped his fingers. 'You are right. Get hold of
Flight Captain Gebhardt and tell him to destroy that bridge.
Both bridges, the railway as well as the road.'

'Ah . . . we will have to wait until the Italians have
completed their crossing.'

'Very good. He can commence bombing in three days.'

'I think we have to wait until we get the all-clear from
General Frasciatti.'

'Why?'

'The Italians may still be using it in three days' time. And
there are the people holding it to be considered. Besides,
might it not be better to wait until the Partisans are committed
to crossing the river? If the bridge is blown too soon, they
may turn away.'

Wassermann gazed at him for several seconds while
Weismann held his breath. Then he said, 'Very well. Gebhardt
will monitor the situation. But once the Partisans are within
forty-eight hours of the river, if they have not by then been
checked by the Italians, I want that bridge blown, regardless
of how many of Frasciatti's people may be on it. At that
time he is also to commence strafing the Partisans, and keep
bombing them until further orders.'

'Ah . . . they are being shadowed by the Cetniks. If they
also become closely engaged with the Italians—'

'I am not going to lose any sleep if a few Italians or
Cetniks get hit by mistake. They caused this fuck-up in the
first place.'

Weismann gulped. 'Am I to inform General Frasciatti of
our intentions?'

'Certainly not. He will only complain. You will inform
General Frasciatti that I am assuming that it is his intention
to engage the enemy at the earliest possible moment, and
either destroy them or hold them until our forces come up.
That will be in ten days' time.'

'Ten days, sir?'

'We are going to have to hurry, Weismann. Have the same message sent to General Mihailovic.'

Weismann hesitated for a moment, then saluted and hurried off.

'There,' Mathilde said. Sasha and Rosa were being brought out of the wreckage of the town by four soldiers. Mathilde got out of the car to stand beside Wassermann. Sasha was still naked from the waist down except for her boots; the fluttering tails of her shirt offered very little protection. But her gaze was as defiant as ever. Rosa was, as always, a bundle of nerves.

'Herr General!' she cried. 'It is so good to see you, so good to be rescued.'

'Why were you fighting with the enemy?' Wassermann asked.

'They made me. I had no choice. But I delivered your message. And the army fled. Is that not what you wished?'

'That is what I wanted. You have done very well, Rosa. But now you have outlived your usefulness. I have no more employment for you.' He glanced at Mathilde. 'Have you any use for her?'

'I have never seen her before in my life, except for that day in your office.'

'Ah. Yes.' He addressed the waiting guards. 'Put her with the other women.'

'You mean we are to be set free?' Rosa asked.

'I am sending you to Captain Halbstadt,' Wassermann told her. 'He will be pleased to see you, and he will tell you what is going to happen to you.' He watched her being marched off, and then turned to Mathilde. 'That should be very amusing. He has been fucking her for the past year.' He looked at Sasha, who waited, her arms held by the two soldiers. 'The famous Sasha Janitz. You seem to have had a busy afternoon.'

Sasha stared at him. 'Do you remember me?' Mathilde asked. She touched the scar on her cheek. 'You gave me this.'

'I did not hit you hard enough,' Sasha said in a low voice.

'So you *can* speak,' Wassermann said. 'Can you also scream?'

'Not for you.'

'We shall see. I assume you do not wish her shot with the others?' he asked Mathilde.

'I am sure someone as famous as Sasha Janitz will have valuable information for us,' Mathilde said.

'Of course. I will let Halbstadt have her.'

'No,' Mathilde said. 'I would like her.' She flushed. 'Do I not deserve that?'

'Why, yes,' Wassermann said thoughtfully. 'But would you know what to do with her?'

'I will think of something.'

'What an exciting thought. Unfortunately, we don't have the time right now. Thanks to the incompetence of those Italian bastards I must get down there with all of my people right away.'

'Do you need me?'

'Yes. Yes, I need you.'

They gazed at each other. Like I need a hole in the head, Mathilde thought. If she had to go through that too often she would go mad. But she had made this bed, and she had to lie in it – certainly if it would give her what she wanted. 'You say it is not going to be a very long campaign. Can she not wait until we are finished?'

Wassermann considered. He remembered how, nearly two years before, he had captured an even more valuable prize: Sandrine Fouquet herself. Then too he had been engaged in a campaign, and thus he had sent her back to Belgrade to await his return. But that had been only a few days before he had been shot. By the time he had recovered she had been long gone, exchanged for Angela. But that could not happen this time. Angela was safely in the governor-general's house, and was not going anywhere. And there was no prospect of any exchange. 'I think that should be possible. You . . .' He pointed at an orderly. 'Send Sergeant Jalmar to me.' The orderly hurried off. 'And you . . .' He addressed the men holding Sasha. 'Bind her arms behind her back. Securely.'

'Who is Sergeant Jalmar?' Mathilde asked.

'Someone I can trust to deliver the woman safely to Ulrich, to be held until our return. He is a homosexual, and is not likely to fall for any of her tricks.'

Mathilde raised her eyebrows. 'I though it was the Führer's command that all homosexuals should be placed in concentration camps.'

Wassermann smiled. 'I am sure that is where Jalmar will wind up. But for the time being he is useful to me.'

'He is not to harm her.'

'He will deliver her to Ulrich with written instructions from me. She will be waiting for you.'

Mathilde stepped past him to stand before Sasha, whose arms were now secured behind her back. 'She must be given something to wear. She is indecent.'

'Jalmar will see to it.'

Mathilde stared at Sasha, who stared back. 'I am going you make you pay for this.' She touched her scar again. 'And for the death of my husband. I am going to make you scream for mercy before you die.'

Sasha spat at her.

Halbstadt watched the women being assembled in front of him. Quite a few of them were clearly dazed and had little idea where they were or what was going to happen to them. Several others were bleeding from various undressed wounds, and others were half naked.

Halbstadt loved women. All women, but certainly those who were young and pretty. All his adult life he had pursued them with relentless lust, aided by the black uniform and his undoubted good looks. He even enjoyed the dangers involved in seeking out married women. Of course he knew now that allowing himself to be seduced by Angela Wassermann had been an unacceptable risk – but what an experience it had been. And it did not appear as if Wassermann was intending to do anything about it, save give him every unpleasant task he could think of. Such as now. The sight of so many exposed legs and breasts, so much fluttering hair, about to be destroyed, made him feel at once sick and sexually aroused.

'It is a shame, sir, isn't it?' asked the sergeant in charge of the firing squad. 'You need to remember what these beauties would do to you, if you were *their* prisoner. Hello, here's another one.'

Halbstadt turned, and looked at Rosa, being marched towards him by two soldiers. Rosa had already seen the women standing against the wall, and knew what was going to happen to them. Now she gave a shriek. 'Erich! Save me!'

Halbstadt looked at the sergeant, who tactfully looked at the sky. Then he addressed the corporal holding Rosa's arm. 'There must be some mistake. This woman works for us.'

'Yes!' Rosa moaned. 'Yes. I work for you.'

'The order was given to me by General Wassermann personally,' the corporal said.

'I must speak with the general,' Halbstadt said. 'Wait for my return, Sergeant.'

'The general has already left, Herr Captain,' the corporal said.

'Damnation. What did he say was to be done with the woman Janitz?'

'She is to be returned to Belgrade.'

'Under whose escort?'

The corporal grinned. 'Sergeant Jalmar.'

Halbstadt considered for a moment, while both NCOs watched him and Rosa trembled. He really did not know what to do. But he knew he could not possibly stand here and watch Rosa being shot to pieces in cold blood. There simply had to be a mistake, or Wassermann had to be given time to cool down. He came to a decision. 'Take this woman to Sergeant Jalmar, and tell him that she also is to be returned to Belgrade, and held under exactly the same conditions as Janitz.'

'Sir!'

'Oh, Erich,' Rosa cried. 'I knew you would save me. But . . . you cannot send me with Janitz. She will kill me.'

'I am doing all I can,' Halbstadt said. 'Corporal, you will tell Sergeant Jalmar that the two women are to be kept apart at all times, and that Janitz is to be handcuffed, at all times.'

'Can't you come with us?' Rosa begged.

'I cannot. As soon as I have finished here, I must rejoin the army. Now go.'

The corporal pulled Rosa's arm, and she reluctantly turned away. Halbstadt drew a deep breath, and turned back to the sergeant. 'Commence firing.'

Hermann Ulrich looked at the order which had just been placed on his desk. Shit, he thought. But it was in Wassermann's own handwriting, even if he concluded that it had been written under some stress: Wassermann was usually meticulous about his grammar, but he had left the 's' off the end of the word 'prisoner,' although the secretary had said there were two of them awaiting him. And the instructions were perfectly clear.

Ulrich sighed; he had a strong sense of déjà vu. In November 1941 he had been sent Sandrine Fouquet, with virtually the same requirement: that she was to be held incommunicado and secretly until Wassermann's return. But his boss had learned some things over the intervening period, and the order had a rider: *Under no circumstances is my wife to be informed of the identity of this prisoner, nor must she ever be allowed to see her or visit her cell.*

Once again the suggestion of stress. It was impossible to decide which of the prisoners he was speaking of. Angela certainly hated her erstwhile maid, even if Rosa had saved her life. But he also clearly remembered how Angela, discovering that Sandrine was in the Gestapo cells, had set out to torment her for being at least partly responsible for her mother's death, and had then fallen hopelessly in love with the beautiful Frenchwoman. Of course there was no chance of Angela, however desperate she was for sexual companionship, forming a relationship with Sasha Janitz. But there was an even more compelling reason for keeping them apart: when Angela had been a prisoner of the Partisans, Janitz had been her gaoler, and had apparently given her a very hard time. What she might do if she ever found her erstwhile tormentor bound and helpless before her did not bear contemplation.

'Sir?' asked the secretary. 'Will you see the prisoners?'

'No,' Ulrich said.

'The woman Malic is requesting an interview.'

'If she is a prisoner by General Wassermann's order, she has no right to request anything. Lock them up. And see that the instructions as regards segregation and secrecy are carried out.'

The Partisan army tramped through the valleys, splashed across streams, looked up at the towering peaks to either side. The weather remained fine, but the very altitude with which they were surrounded brought rain clouds almost every morning.

The advance guard consisted of scouting patrols, although the way ahead seemed clear enough. The main body of the army, the male regiments, followed, with their mortars and machine-guns being drawn by horses; to either side a company was thrown out to act as flank guards. Next came the non-combatants, a huge crowd of women and children, mule-drawn carts carrying the badly wounded, surrounded by those able to walk, and accompanied by other carts loaded with the steadily dwindling store of medical supplies. The doctors were with these. Behind them came the mules drawing the supply wagons. These were guarded by soldiers, because the army was on strict rations; there was little food to be found in these mountains, and no one, not even Tito, knew how long it would be before they reached shelter. Behind the supply wagons came the five German prisoners, also under male guard.

The women brought up the rear, at a distance of about a mile from the centre. Theirs was the most dangerous situation, for although it seemed evident that they had left the Germans and their allies far behind, they knew they were under constant surveillance from the Cetnik patrols, who ranged from side to side, every so often exchanging fire. Tony indeed had to exercise tight control to keep his women from attacking their enemies. 'We can't afford the time,' he told them. He and Sandrine, together with his adjutant, a dark-haired Jewish girl named Judith Hanisch, stayed with the last regiment, where they could exercise the most control. Sandrine was always with Charles in her arms or strapped to her back. The child remained amazingly cheerful, despite the fact that the rest of them were exhausted, their clothes torn and their bodies filthy, even their new boots becoming holed.

Sandrine, of course, indulged in some grumbling; it was her nature. 'We have been walking forever,' she remarked as the command to halt came down the column. Most of the women immediately sank to the ground.

'We have been walking for twelve days,' Tony reminded her.

'And now we are going to walk for another twelve days. I do not believe Montenegro actually exists.'

'Let's worry about the river first. I reckon we should be there in another day or so. In fact . . .' He watched a lieutenant coming down the line towards him.

The boy saluted. 'The general requests your presence, sir.'

'Maybe we're there,' Tony said. 'Mind the fort.'

He accompanied the lieutenant, a long walk through the many exhausted people, most of whom had already fallen asleep, to the head of the column, where Tito waited, surrounded by his senior officers. And frowned at the air of tension. Even Tito's features were tight. 'It appears that you were right, Tony,' he remarked.

'Sir?'

'That little bitch was a plant, after all. A patrol has just come in to say that there is a large Italian force not twenty miles away.'

Five

The Disaster

'We must retreat,' said Brigadier-General Doedjic.
'Retreat where?' asked Brigadier-General Gronic.
'The Germans are too close behind us.'

'We do not know that. They could still be at Bihac. Astzalos' last radio message said they were still holding out.'

'That was a week ago, and we have heard nothing since. Bihac has fallen.'

'General Davis?' Tito asked.

'Have we any idea of the force opposing us?' Tony asked.

'It is considerable. I sent out three probes. One to the right, one to the left, and one straight ahead of us, towards the river. The right-hand probe reports an Italian concentration of at least divisional strength, here, astride the railway line.' He prodded the map. 'It has tanks and artillery. The left-hand probe has made an almost identical report, here.' Another prod.

'And the centre probe?'

'No contact. They have actually reached the railway line. You'll see that in this side it runs roughly parallel to the river for several miles before turning north.'

'That is very obviously a trap,' Doedjic remarked.

'I wonder,' Tony said. 'These are Italian troops. Oh, they are brave enough when face to face with an enemy, but they are not the most energetic of armies, as they have proved against us British in North Africa. There is at least a possibility that in crossing the river, their two divisions have become disconnected, as it were. Thus they will be meaning to link up as soon as possible. If we advance strongly now, in the centre, we may well break through and gain the river before they can complete their concentration.'

'And if it is a trap?' Tito asked.

'Well, sir, I know you are a good chess player. Is there not a saying in chess, that the best way to refute a sacrifice is to accept it?'

'That is one of Grandmaster Tartakower's witticisms,' Gronic said. 'I don't know that he believed it himself. And if we fail to break through . . .'

'We will be destroyed,' Tito said. 'But so will we be destroyed if we remain here, and allow ourselves to be surrounded by the enemy. You know that we are constantly being shadowed by the Cetniks, and the Luftwaffe. But they have not attacked us, although it is obvious that they, or at least the Cetniks, are in some strength. This is clearly because they have been shepherding us, one could say, in the direction General Wassermann wishes us to go: that is, into the arms of the Italians. If, having encountered the Italians, we now turn aside and attempt a march either to east or west, we will be pinned down in the mountains, and surrounded by a huge Axis combination. But if, as General Davis has said, we take our fate into our own hands, and break through the Italians, and thus cross the river and gain Montenegro, we will have thrown his plan back in his face.'

His officers did not look convinced, but no one was going to argue. 'When do we carry out this attack?' Gronic asked.

'Now.'

'But . . . in broad daylight?'

'Yes. It is essential that we move through that gap before it is sealed. Besides, we have established a pattern: move by night, rest by day. That is what they expect us to do, which is why they are not hurrying their concentration. To attack now will take them by surprise.'

'Our people are exhausted.'

'They are tired, General; they have marched all night. But it was only for eight hours. Now is the moment for a supreme effort. Their lives are at stake.' He bent over the map. 'General Gronic, your brigade will form the right wing. Your business will be to repel any move against us by the Italian left-hand division. You will be outnumbered by at least five to one, but while you will move steadily south, you will not let them close on us.' Gronic swallowed, but nodded.

'General Doedjic, you will command the left wing. Your orders are the same: steady movement south while holding off any counter-attacks. The odds against you will be roughly the same. I will command the centre and the main thrust through the gap. I will have the remaining three men's brigades. General Davis, you will continue to command the rearguard with the women's brigade. You will follow my advance in the centre, but your main task will be, firstly, to repel any attempt by the enemy to close in on our rear, and secondly, to round up and bring along all stragglers, protect the non-combatants and wounded, and control as many of the animals as you can. Thank you, gentlemen. The river, and safety, is only a few miles away. Prepare your people, and make sure they have a meal. We move out in two hours' time. I will see you at the river.'

'So there it is,' Tony told his regimental commanders. 'This is an all or nothing business. You must keep your people moving at all times, regardless of casualties, but you must also bring your wounded with you.' He handed the sheet of paper round. 'I will be in personal command of the Foca Regiment, which will bring up the rear. Major Hanisch, you will be with me.'

'That is my regiment,' Sandrine objected.

'No mother is required to fight, except as a last resort.'

'You have just told us that this is the last resort. Anna Spejic will look after Charles. I will command my regiment.'

Tony knew he could not argue before all the other captains and colonels. 'Very good. Feed your women, and prepare to move out in two hours' time.' The women filed away, but he held Sandrine's arm. 'You don't have to,' he said. 'No one will criticize you. No one will dare.'

'That is why I must fight with my regiment. Where I lead, they will follow.'

'Well . . .' He hugged her. 'I'll be glad to have you beside me, as always.'

It took Tony all of the two hours to get the rearguard organized. He had five regiments, each of approximately eight hundred women, and each named after the town where it had originally been recruited.

The Sarajevo Regiment, commanded by one of his most trusted aides, Martina Drozic – she had been with him in the assault on Bihac the previous year – he sent out in front. He knew that the rearguard, because of its extra burden of animals and non-combatants, would inevitably fall behind the assault troops, and he also knew that it was essential to keep in touch. The Bihac Regiment he placed immediately behind Martina's, both to act as the front section of the hollow square he was creating, and to support Martina should an enemy force get between the rearguard and the main body. The Zagreb and Uzice Regiments were thrown out one on either side, while Sandrine's regiment formed the back of the square. In the centre were herded the non-combatant women, who had with them the children, together with the wounded – fortunately there were as yet only a few of them – the supply wagons, drawn by mules, and the five German officers, under their male guards.

Thus far Tony had shown little interest in them, nor was there any reason for him to do so. He did, however, visit them before the march commenced. 'I'm afraid you are in for a hectic couple of days, gentlemen,' he told them.

Amazingly, after well over a month in Partisan hands, they still managed to look remarkably spic and span; they had all shaved that morning, and had clearly breakfasted well. Nor had they lost any of their arrogance. 'You are mad,' said the brigadier. 'You are surrounded by immensely superior forces. You will be wiped out if you do not surrender.'

'Ah, but you see, General, we will be wiped out if we do surrender, so we really have nothing to lose. I would keep your heads down.'

A woman hurried down from the front. 'The army is moving, sir.'

'Very good. Tell Colonel Drozic to follow as closely as she can; under no circumstances is she to lose touch with the rearguard. Tell her also that I am to be informed the very moment she comes into any contact with the enemy.' The woman saluted and hurried back. 'Start your people moving, Major Bladic,' Tony told the commander of the escort, who also had responsibility for the non-combatants. He turned back to the German officers. 'I would hope to see you at the bridge, gentlemen. Please remember that you have given me your parole, and please also bear in mind that my women have orders to shoot anyone attempting to leave the column, or to disrupt its movement in any way.'

He went to the rear, where Sandrine's regiment were sitting or lying on the grass. 'Time to go.'

'They're watching us.'

Tony looked at the half-dozen planes circling above them. 'As long as they watch.'

'And those?'

She pointed, and he levelled his binoculars. There was movement on a low ridge, perhaps half a mile away. 'Still Cetniks.'

'How do you know they are not Italians, closing in?'

'Simply that for them to be Italians they would have to have wings.'

'We can drive them out of there in half an hour.'

'And then half an hour back, and another half an hour to bury your dead and get organized. There's no time for that. We must keep up with the army. So we'll let them come to us, if they wish to. But keep an eye on them.'

She nodded, gave her orders, and her people fell in. 'Will you stay with us?'

'I'll come back to you in an hour or so. I just need to make sure everything is going according to plan.'

She caught his hand for a squeeze. 'Will we make it?'

'We'll make it,' he promised her.

He made his way back to the centre, where the movement was the slowest and most cumbersome, as the wagons creaked, the mules neighed, the wounded groaned, the children shouted, and the women inevitably chattered. But they were moving. He left them and went out on to the open ground to his right, where the flank regiment was proceeding, again slowly, as it was required to keep pace with the centre. 'Nothing yet,' the colonel told him.

'There are Cetniks all around us,' he warned her.

'Just let them come,' she promised him.

It was the same on the left wing, while out in front Martina was chafing at the bit. 'Can't they move faster?'

'I'm afraid not.'

'The enemy must know we're advancing by now.'

'Sure they do. They're working to a plan. And we can only wait to see what it is.' As he spoke they heard the growl of gunfire from in front of them. A ripple of excitement went through the marching women. 'Keep them in hand,' Tony reminded Martina. 'Our business is to get the non-combatants to the river, and prevent the army from being encircled until we do.' She grunted, still itching for action.

Throughout the day the sounds of firing increased, but they

were coming mainly from the flanks; it seemed entirely likely that the Italians had still not closed the gap, and as yet the rearguard had not been engaged. Tony was back with Sandrine's regiment, where she was having difficulty restraining her rear company from firing at the still visible Cetniks, when they saw the planes. 'Stukas!' someone said.

'And Heinkels,' Tony observed.

'They are ignoring us,' Sandrine said.

Certainly the Stukas were flying straight by, although the Partisans, now in open country with only a scattering of trees, had to be clearly visible from the sky. 'They are going after the army,' Tony said. But the aircraft continued out of sight to the south, still without dropping any bombs. Tony began to have an uneasy feeling in the pit of his stomach, but he kept his thoughts to himself. They moved on, crossing the railway line, now definitely closing the battle in front of them. It was late afternoon, and he was with Martina when there came a flurry of shots from behind them. 'Hold your line of march,' he told her, and hurried to the rear, where Sandrine's regiment had ceased marching and assumed a defensive perimeter, facing a large body of troops. 'Guns?' he asked.

'I have not seen any. Or heard any explosions,' Sandrine said. 'But there are a lot of men.'

Tony studied them through his glasses. 'A couple of thousand,' he agreed. 'Cetniks. They have been ordered to slow us down.'

'Now can I attack them?'

'Then they would have achieved their objective. We must get our people to the river.' He squeezed her hand. 'War is not always death and glory.'

'I know,' she said. 'Sometimes it is only death.'

'Just remember, you're taking Charles to safety.'

She made a face, but he knew she would keep her cool, and went forward again. Now the distant firing was very fierce, both from in front of them and to either side, and they could see the explosions of the Italian artillery, but as yet there did not seem to have been any infantry or tank attack, and in front of them, as it was now relatively open country, he could see the Partisan columns pressing onwards towards what looked like a fairly thick wood, which could provide some shelter – if they got there.

'How far to the river?' Martina asked.

'Only a couple of miles. In fact' – he levelled his binoculars – 'I think that wood hides the river valley.' Then he added, 'Shit!'

'What is it?'

'That's where the planes are. They're circling over the valley.'

'But we haven't got there yet.'

'And they don't care if we do. They're bombing the bridge.'

Others had noticed the looming catastrophe. The lead regiment of the rearguard had always, as Tony had ordered, kept in visual contact with the main body, at a distance of about two miles. Now the gap had narrowed to under a mile as the men in front of them came to a halt. 'Hold your ground,' Tony told Martina.

'Then they will attack us.'

'I'm not sure they will, right now. It'll be dark in a couple of hours. Send runners to the flanking regiments and tell them to come in and prepare defensive perimeters. Send another back to Sandrine, and tell her to do the same, but also tell her to place Major Hanisch in command and join you here, because she is required to take command of the brigade until I return.'

'Where are you going?' Martina's voice took on a note of concern.

'To find out where *we* are going. Haste, now.' He kissed her on the cheek. 'Don't worry. I'm coming back.'

*   *   *

He felt singularly exposed as he crossed the open ground to join the main body. The firing had died down, but there were several shell craters and clumps of dead bodies, although, in accordance with Tito's instructions, all the wounded had been carried forward.

When he joined the men he was greeted vociferously while questions were shouted at him. They were totally bewildered. 'You'll receive orders in a little while,' he told them, and hurried on into the wood, which was also crowded with men. On the far side, perhaps a quarter of a mile further, he came up with Tito and his staff, standing on a ridge looking down at the river valley and the wreckage of the bridge, now nothing more than a few stone uprights sticking out of the fast flowing water.

'Are you under attack?' Tito asked, his voice calm as always, although Tony knew his stomach had to be churning with despair.

'Surprisingly, not at the moment.'

'Not so surprising,' Tito said. 'They see no necessity for it. They think we are trapped, and they will let the bombers do as much damage as possible while they wait for Wassermann to come up.' Tony looked up at the now empty sky. 'They've gone off to re-arm,' Tito said. 'They'll be back tomorrow.'

'And then?' someone asked.

'We must get across the river,' said someone else.

'You wish us to swim?' asked another officer.

'We must move to the left, back into Bosnia,' declared the first speaker.

'Against an Italian division? That is what they wish us to do.'

'We are trapped!' Tony watched Tito, who was listening, face impassive as always, but his jaw was tightly clenched. He wanted to speak, but there was nothing to say: if this had been planned by Wassermann, then he was far more able than they had supposed.

A captain staggered up to them, panting: he had clearly

been running for some distance. 'We have found another bridge, General.'

'Ah,' Tito said, and Tony realized that he had been waiting for this report, having obviously sent out a reconnaissance the moment he had seen the bombers and discerned their target. 'How far?'

'A mile downstream.'

'And the bombers did not strike it?' demanded a staff officer.

'I do not think they would have considered it worth their while, sir.'

'What is the matter with it?'

'It is a rope bridge, sir.'

'A *rope* bridge?'

'We are lost!'

'It is not too bad. It is planked. It is the suspension and the rails which are rope.'

'Will it take wheeled transport?' Tito asked.

'No, sir.'

'Mule?'

'I think so, sir.'

Tito looked around the gloomy faces, then up at the darkening sky. 'It will be too risky to attempt a crossing in the dark. The army will bivouac for eight hours. They need the rest, and they will need all their wits tomorrow. We will begin the crossing at four tomorrow morning. It will not be easy, but it must be done, and as quickly as possible. We must be across the river before the main German force gets here. General Davis, at three you will bring forward your non-combatants and wounded. They must cross immediately behind the advance guard. Your brigade will follow. Colonel Martinovic, send a runner to General Doedjic to inform him that he is to move along the river bank for a mile beyond the bridge, and hold his position. Send another runner to General Gronic and tell him that he is now the rearguard of the army, and must hold off the Italians while he retreats towards us.'

'If he is attacked by a division . . .' someone said.

'He will have to do the best he can.'

'My women are already in position, sir,' Tony pointed out.

Tito hesitated for a moment, then nodded. 'Very good. Detach one regiment to escort the non-combatants and the wounded. Form the remainder into a perimeter one mile from the river. I will send two of my regiments to support you. And tell Gronic to link up with you. You must hold your position until the bulk of our people are across.'

Sandrine lay in his arms, Charles between them. They were too exhausted to wish to do more than just enjoy the comfort of each other.

'Are we done?' Sandrine asked.

'We'll make it. Some of us.'

Her hand was tight on his. 'Tony . . .'

'We can't foresee the future, my dearest love. Our best, our *only* hope of survival, is to do our duty without looking to left or right, or worrying about each other, until we are across. Promise me that.'

She sighed. 'And after we are across?'

'We continue fighting.'

He awoke on time, kissed Sandrine, and hurried up the column to get Martina's people moving. Then he went on to the ridge overlooking the river valley. Tito was there with his officers. Below them there was nothing but darkness, but they could hear the rustle of the flowing water. Then the first light appeared over the eastern mountains. 'It is going to be a great day,' Tito said, looking up at the clearing sky. 'That is bad luck. Get your people up, Tony.'

The sun was bright by the time Tony regained the brigade. He hurried through the restless ranks, and rejoined Martina and Sandrine. 'They have stopped attacking,' Sandrine said. 'What is happening?'

'They have one thing in mind; we have another. Sandrine, bring forward the women and children, the wounded and the animals. When you reach the river, you will be given instructions.'

'You mean the bridge is intact?'

'I mean there is a bridge. Hurry, now. Martina, your regiment will support and assist.'

'Hold on,' Sandrine said. 'What are you going to do?'

'Form a perimeter and hold off the enemy until you are across.'

'Oh, no,' she said. 'Oh, no, no, no. Martina can command the evacuation. I am staying with you.'

'You are going to obey orders,' Tony snapped. 'Or I will have you placed under arrest.'

She gazed at him, eyes filling with tears. 'Tony . . .'

He took her in his arms and kissed her. 'I'll be with you in a couple of hours. I promise. Now do your duty.' He ran for the rear, summoning the second regiment to follow him.

Sandrine watched them go. She knew he wanted to save her life, no matter what happened. And there was Charles to think of. But it was impossible to consider life without Tony. She drew a deep breath and gave her orders, telling Martina to stand fast until she had organized the non-combatants. Then she went into the excited and frightened throng, and was surrounded by shouted questions. 'Move out,' she bawled. 'Move out to the river. You will be escorted.' She reached Anna Spejic, who had Charles cradled in her arms.

'You would like to have him back now?' Anna asked.

'Yes. But I cannot take him. Carry him with the rest. I will be with you shortly.'

She told the muleteers to get their animals moving. There was neighing and braying, and barking. And at the rear was the cart in which sat the five German officers. 'We should leave them behind for their friends to find,' the guard sergeant muttered, fingering his pistol.

'Having brought them this far,' Sandrine said. 'Get down,

gentlemen,' she said in German. 'You are going to walk for a while.'

Brigadier-General Marwitz peered at her; she wore no insignia, thus all he saw was a very pretty, heavily armed young woman. 'Who are you?'

'I am Colonel Fouquet, and I am in command. Hurry now.'

'Fouquet?' Major Klostermann climbed out of the cart. 'You are Sandrine Fouquet?'

Sandrine looked at him, and frowned.

'Karl Klostermann.'

'My God!'

'Do you know this woman?' Marwitz inquired.

'She was my brother's fiancée.'

It was the general's turn to say, 'My God!'

'That was before the war,' Sandrine told him. 'I am sorry about your brother, Herr Major. Now you must hurry.'

'Do you know how he died? I know his body was found in Uzice after the first Partisan raid. But nothing more than that.'

'He died well, leading his troops,' Sandrine said.

'You know this?'

'I was there,' Sandrine said. 'I shot him.' Klostermann stared at her with his mouth open. 'Now move out,' Sandrine told him. 'And remember that you are on parole.' He stumbled behind the other officers. 'Keep a close eye on them. *Him* in particular,' she warned the sergeant.

Sandrine hurried back to the front of the column, which was now entering the wood, shepherded by the women of Martina's regiment. The men and women, as always, exchanged quips, but the women were hurried through, to reach the bank of the river. Apart from the hubbub of twenty thousand people all apparently talking at once, the morning was strangely quiet, with no sound of gunfire. 'Turn left,' a major told her. 'Follow the bank. The bridge is not far.'

She marshalled her people, all of whom gazed fearfully at the rushing water, now clearly visible beneath them, and the wreckage of the bridge. She caught her breath when she saw the next bridge. So did Martina. 'We are to cross *that*?'

'It looks like it.'

The space before the bridge was crowded, but Sandrine saw that there were already quite a few men on the far side, and more crossing as she watched, while the narrow bridge swayed to and fro and the water rushed by beneath it. 'Ugh!' Martina commented.

Tito saw them and came through the throng. 'Are your people ready?'

'They're here,' Sandrine said. 'I would not say they are ready.'

'Well, they must start crossing now. Send a senior officer across first, and then get the wounded over. Then the women and children.'

'And the animals?'

'After the women and children.'

'And the prisoners?'

'Them last. Move it.'

'One question, General. How many on the bridge at once?'

'Single file, four feet apart.'

'The bridge will take it?'

Tito's smile was grim. 'We must believe that it is going to.'

He went off, and Sandrine turned to Martina. 'You first.'

'Why me?'

'Because you are my senior officer. There is nothing to be afraid of. Look at all those men on the other side, the men on the bridge now.'

'I am going to be sick,' Martina said. 'I know I am going to be sick.'

Sandrine felt the same way, but she wasn't going to show it. She patted Martina on the shoulder, and went back to marshal the wounded. When she regained the river bank, she saw Martina half-way across, escorted by two soldiers, hanging on to the rope rail with every step. 'Stretcher bearers,' she commanded.

The men went forward, two to a stretcher, followed by the other wounded, some crawling, others holding on to each other for support. So much for single file four feet apart, Sandrine thought. She moved up and down the ranks, chivvying and exhorting. These were all older women, who had taken no part in the fighting of the past two years, and were clearly terrified, but the men guarding the bridgehead, in many cases their husbands or sons, encouraged them and they took cautious steps on to the swaying platform, while the children screamed and clung to them, and their dogs barked; some had already jumped into the water to swim across. It was a slow business, but the bulk of them were over by mid afternoon.

But now they heard the planes. At the same time there was heavy firing from behind them. A wave of anxious sound rippled through the people on the bank, while those on the bridge stopped moving. 'Keep going,' an officer bellowed, and, reluctantly, they resumed shuffling forward. Then the bridge snapped.

It parted close to the far bank, the whole length plummeting down into the water. People screamed as they went in, and to Sandrine's horror she saw that the last of the women and children were amongst them. Above them men were clinging desperately to the ropes. A moan of desperation rose from the men on the north bank, but Tito was instantly there, exhorting and encouraging. He had had the fore-sight to attach loose retaining lines to both ends of the bridge, and using these the men on the south bank slowly dragged it back into position, several risking their lives to crawl out on to spurs of rock to secure the lines. It was impossible to estimate how many people had been thrown into the water, or to guess how many of those might have survived. Nor was it possible to identify any of them.

Sandrine turned round in despair, and listened to the rattle of rifle and machine-gun fire, the boom of the guns, the sharp explosions of the mortars. Tony was fighting for his life back there. All of their lives. While she . . .

She again felt quite sick when she discovered Anna at her elbow, with a bawling Charles. 'Why aren't you with the others?'

'I wished to stay with you.'

'Thank God!' She squeezed her hand and kissed Charles on the cheek. And then chewed her lip. All of the other women and children were across, or had drowned in the river, and the mules were being lined up as the bridge was slowly reconstructed. If it had parted under the weight of human bodies, how could it possibly stand up to the weight of the mules? This was going to be the most dangerous part of the operation, especially as the bombs were starting to fall. At the moment they were not being very accurate – Sandrine supposed that from any height the rope bridge would be just about invisible, although presumably the line of people and animals could be seen. But the masses of people on the bank were clearly visible, and now a bomb exploded amongst them, sending pieces of humanity flying in every direction. 'Shit!' Sandrine said. 'All right, Anna. Take cover under those trees. You'll come with me when I go.'

She found the German officers beside her. 'It would be ironic for us to be blown up by our own bombs,' the general said.

'I think it would be very appropriate,' Sandrine remarked, and turned again as there was an upsurge of noise from the bridge and she saw that one of the mules had got out of control and kicked its way through the rope handrail to go plunging down into the water beneath, carrying its load and its driver with it. Immediately men hurried forward to repair the broken rail, but the thought that

Anna and Charles might have been there made her skin crawl.

'Move up, move up,' shouted a staff officer.

Bombs were now falling all around them. Sandrine remembered what Tony had told her of the beaches of Dunkirk. He had not been there himself, having been wounded and returned to England a fortnight earlier, but several of his friends had been, and had been able to give him a vivid description of what it had been like. But as she recalled, the sand had absorbed a lot of the bombs. Here it was mostly rock, and from the noise the casualties were terrifying. But there was nothing for it. The bombers had gone again and the afternoon was drawing in. All of her people were across. She beckoned Anna to her side, and indicated the bridge to the Germans. 'After you, gentlemen.'

'Should not ladies go first?' asked the brigadier.

'There are no ladies left around here,' she reminded him.

He grimaced, and stepped on to the swaying platform. His officers followed him, Klostermann bringing up the rear. Sandrine looked around her, but there were only men, waiting to follow her. And Anna and Charles.

'Off you go, Colonel,' the staff officer invited.

'You first, Anna. Give me the child.'

Anna was happy to do so, and followed the German officers on to the bridge. Sandrine held Charles close. He was bewildered and frightened by the noise, but he knew her smell, and his face snuggled against her neck. She held him with one hand, grasped the rope rail with the other, stared at Anna's back as she made her way forward, and heard the roar of engines and the *crump* of bombs; the planes were back. Anna checked, looking over her shoulder.

'Keep going,' Sandrine told her.

She moved forward, and was showered with water. A bomb had plunged into the river almost immediately beneath the bridge. Instantly a tremendous ripple travelled along the swaying pathway, sending people staggering to and fro. The man immediately behind Sandrine lost his footing and his grip on the rail, and, falling forward, threw both arms around her waist. His flailing hands struck Charles and swept him from her grasp to go flying down into the water. Sandrine gave a shriek, and without a moment's hesitation ducked under the rail and leapt behind him.

'My God!' a German colonel shouted. 'The babe!'

'The woman,' Karl Klostermann cried, and jumped behind her.

As the light began to fade, the enemy came again. Their tanks were split up, as support for the infantry rather than assault weapons in themselves. So accurate had the Partisans' mortar fire been earlier that four of the iron monsters still burned: these were not panzers, but inferior Italian machines.

But yet the women had been forced back from their original position, leaving too many of their number dead on the ground. Now they had been stiffened by the arrival of three regiments of men, but Tony knew they would not be able to hold on much longer; he calculated that there was a whole division out there, not including the Cetniks. In fact, he had no doubt that had their opponent been Germans, they would have been overrun by now. But neither the Italians nor the Cetniks seemed keen on getting to close quarters. Their ground forces waited for each artillery barrage, and then moved forward a short distance, supported by their tanks, before halting again.

Gronic arrived beside him. 'My men are in position.'

Tony stared at his fellow brigadier in amazement. Gronic had lost his hat, his uniform was torn and bloodstained, his face grimy with dust. Then he realized he could hardly look any different. 'Thank God for that,' he said. 'Are you hurt?'

'I do not believe so. But I have to inform you that my people are exhausted; they have been engaged all day.'

Tony looked along the backs of the women, lying or

crouching behind the slight rise they had taken as their new position. Exhausted, he thought.

'Also,' Gronic went on, 'we have expended our mortar shells, and we are short of ammunition.'

'Join the club. Our mortars have a few left.'

'We must withdraw.'

'We have already done that, more than once. Our orders are to hold a perimeter.'

'I am sending to Tito for instructions.'

'Good luck.'

But at that moment a runner arrived, panting. 'Message from the general, sir.'

'Yes?' Both brigadiers spoke together.

'It is time for you to cross the river.'

'You mean the bridge is still intact?' Tony could hardly believe his ears.

'It has been repaired more than once, sir. But it is still usable. It is too narrow to be hit.'

'Hallelujah! Major Hanisch.'

'The withdrawal must be in good order, sir. The enemy must be kept at bay.'

Tony nodded. 'Take your men out, Gronic. We will cover you.'

Gronic looked embarrassed. 'If we had sufficient ammunition . . .'

'But you do not. To run out of ammunition is no disgrace. Now, go, go go.'

'General?' Judith stood before him. She was also hatless, her dark hair fluttering in the evening breeze. And her blouse was also bloodstained; she had a bandage round her right shoulder.

'Are you all right?'

'Yes, sir.'

'Very good. We are ordered out.'

'Thank God for that, sir.'

'But it is to be a retreat, not a rout. Organize your wounded and send them off. Then return here, and I will give you our order of march.'

She saluted with her left hand, and hurried into the gloom. The gloom, Tony thought, and looked at his watch. It was a quarter to eight. Which in April meant that it would be dark in an hour. Their lifeline; he did not think the Italians would continue to attack in the dark. As for the aircraft, they had again vanished. Perhaps they were merely re-arming. But if they came back in the darkness, while presumably they would be able to see the river they would hardly be able to hit the bridge, having not succeeded in doing so in daylight.

He went forward to join the women immediately in front of him. The firing had died down, although the odd shell still screamed over their heads and burst behind them. 'Will they come again, General?' asked one of the women.

'Not tonight,' he assured her.

'But tomorrow . . . I have only twelve cartridges left.'

'We won't be here tomorrow. Just sit tight.'

The minutes passed with agonizing slowness. The women were not only exhausted, they had run out of food and water as well as ammunition. Yet not one of them had cracked. He thought they had the making of the best troops in the world.

At last Judith came back. 'The wounded are on their way, General.'

'Right. We will withdraw as follows. The Uzice Regiment first. The Sarajevo Regiment second. The Foca Regiment third. The Zagreb Regiment, this one, will bring up the rear. Machine guns and mortars will be dismantled and carried in sections. All movement is to be as quiet as possible, but all commanders must be prepared to halt and face the enemy if we are attacked.'

'Yes, sir. Will you lead?'

'I will stay with this regiment.'

'Yes, sir. I will come back to you.' She vanished into the gloom.

*   *   *

It was ten o'clock before the Zagreb Regiment could move out. Now the night was quiet, although always with the suggestion of distant sound; the enemy were resting, no doubt confident of completing the destruction of the Partisan army in the morning.

And who was to say that their confidence was misplaced? Tony wondered as he led the remnants of his command through the trees to the river bank. Whole swathes had been cut down by the bombs, and dead bodies lay everywhere. It was worse on the bank itself, but at least the numbers of people on the north side had dwindled conspicuously. The bridgehead was being held by Doedjic's brigade.

Tito was with him. 'Well done, Tony. Well done.' the general said.

'How many got across?'

Tito made a face. 'Not enough. And we have had to abandon all of our equipment. But we still have an army.'

'Sandrine?'

Tito sighed. 'There was a panic . . . Well, there have been several panics.'

'Sandrine?' Tony's voice rose an octave.

'She went in.'

Tony stared at him in the darkness, unable to believe his ears. 'And?'

'I do not know what happened to her. Several of the people who went in have been recovered. So . . .'

'But not her, as yet.'

'No. Now take your people across.'

'I will do that, sir. Then I request leave of absence.'

'To go looking for her?'

'Yes, sir.'

Tito hesitated. But he knew how valuable Tony was to his command. 'The army has got to keep moving,' he said. 'We have bought ourselves some time, but it is probably only a matter of hours. You may have four hours.

After that I expect to see you at the head of your brigade.'

The last of the women having crossed, Tony took Martina aside; she had remained at the southern bridgehead all day, directing her people as they came across. 'Do you know what happened?'

'I saw her fall. But Tony, one of the Germans—'

'Those bastards pushed her?'

'No, no. They were in front of her. But one of them went in after her. It was very gallant.'

'And what happened?'

'I do not know. They were both swept away. As for the babe—'

Tony's head jerked. 'The babe?'

'Sandrine was carrying him. They went in together.'

'Right. Take command. I am going down the river.'

'In the dark? You have no chance of finding her.'

'I am going to look. Have all our people rest up. You will receive orders to move out in about four hours. Follow them. I will come back to you.'

She grasped his hand. 'If you do not . . .'

He gave a savage grin and kissed her. 'Don't I always?'

But in the dark it was an impossible task. He made his way along the bank, slipping and falling on the various stones, more than once nearly tumbling into the river himself. He gradually became aware of how weary he was, his exhaustion compounded by his growing despair. He found several people on the bank, and several more bodies. The living he directed back to the army, the dead he examined carefully, but none of them was either Sandrine or a German officer. Nor did he find the body of any child. All gone, he thought. All gone. The two most glorious years of his life, all gone.

After two hours he retraced his steps to join the army. It was all he had left.

Six

The Victors

General Wassermann stood on the banks of the River Neretva, gazed at the water, the wrecked road bridge, and the suddenly famous rope contraption. 'They got across *that*?'

'Well,' said General Frasciatti, 'some of them.'

'How many?'

'We estimate they suffered at least eight thousand casualties.'

'You *estimate*? My information is that the Partisan army numbered well over twenty thousand combat troops. They were to be destroyed, here. And you say they may have suffered the loss of a third of their people? A *third*?'

'It has been a great victory,' Frasciatti protested. 'Any battle in which the casualties inflicted amount to a third of the opposing army is a great victory.'

With great difficulty Wassermann kept his voice under control. 'Our aim was the annihilation of the enemy, not simply to beat him. This is virtually a defeat. Has a pursuit been mounted?'

'No pursuit is possible until the road bridge has been repaired. That bridge, I remind you, Herr General, was destroyed by your bombers.'

'To prevent the enemy's escape. But he did escape, across *that* bridge.' He pointed. 'According to your own estimate he took more than fifteen thousand people across that bridge. And you have not been able to send one.'

'The enemy destroyed the bridge. We repaired it, and I sent a patrol across. And it was fired upon, so they withdrew.'

'After a few shots?'

Frasciatti's face froze. 'Are you impugning the courage of my men? To have attempted a crossing in force under fire would have been to send them to certain death.'

'I am suggesting that you, and your men, are not treating the situation with sufficient urgency, General. Tito still has at least those fifteen thousand effectives. That is a sizeable force. He must be harried to disintegration before he can regroup.'

'My intention is to repair the road bridge, and then take my men back to Albania. I was told this was to be a short, sharp operation. Well, I have ended the campaign by my victory. My men are not equipped for a long campaign against guerillas in these mountains. Besides, I have received orders to return to Albania with all possible haste. I will wish you good day.' He stamped off.

'Italian swine,' Weismann remarked.

'Oh, let them go,' Wassermann said. 'I should never have relied on them in the first place.'

'What do you intend to do?'

'It is sometimes best to float with the tide,' Wassermann said. 'Frasciatti has told us what he intends to do: declare that he has gained a great victory. Well, we will make the same claim. After all, eight thousand Partisans killed represents quite an achievement.'

'But we did not take part in the battle.'

'Oh, come now, Weismann. The Partisans entered the trap because they knew we were coming. Had they known we were *not* coming, they would probably have turned on the Italians and cut them up. And the victory would in any event have been impossible without the Luftwaffe. It is our victory, Weismann. I will make sure that everyone knows that. I will dictate a despatch this evening.'

'And then?'

'In the circumstances, I am entitled to demand more troops.

More German troops. And in the circumstances, I do not think we will be denied reinforcements to finish the job. However, as soon as that bridge is repaired we will cross and see what we can find. We will camp downstream tonight. Away from all of these bodies.'

Wassermann's tent was pitched, but as it was a pleasant spring evening he sat outside to dictate his report. 'One copy to Reichsführer Himmler, one to OKH, and one to General Hartmann,' he told his male secretary. 'In the meantime, has the radio been set up?'

'Yes, Herr General.'

'Very good. I wish to communicate, personally, with the Reichsführer. Set the call up.'

'Yes, Herr General.' The secretary hurried off.

'Schnapps?' Mathilde emerged from the tent carrying a tray, on which there was a bottle and two glasses.

'Thank you.'

She sat in the other chair, poured, and gave him a glass. 'I toast your success. Is it a success?'

'Not as much of one as I would have liked. Our friends are apparently still at large. At least, their bodies have not been found. But they have suffered enormous casualties. I would say they are broken.' He looked up as two men approached. One was Weismann, the other was a caricature of a German officer: his uniform was torn and he had clearly recently been immersed in water; he had neither cap nor belts nor side arm. 'What the devil . . .?'

'This is Major Klostermann, Herr General,' Weismann explained.

'Karl!' Mathilde started to her feet.

'Do you know this man?' Wassermann inquired.

'He was in the troop convoy with us. The Partisans took him away. I presumed he was shot.'

'And now you are here?' Wassermann asked. 'You have been with the Partisan army?'

'Yes, Herr General.'

'And survived?'

'They treated us very well.'

Wassermann did not pick up on the plural. 'And you have escaped? You are to be congratulated. Mathilde, give the major a glass of schnapps. Oh, and one for General Weismann as well.'

Mathilde hurried back to the tent for two more glasses.

'Now, tell me how you got away,' Wassermann invited.

'I jumped off the bridge when we were crossing it.'

'You mean you were not restrained in any way. Not even handcuffed?'

'Well, no, Herr General. They asked for our parole, and we gave it to them.'

'But you broke your word at the first opportunity. That is not the conduct expected of a German officer. But nonetheless I am proud of you. I drink to your health.'

Mathilde had returned and the four of them raised their glasses.

'But that is not how it happened,' Klostermann protested.

'You are not going to say they released you?'

'No, no. But one of their senior women fell off the bridge, and I went in behind her. She was carrying a small child, you see, of which I think she was rather fond. It went in, and she went in, and I went behind her.'

'And no one tried to stop you?'

'Well, no. They thought I was trying to save her from drowning. Well, actually I was.'

'You wished to save a Partisan commander from drowning?'

'Well, actually, she was a Frenchwoman. A rather beautiful Frenchwoman. She also happened to have been my brother's fiancée before the war. She claimed to have shot him in the first battle for Uzice, but I did not believe her. So . . .'

'My God! Fouquet!'

'That was her name, yes. Do you know of her?'

'Know of her? She is one of the three most wanted people in Yugoslavia. And you say you drowned her? I shall recommend you for the Cross.'

'I did not drown her,' Klostermann said coldly. 'It was my intention to save her life.'

'But she *did* drown?'

'No, Herr General. Actually, she did not need my help; she is a very strong swimmer. But she was handicapped by her distress over the child, so I assisted her to the bank.'

'And you have brought her in? But that is brilliant.'

'I did not bring her in, sir. But she released me and let me go.'

'*She* released *you*?'

'Well, sir, when we reached the bank, well . . . She had both a pistol on her belt and a tommy gun slung on her shoulder.'

'And you could not disarm her? You said she was distraught.'

'She was, sir. But she was still too quick for me. I think she came close to killing me. But when I explained that I had been trying to save her, she told me I could swim back across the river and rejoin my comrades.'

Wassermann stared at him for several seconds, while Weismann shuffled his feet uneasily and Mathilde sat down. Then Wassermann pointed. 'You, sir, are both a coward and a traitor. Your behaviour is a disgrace to the Wehrmacht. General Weismann, place this . . . this *creature* under arrest.'

'But . . .' Klostermann tried to speak. 'What is my crime?'

'In the first place, collaborating with and aiding and abetting the enemy while in battle.'

'I felt it was my duty to regain your army if possible, because I have information.'

'Oh, yes? What information?'

'There are four other German officers held captive by the Partisans. Including Brigadier-General Marwitz.'

Wassermann looked at Mathilde, who nodded. 'General

125

Marwitz was in command of the brigade. We assumed that he also had been shot.'

'So he is a prisoner. Well, he had better hope he survives until we catch up with those swine.'

'Surely he should be exchanged?'

'I have no intention of dealing with the Partisans on any subject except at the point of a gun.'

'I protest most strongly, Herr General,' Klostermann said. 'I demand that General Marwitz's situation be forwarded to a higher authority.'

'You *demand*?' Wassermann looked at Weismann, who wagged his eyebrows. 'Take him away.'

Weismann touched Klostermann on the shoulder, and the two officers marched off. 'Can he make trouble?' Mathilde asked.

'He can try. Yes, Otto.'

The secretary stood to attention. 'We have contact with the Reichsführer, Herr General.'

'Ah!' Wassermann hurried to the radio tent. 'Herr Himmler?'

'I will tell him you are there, Herr General,' said the voice on the other end of the signal.

Himmler came on the mike a few moments later. 'Wassermann? What is your situation?'

'I have to report a great victory, Herr Reichsführer. Bihac has been recaptured, and the Partisan army has been annihilated. We have counted eight thousand dead. Our own casualties are virtually nil. Less than a hundred dead, and a few hundred wounded.' He saw no point in reporting the Italian or Cetnik casualties, which he knew had been considerable.

'Eight thousand? I thought there were many more Partisans than that.'

'We are still counting, sir. Although my estimation is that their original numbers were exaggerated. However, a few scattered elements have managed to get down into Montenegro. I would have supposed their final destruction could have been left to the Italians, but I am afraid that General Frasciatti is no longer willing to take part in the campaign. He says he is under orders to withdraw to Albania.'

'I have no doubt that he is under orders to withdraw to Albania,' Himmler said.

'Ah. Well, sir, I am sure we can manage on our own. However, I would like to request a continuance of air support and if possible a division of regular – I mean German – troops to complete the campaign.'

'There will be no reinforcements, Wassermann. And no further air support. The Luftwaffe is being withdrawn from Yugoslavia.'

'But . . . what has happened?'

'What has happened, Wassermann, is that General von Arnim has laid down his arms. Every soldier in North Africa – and we are talking of something like three hundred thousand men – is now a prisoner of the Allies. North Africa is lost.'

Wassermann was speechless.

'We can therefore expect, this summer, an Allied invasion of Fortress Europe. This will take place either in the toe of Italy, or more likely, on the Adriatic coast, perhaps of Italy, but as there are few good harbours on that coast, on the coasts of Yugoslavia and Albania. Albania must be left to the Italians, but the defence of the Dalmatian coast involves the troops under your command. You will redirect them to the north-west, where they will receive their orders. All available aircraft are being relocated to airfields in the south of Italy. All available Wehrmacht units are being redeployed with a view to defending either Italy or the Dalmatian coast. I know that strictly speaking this falls into your command, but that command is now terminated. This has become a Wehrmacht matter, and will be in the hands of OKH.'

'But Herr Reichsführer, the Partisans . . .'

'I congratulate you on your success, Wassermann. And I am not withdrawing you. But if they have been totally denigrated all you have to do is keep an eye on them. For this purpose you may retain your brigade of the Waffen SS. In all other matters you will be under the command of the Wehrmacht. Do not be discouraged. The GOC is to be your own father-in-law.'

'Blintoft?' Wassermann shouted into the mike. 'He was sacked two years ago.'

'He has been recalled because of his knowledge of the country and the people. As were you, Wassermann. Therefore, working together, you should achieve even greater success. Again, my congratulations. Good morning.'

Tito stood with his generals and watched his people trudging by. The Partisans were in surprisingly good spirits. They had survived, although there was not a man or a woman amongst them who had not lost at least a close friend in the Neretva disaster. But they were still a viable fighting force – barely. Only Tito himself, and his closest associates, knew just how serious a defeat they had suffered. Apart from the more than eight thousand casualties, all their heavy equipment was gone, together with most of their spare ammunition. They were no longer capable of fighting even a defensive action, much less considering an offensive, not even another raid like the so successful venture into Serbia only two months before.

Tony watched the last of the rearguard come in. The women were much less happy than the men. They were exhausted; they too had suffered very heavy casualties, and they counted one of those casualties as perhaps more important than all the rest put together. Their commander certainly did.

'Well?' Tito asked.

Tony saluted. 'Nothing of importance. The Italians repaired the rope bridge and sent a patrol across but when we fired on them they withdrew in haste. Now they are working on repairing the road bridge.'

'Wassermann?'

'The Germans and their allies have certainly come up. I

presume Wassermann is with them. But they have merely pitched camp. They are making no attempt to cross the river.'

'And there have been no planes today,' Gronic observed.

'It is a miracle,' Doedjic suggested.

'Miracles usually have a very logical basis,' Tito remarked. 'Whatever that basis is, we must take advantage of it.'

'To do what?' Gronic asked. 'My men are exhausted.'

'We are all exhausted, General. But we must keep moving, into the mountains. We need time to rest and regroup. And hope that we can re-arm.'

'We are too numerous to hide when the planes come again,' Gronic said.

'We will have to split into several smaller groups. But we must keep in close touch. This army must not disintegrate.'

'Keeping them together, in these circumstances and with no prospect of victory, will be very difficult,' Doedjic pointed out.

'That is why you are a general, General: to carry out tasks other men would consider too difficult.' He took Tony aside. 'But it is all true. Your people simply have to re-arm us, Tony.'

'Or your people.'

Tito gave a grim smile. 'I am more inclined to put my faith in London than in Moscow on this matter. When this brigadier arrives, *if* he arrives after what has happened, you simply have to make him believe in us.'

'I will do my best, sir.'

'I know you will.' Tito looked into his eyes. 'Are you all right?'

'I am still capable of fighting and killing. That is all I have left to do, now.'

Tito hesitated, looking as if he would have said more, then changed his mind. 'Your women have fought magnificently,' he said. 'Give them my thanks. Now they may camp for twelve hours.''

Tony joined Martina and Judith. 'Halt the march,' he told them. 'And make camp. Twelve hours.' He looked at his watch. 'We move out at four tomorrow morning. But sentries must be posted, just in case there is a pursuit.'

'Where are we going?' Martina asked.

'Further into those mountains. Count your blessings. It's summer.'

He chose a position removed from the main body of women as his bivouac, and lay down. His clothes were damp, his boots seemed filled with water, but he had no desire to undress. Throughout the preceding two days he had refused to allow himself to rest, because to rest would have meant to think. Now he was so tired he hoped to be able to sink into a deep sleep. But he knew that was not going to be possible.

He had supposed her lost once before. Incredible that that was only eighteen months ago. It seemed like light years away. Then too he had known despair. But then he had been able to share his despair, with Sasha. Now she was also gone. Now . . .

He opened his eyes at a movement close beside him. 'Is there anything I can do for you, General?' Judith asked.

She was offering herself, because she loved him. They all loved him, not so much as a man, but as a symbol, at once of their survival and their victories in the past, but equally of their survival in the future. But none of them could replace Sandrine. 'Thank you, Judith. All I need is a few hours' sleep.'

'Yes, sir.' She turned away, and checked as there was a sudden outburst of noise. 'We are being attacked.'

Tony sat up and reached for his guns, then realized that the sound was not shouts of alarm, but cheers. He scrambled to his feet and watched Martina coming towards him. Walking beside her was Sandrine.

It seemed the entire brigade gathered round Sandrine, to hug her and pat her back, to give her food and water. She had in fact not eaten for two days, as she had desperately tried to catch up with the retreating army, but she was too exhausted to take much sustenance before collapsing into Tony's arms.

He stroked her hair, her shoulders, held her close. Her clothes were in rags, and she was a mass of bruises. But none so severe as the bruise in her mind. 'I held him in my arms,' she said. 'I could feel his heart beating. Then we were swept under the water again. I had to use an arm to get back to the surface. He slipped out. But Klostermann was with us, and he held him, and got us both to the bank. Then he gave Charles to me, and I held him close again. But his heart had stopped.'

Tony could only hold her close as well. This was not something about which he could ask questions. She would tell him whatever she wanted to tell him.

'So I let him go again. I was sitting in the water. I just let him go, and it took him away. Oh, Tony . . .'

She was weeping. He kissed her eyes. 'You did everything you could. You risked your life to save him.'

'So did Klostermann. Tony, I let him go as well. After Charles, I just wanted to be alone. I told him that if he could get back across the river he could rejoin his people. He tried to help me, after I had killed his brother. Did I do wrong?'

'No. You did absolutely right. There is always room for heroism and magnanimity in war. Even this war.'

'But Charles . . .'

'There'll be another Charles. Our very own.'

'When, Tony? When?'

He pulled his head back to look at her.

'Yes,' she said. 'Yes, yes, yes. Now.'

'Aren't you too tired?'

'Not for that.'

Suddenly he wasn't too tired, either.

Mathilde Geisner lay on her face and moaned as the belt

slashed into her bottom. Her fingers were dug into the earth beyond the ground sheet on which she lay, arms outstretched. Her legs were pressed together, her buttocks clenched, but that in no way mitigated the pain of the blows. She panted, and wept, and hated, but she knew better than to attempt to move until he had exhausted himself, and hopefully, his rage.

The blows ceased. Cautiously she turned her head. Wassermann knelt beside her, the belt fallen from his fingers, his chin on his chest. At her movement he raised his head. 'Do you hate me?'

'I am trying to understand you,' she said. 'What has happened that is so terrible? You have been congratulated by Himmler personally. You are still in command . . .'

'Of a single brigade. I am a general. Yesterday I had an army. And those swine are still out there. Keep an eye on them! How am I supposed to do that without aircraft? All that will happen is that they will recruit and re-arm. As for having that fool Blintoft back again . . . I am being treated with contempt.'

Slowly and carefully, Mathilde moved, reaching for her knickers.

'What are you doing?' Wassermann demanded.

'I am going to get dressed.'

'I do not wish you to get dressed. I wish you to lie there. Is your ass not sore?'

'Yes, it is sore.'

'Well, I will rub it for you. Would you not like that?'

Actually, his hand, now gentle, was soothing. 'What will you do now?' she asked.

'I cannot pursue the Partisans with less than five thousand men, no tanks and no aircraft. I cannot even "keep an eye on them". I will return to Belgrade and see if I can knock some sense into Blintoft's head.'

'I will come with you.'

'To get home to Germany?'

'I will stay with you, if you wish.'

'Of course I wish. But you will do this? Despite . . .'

'What you do to me? Yes. If – when we get back to Belgrade, you will let me have Janitz.'

'Ah, Janitz. Yes. You may have Janitz. We will have her together. Perhaps the Partisans will hear her screams even in Montenegro.' He got up and went outside. 'Otto! Has Captain Halbstadt come in yet?'

'He arrived an hour ago, Herr General. He is changing his clothes.'

'Tell him I wish to see him right away.'

'General Mihailovic is also here.'

'I will see him after I have seen Halbstadt.' He went back into the tent. 'Dress yourself.'

Mathilde raised her eyebrows, but obeyed. She was tying her tie when Halbstadt arrived. 'May I offer you my congratulations on your victory, Herr General.'

'Thank you. Yes, it has been complete, as you can see. The enemy has been annihilated. So you will be pleased to know that we are now returning to Belgrade.'

Halbstadt glanced at Mathilde. He wondered if that meant she would soon be available. For all her scarred face, she was a most attractive woman.

'So tell me,' Wassermann said, 'were my orders carried out?'

'Yes, Herr General.'

'The woman Janitz has been sent back to Belgrade, under guard?'

'Yes, sir. And Malic.'

'Eh? I sent Malic to you to be shot.'

'I felt sure there had been a mistake, sir. Malic was working for us.'

'You fool! She was fighting with the Partisans.'

'She said she was forced to do that, sir.'

'And you believed her? You are a cretin, Halbstadt. A cretin! Now you will tell me that you let her go.'

'I did not let her go, sir,' Halbstadt said with dignity. 'I returned her to Major Ulrich with the same instructions as those regarding Janitz: that she was to be held in solitary confinement until your return.'

'Well, then,' Matilde said. 'She is waiting for you, for us. We can deal with her when we deal with Janitz.'

'Herr General!' Mihailovic saluted. Unlike Wassermann, who was, as always, immaculately dressed in his black uniform, the Cetnik leader was travel-stained and untidy.

'Mihailovic,' Wassermann replied with a deliberate lack of courtesy. Mihailovic looked at Mathilde, also seated at the table outside the tent. He knew who she was, but he clearly did not wish her to be present. 'You have something to say?' Wassermann asked.

'I am reporting.'

'Very good. You have reported.'

'You have no orders? Are we not to cross the river and pursue the Partisans?'

'Whether you cross the river or not is up to you. I have no orders for you.'

'But—'

'The campaign is terminated. The Partisans have been annihilated.'

Again Mihailovic glanced at Mathilde. 'In that case, Herr General, our arrangement—'

'That also is terminated.'

Mihailovic stared at him. 'I have done everything you required. My people have suffered very heavy casualties keeping the Partisans on the run.'

Wassermann nodded. 'I accept that.'

'Then—'

'For that reason, I am not placing you under arrest as an enemy of the Reich.' Mihailovic's jaw dropped. 'Nor am I having your people rounded up and shot. But our agreement has been overtaken by events. There are more important matters to be dealt with. There is to be a new commander arriving in a day or so, and he will certainly regard you as an enemy of the Reich. My advice to you is to take your people home and disband them, and keep out of sight. You are dismissed.'

'That is a betrayal of our agreement.'

'Show me this agreement. Do you have it with you?'

'Well, of course I do not. Nothing was written down.'

'Then we have only your opinion that there ever was an agreement. I cannot remember one.'

'You, sir, are—'

Wassermann raised a finger. 'I would not say anything you might regret, or I may have to arrest you after all.'

'I shall protest.'

'By all means do that. Tell me, who are you going to protest to?'

Mihailovic continued to stare at him for several seconds. Then he turned and walked away. 'Was there an agreement?' Mathilde asked.

'I did suggest that if the Cetniks fully supported me, and if the campaign was a success, he might be given a pardon and the right to establish a civilian government in Serbia.'

'Did you have the power to do that?'

'No.'

'Then you never meant to honour your word.'

'I did not give my word. I suggested that it might be possible.'

'And he believed you.'

Wassermann shrugged. 'The man is a fool. Worse, he is a traitor to his country for agreeing to work with us at all.'

'Then should you not have shot him anyway? He will now be your enemy.'

'The Cetniks are finished. I do not think we will hear from them again.'

*   *   *

135

'Papa?' Angela stared at the tall, robust man standing in front of her. Anton von Blintoft had always possessed a commanding figure, a blandly handsome face. Perhaps his hair was greyer than when last he had been in Belgrade, his stomach larger, but he wore his considerable breastful of medal ribbons as proudly as ever, and the Iron Cross First Class with the oak leaves cluster still hung about his neck. Angela had not seen him for four months, not since her last visit to the family home in Baden where he had been living in retirement, and she was delighted that he was looking so well. But to have him here in Belgrade, and wearing uniform . . . 'What has happened?'

'I have been returned to command.' He held his arms open and she went forward for a hug.

'You are again governor-general?'

'No, no.' He smiled past her at General Hartmann, who had accompanied him into the room. 'I am to take command of the Wehrmacht here in Yugoslavia. And beat the British. And the Americans, to be sure.'

'Here in Yugoslavia? I don't understand. There are no British here in Yugoslavia. Except for that devil Davis.'

'Ah, yes. Davis. Him certainly. But there may soon be others. Now tell me, how is Fritz? I gather he has been covering himself in glory.'

'So we are told. As to how he is, I have no idea. I haven't seen him in a month. But I believe he is returning to Belgrade shortly.'

'So I understand. Well, my dear, I have a lot to do. Kurt, it is very good of you to offer me a room while I'm here. But I must get down to headquarters and see the situation for myself. I will see you at dinner.'

'I shall look forward to that. Yes?' Hartmann asked the orderly who had appeared in the doorway.

'Major Ulrich is here, Herr General.'

'You'll excuse me, Anton. This will be some domestic matter. You know what these policemen are like.'

'But I should like to see Ulrich again.'

'And I would like to show you the garden,' Angela said urgently.

'I know what the garden looks like,' her father reminded her. 'You can show it to me later.' Hartmann was already at the door. Blintoft followed him into the office, where Ulrich stood to attention.

'Herr General! My best congratulations.'

'Thank you, Ulrich. Thank you. Let us hope it will not be a poisoned chalice like the last time, eh?'

'I am sure this time you will triumph, Herr General.'

'Why, so am I. *If* they come, eh? If they come.'

'You wanted to see me, Major,' Hartmann said.

'Yes, sir. It is a difficult matter.'

'Well? I am sure it need not be a secret from General von Blintoft.'

'No, no, sir. It concerns a Major Klostermann, who has just arrived in Belgrade under close arrest.'

'Klostermann? The name is not familiar.'

'He has never served in Yugoslavia, sir. Although his brother did, and was killed by the Partisans. This brother was a member of the troop convoy that was overrun by the Partisans in March.'

'And what has he been doing since then?'

'Apparently, he has been a prisoner of the Partisans. You may remember that five senior officers in the convoy were captured.'

'Were they not executed?'

'That was our assumption, sir. But apparently they are all alive, and if Major Klostermann is to be believed, have been very well treated. One of them is the commander of the convoy, Brigadier-General Marwitz.'

'Not Joachim Marwitz?' Blintoft asked.

'I believe so, sir.'

'He was gazetted a few months ago as killed in action.'

'That is what I am explaining, Herr General,' Ulrich said

patiently. He was remembering that Anton von Blintoft had never been very quick on the uptake. 'We assumed that all the officers taken by the Partisans would have been executed. Are you acquainted with General Marwitz, sir?'

'We are old friends. You remember Joachim, Kurt?'

'Yes,' Hartmann agreed. 'And you say he has been a prisoner of the Partisans for several months?'

'We must get him out,' Blintoft said.

'That is what Major Klostermann says,' Ulrich agreed.

'I am confused,' Hartmann said. 'You say Klostermann was also a prisoner of the Partisans, but has escaped, and is now here under arrest. Explain this to me.'

'Well, Herr General, General Wassermann has charged him with collaborating with the enemy. Major Klostermann claims that such collaboration was necessary in order to make his escape.'

'And I would say he is right. Have him released.'

'Yes, sir,' Ulrich said thankfully.

'And General Marwitz?' Blintoft inquired.

'Hm. Yes. That is a difficult one.'

'Surely if they have kept him alive and in good health for so many weeks, they will be prepared to exchange him for one of theirs?'

'I imagine you are right. But they will only exchange him for someone of equal rank, or at least equal importance to them.'

'And we have no one to offer them?'

'Not to my knowledge. Ulrich?'

'Ah . . .' Ulrich considered. Wassermann had to be obeyed when he was in command, because he did not forgive those who he considered had let him down. But now he was no longer in command. Ulrich had no feelings of loyalty towards the man who had been his immediate superior for so long: he heartily disliked him. And how could Wassermann's sadistic desires, which he was obviously intending to indulge on Sasha Janitz and Rosa Malic when he returned to Belgrade, be allowed to matter before the opportunity to free a general, and more importantly, to please *these* two generals?

'Well?' Blinoft demanded. 'You know of someone?'

'I am holding the woman Janitz in my cells at this moment, sir.'

'Who?'

'You would not know her,' Hartmann said. 'She came to the front after you had left Yugoslavia. But she is a close associate of Davis, and has almost as great a reputation as a terrorist. And you say you have her in your cells, Ulrich? When did this happen?'

'Some weeks ago, sir. She was taken prisoner at Bihac.'

'Why was I not informed?'

'Well, sir, she was sent here on General Wassermann's orders to be held in strict secrecy until he returned. He gave the same order regarding the woman Rosa Malic.'

'What a strange thing to do, when the announcement of her capture would have been such a propaganda coup.'

'He is merely being Wassermann,' Blintoft observed. Hartmann looked at him in surprise; he was speaking of his own son-in-law. 'He has done this sort of thing before,' Blintoft explained. 'But what is Rosa doing in our cells with her?'

'Yes, tell us,' Hartmann said. He was well aware that Rosa had been Angela's maid, and that she had given evidence on her mistress's behalf at her murder trial.

'It would appear that she also was taken prisoner at Bihac, fighting with the Partisans. It is unclear whether or not she was acting under cover for General Wassermann. I know he was intending to use her, but I do not know if she betrayed him or not. However, his instructions were that she should be held in the same conditions as Janitz.'

'Have they been, ah, interrogated?'

'No, sir. Those again were General Wassermann's instructions.'

'And you think this woman . . . What did you say her name was?' Blintoft asked.

'Sasha Janitz, Herr General.'

'You think she may be sufficiently important to the Partisans for them to exchange General Marwitz for her? What rank does she hold?'

'She is a major, sir.'

'Hm.'

'But as General Hartmann has said, she is a close associate of Davis and Fouquet, and therefore of Tito himself. She is also famous in her own right as a leader of terrorist activities against the Reich. I think they would be very anxious to have her back, especially as they do not know she is alive and in my hands. All the other prisoners taken at Bihac were shot.'

'It goes against the grain to release such a woman,' Hartmann remarked. 'When you think of the propaganda value of showing her to the press, having her tried and condemned in open court, and then publicly executed . . .'

'If the Partisans think she is dead,' Blintoft said, 'and suddenly learn that she is alive and soon to be publicly executed by us, they will almost certainly execute General Marwitz in retaliation.'

'Yes. Yes, I take your point. Well . . .'

'Besides,' Blintoft said, 'I have a plan.'

Oh, shit, Ulrich thought. He remembered Blintoft's plans from the last time they had worked together, nearly every one of which had gone disastrously wrong, and never more so than the attempt to hijack the last exchange of prisoners. 'I do not think we could risk any, ah, subterfuge with this, Herr General. After what happened at Foca, the Partisans will be on their guard. In any event, it is very unlikely that Tito would personally attend the exchange after that business.'

'I am not thinking of any subterfuge, as you call it, Major. I am considering how we may turn this exchange to our advantage.'

'Well, I will leave you to hammer out the details,'

Hartmann said. 'I take it you are able to contact these people, Ulrich?'

'I think so, sir. We know they listen to our radio broadcasts.'

'Well, then, set it up.'

'There is just one thing, sir.'

'Yes?'

'General Wassermann will shortly be returning to Belgrade. He is under the impression that Janitz and Malic are prisoners of the SS. If they are actually now prisoners of the Wehrmacht, I will require that in writing.' He glanced at Blintoft. 'General Wassermann can be a difficult man.'

'You will have the order, in writing, this afternoon,' Blintoft said. 'As of this moment, Janitz and Malic are prisoners of the Wehrmacht. If General Wassermann raises any objection, refer him to me. I look forward to seeing him again, anyway.'

'And if he decides to go to a higher authority?'

'You mean Reichsführer Himmler? That too can be referred to me. I am taking responsibility for everything to do with the recovery of Brigadier-General Marwitz and his colleagues.'

'Very good, Herr General. Herr General.' Ulrich saluted them in turn and left the room.

'I hope you are not putting yourself in a difficult position, Anton,' Hartmann remarked. 'Himmler appears to have a certain affinity for Wassermann.'

'Herr Himmler,' Blintoft said, 'has no affinity for anyone, not even, in my opinion, for the Führer. He is the coldest fish I have ever encountered. As for Wassermann, I very much doubt he will go to his boss complaining about the loss of a woman he wants less for her political or propaganda importance, or for any information she may have, than for the satisfaction of his own peculiar lusts.' Hartmann scratched his head as he again refleted that this man was speaking of his son-in-law. 'Besides,' Blintoft went on, 'I anticipate his entire support when I outline my plans to him.'

* · * *

Ulrich had gone down the stairs and was in the covered gallery that fronted the palace when he saw Angela coming towards him. 'What is all the fuss?'

'No fuss, Frau Wassermann. Just technical matters. I must say, your father is looking very well.'

'Yes, he is. But to have him here, and with Fritz coming back . . . You will have to tell Max I will not be able to see him for a while.'

'Max is not someone I care to contact.'

'You found him for me. You know where and how to reach him, even if it is in a brothel. Just do it. I will let him know, through you, when it will be safe again.'

'You do realize that one day this vicious little private world of yours is going to blow up in your face?'

'You should listen to the news,' Angela recommended. 'Our public world is likely to blow up even quicker than that. So let me get on with my private vice as long as I can.'

'And then?'

'I think we will all have to die laughing, Hermann.'

Seven

The Trap

'Ah, Ulrich,' Wassermann said, stripping off his gloves as he entered the office. 'Is everything under control?'

'I think so, Herr General.' Ulrich gave a brief bow in the direction of Mathilde, who had followed Wassermann in. 'May I congratulate you on your triumph?'

'You may. However, my campaign is not yet over; its completion has been delayed by the unfortunate events in North Africa. So I am afraid you will have to put up with me for a little while yet.'

'Of course, sir. Have you been to the palace yet?'

'No, no. I came straight here. There is a lot to be done.'

'Your father-in-law is anxious to speak with you.'

'Well, he can wait. Now, I take it you have Janitz and Rosa downstairs?'

'Well, sir, yes and no.'

Ulrich had come round the desk to greet his superior; Wassermann now seated himself behind it. 'What the devil do you mean by that stupid answer?'

Ulrich did not take offence. 'What I mean is, Herr General, that while Janitz and Rosa are in my cells, this is a matter of convenience. They are no longer my prisoners. Or yours.'

'Have you gone mad? Whose prisoners are they?'

'They are claimed by the Wehrmacht.'

'They are *what*? What does the Wehrmacht have to do with it?'

143

'I think you should take the matter up with the GOC, Herr General. Your father-in-law.'

'That bumbling oaf!' Wassermann flushed, and looked at the open door.

'I have the written order here.' Ulrich took the paper from the desk.

Wassermann scanned it. 'What does he mean, he requires these prisoners for military matters? What military matters?'

'I understand that he intends to offer Janitz to the Partisans in exchange for Brigadier-General Marwitz and the other officers held by them.'

'How did he learn about that?'

'Major Klostermann brought in the information.'

'That swine? I suppose you are going to tell me that he is not under our jurisdiction either. Even if he is in our cells.'

'That is exactly correct, sir. Actually, he is not in our cells at all. On General Hartmann's order the charges against him were dropped, and he has been returned to duty.'

For a moment Wassermann was speechless. Then he shouted, 'Get out. Out!' Ulrich clicked his heels. Mathilde waited for further orders. 'You stay,' Wassermann said. 'I am going to sort this out.'

'As you wish, Herr General.' Ulrich left the room.

'Will the Partisans make the exchange?' Mathilde asked.

'Of course they will, if they are given the opportunity. Janitz is much more important to them than an itinerant brigadier-general is to us.'

'You mean you will just let her walk away, unharmed, after . . .' She touched her cheek.

'What she did to you,' Wassermann pointed out, 'is the very least of the crimes of which she is guilty. But she is not going anywhere, except to the hangman's noose, when we are finished with her.' He picked up the phone. 'This is General Wassermann. I wish to place a call to Berlin. To Reichsführer Himmler, personally.'

'I will leave you to it,' Mathilde said.

'Where are you going?'

'I wish to have a bath. I will be at my quarters. I presume they are still mine?'

'Of course they are.'

'Well, then, are you allowed to enter the women's hostel?'

'I am allowed to enter wherever I please. I am General Wassermann.'

'Then I will wait for you to come to me, and bring me up to date.' She closed the door behind her, and stood there for a moment. She was unsure of her emotions. But the main one was simmering anger. That anger had simmered for more than three months now. Three months ago she had been a happily married woman, who had spent a pleasant year in Athens, delving into antiquity, enjoying the pleasure of having her husband come home to her every evening instead of spending months away campaigning, but yet looking forward to returning to the fatherland, the company of her parents and her sister. And on one afternoon her life had been torn apart, her husband blown into unrecognizable fragments of flesh and bone, her own beauty destroyed forever. She had sought only vengeance. And to obtain it she had allowed herself to become the plaything of a vicious monster. If after all that she was going to be robbed of her prey . . .

Ulrich was nowhere to be seen. She knew the layout of the building very well, having been shown it by Wassermann before the campaign had begun. She went down the stairs to the ground floor. Secretaries and Gestapo agents looked at her curiously, but as they all knew who she was, no one attempted to question her, or prevent her from going wherever she chose.

She went down the next flight of stairs into the cell level, nostrils dilating to the strong smell of disinfectant. The steps debouched into a lobby which on her left gave access to the tram, the dreaded room where those suspected of crimes against the Reich were kept to await interrogation, forced to sit bolt upright on backless benches for hours, unable to eat or drink or even more for fear of a beating, their misery accentuated by their apprehension of the horror that was just along the corridor.

There were seven people in the tram this morning, and two guards. One of these came to the door. 'Do you wish something, Fräulein?'

'You may address me as Frau Geisner,' Mathilde said frigidly. 'Do you know who I am?'

'Frau Geisner.' The guard clicked to attention. 'General Wassermann's secretary.'

'Very good. Are you in charge?'

'I am in charge of the tram.'

'Who is in charge of the cells?'

'The duty warder.'

'Summon him.'

The guard hesitated, then went to a wall telephone and made a call while he eyed Mathilde's legs and her considerable bust, across which the white shirt stretched tightly. What would he give to have her in the tram, he thought. Generals had all the luck. A woman hurried towards her. She was a blonde, tall and well built, her yellow hair pulled back and secured in a single long swathe by a ribbon. She wore uniform, and although a thick rubber truncheon hung from her belt, she did not look the least vicious. In fact she was quite pretty, save for a curious flatness to her eyes. 'Frau Geisner?'

'I wish to speak with the prisoner Janitz.'

The woman gave the guard an anxious glance, and then retreated several steps. Mathilde went with her. 'No one is supposed to know she is here,' the woman whispered. 'Those were General Wassermann's orders.'

'But I am General Wassermann's secretary,' Mathilde pointed out. 'I am carrying out his orders.'

'Ah. Of course.' The woman led the way along the corridor, past a succession of closed doors. Each door had a small flap covering a spyhole. From one or two there came shouts or cries or groans, but most were quiet.

'What is your name?' Mathilde asked.

'I am Karin.'

'Well, Karin, I may need your help.'

Karin half-turned her head.

'I am to interrogate this prisoner.'

'Ah.'

'But I do not know the layout of this prison. Is there an adequate punishment cell?'

'Our punishment cell is very adequate, Frau Geisner. It contains everything you may need. You wish to have the woman taken there?'

'I will take her there myself. With your assistance.'

'We will require more assistance.'

'To deal with one woman?'

'She is listed as very dangerous. It is better to be safe than sorry. This is the cell. I must ask you not to enter until I return. I will only be a moment.'

She hurried off. Mathilde watched her go round the corner, then opened the little shutter. The cell was illuminated by a single naked and bright electric bulb, dangling from the ceiling, at a height beyond the reach of any normal human being. The furniture consisted of an iron cot with a mattress on it – there were no bedclothes – and a latrine bucket. Sasha lay on the bed. She wore one of the shapeless blue prison gowns, and was on her back, gazing at the ceiling. Clearly Wassermann's instructions had been carefully obeyed; there was no evidence that she had suffered any ill treatment – yet. She was awake, and had heard the slight scrape of the shutter being moved. Presumably she had become accustomed to being overlooked, for her head did not move, although her eyes did.

Karin returned with two other women, each as large and powerful-looking as herself; they also wore uniform and were armed with rubber truncheons. 'We will take her out now,' she said. 'Do you wish to come in?'

'I will wait here.' Suddenly Mathilde had no wish to look into those eyes. She felt that she was in the presence of a power greater than herself. But a power which could be destroyed. Which would be destroyed, in a few minutes.

Karin opened the door. Mathilde stood behind it, listening. 'Up you get, Janitz,' Karin said.

'Where am I going?' Her voice was quiet.

'You are to be asked some questions.'

'Only Wassermann can ask me questions.'

'Do you think you make the rules here? Up!'

There was a rustle as Sasha stood up. Mathilde could imagine her, sizing up the situation, estimating her chances, and no doubt realizing that even she could not take on three women, each of whom was as big and no doubt as strong as herself. A moment later there was a click as her wrists were cuffed. Karin came out first. Sasha followed, the other two women behind her. Sasha half-turned her head, glancing at Mathilde, and then turned away, her features stiffening. She was realizing her position.

It was only a short walk to the punishment cell. Karin unlocked the door, they entered, and she closed it behind them. Mathilde caught her breath as she looked at the various objects hanging from hooks on the walls, the waiting tables and chairs; some of the chairs lacked seats so that anyone seated in them, naked, would be utterly exposed. Then she looked at the hooks suspended from the ceiling, the coiled whips. Karin had been watching her expression. 'These are all yours to play with, Frau Geisner. Tell us what you wish done with her.' She smiled. 'How you would like her positioned.'

Mathilde licked her lips, and Karin's smile became contemptuous; this woman was clearly an innocent. 'Well, you see,' she said, 'we can put her on that frame over there, and you can burn her. Is she to be put on trial?' Mathilde gazed at her. 'If she is to be put on trial, in public,' Karin explained, 'she cannot be visibly harmed. You must use electricity. But that can be most amusing. Or you can put her in the chair,

148

and play with her. That can be very effective with women who, shall I say, have little experience of life. Their shame is as effective as their pain. But somehow, I do not think this one would feel any shame. Do you like playing with women, Frau Geisner?'

Mathilde continued to stare at her, and Karin realized she had no idea what she was talking about. 'And then, of course, there is the lash. Our male superiors have the idea that this is the most effective way of dealing with women. It leaves considerable marking, of course, but if there is sufficient time between the interrogation and the trial these are usually faded.' She paused, questioningly.

'I will use the lash,' Mathilde said in a low voice.

'You would not like to try something else first?'

'I will use the lash,' Mathilde repeated.

Karin shrugged. 'I am going to release the handcuffs,' she told Sasha. 'If you attempt to resist us, we will beat you to a pulp.'

Sasha looked at the two other women, who had drawn the truncheons from their belts. 'Are you not going to beat me to a pulp anyway?'

'I do not think so. I think Frau Geisner just means to tickle you up a little.' She unlocked the handcuffs and took them off. The cell was suddenly filled with tension, but Sasha did not move. 'Take off the dress,' Karin commanded. Sasha unbuttoned the dress and let it slide from her shoulders. She wore nothing underneath. 'Is she not a fine figure of a woman?' Karin asked. 'But she will look even better when she is stretched. Wrists.'

Sasha extended her wrists and the handcuffs were replaced, this time in front of her. One of the women went to the wall and released a rope from round a cleat, and one of the hooks was lowered. Karin extended Sasha's arms above her head, and lifted the handcuffs over the hook. The woman pulled on the rope and Sasha was lifted up until she was on tiptoe. Then the rope was made fast, leaving her helpless, able to move only her feet. The other woman handed Mathilde a whip, a long length of thin leather with a solid stock. 'There,' Karin said. 'Pretty as a picture.' She ran her hands over Sasha's breasts, squeezed her pubes.

'Stop that,' Mathilde snapped. 'You are being disgusting.'

Karin raised her eyebrows, but stepped away. 'When you strike her,' she said, 'she will move. You must wait for the movement to cease before you strike her again. If the lash goes round in front, you could do her a serious injury.'

'Get out,' Mathilde said. 'All of you.'

Karin looked at her fellow wardresses, then shrugged. 'We will be outside if you need us.'

The door closed behind them, and Sasha and Mathilde gazed at each other. 'You are an innocent,' Sasha remarked.

'And you are a bitch.'

'Get on with it,' Sasha said.

Her muscles were tensed. Mathilde drew a deep breath, then thrust the haft of the whip into Sasha's stomach. Sasha gasped and was forcibly relaxed; as she could not bend her body, her knees came up, one after the other. Mathilde stepped behind her, retreating a distance of six feet, and swung the whip. The lash uncoiled, and the end slashed across Sasha's buttocks. She gave a shudder, but uttered no sound. 'Scream,' Mathilde said. 'I want to hear you scream.'

'Fuck off,' Sasha told her.

Mathilde swung the whip again, and again Sasha shuddered, while this time an involuntary moan escaped her lips. 'You will scream,' Mathilde told her. 'You will beg me for mercy, if I have to take the skin from your ass.'

She swung the whip again, and almost lost her balance as the thong was grasped from her hand before it could come forward. 'What are you doing?' Ulrich asked.

Mathilde was staggering; she had not even heard the door open. Now she realized that the three gaolers were standing there, looking highly amused. 'I am dealing with this bitch,' she said. 'Let go.'

150

'This woman is not your prisoner.' Still holding the thong in his gloved hand Ulrich walked past her to look at the red weals on Sasha's flesh. 'You are under arrest,' he said.

Sasha looked at her. 'You should have killed me while you had the chance,' she remarked.

'Who is this woman, anyway?' Anton von Blintoft asked, looking from face to face. Ulrich waited for Wassermann to speak.

'I have been employing her as my secretary,' Wassermann explained. Having been reminded yet again by Himmler that he was now under his father-in-law's command, despite being a general in the SS, he knew he had to pick his way carefully: he could never be certain just how much support the Reichsführer would be prepared to give him. Ulrich looked at the ceiling. 'She has suffered greatly,' Wassermann went on. 'Her husband was killed by the Partisans, and she herself was beaten up and disfigured by Janitz. You cannot condemn her for bearing a grudge.'

'I do not condemn her for bearing a grudge,' Blintoft said. 'But her personal feelings cannot be allowed to interfere with the business of the Reich. Is Janitz badly hurt?'

'I would not say so, Herr General,' Ulrich said. 'In a week or so there will hardly be a mark.'

'Very good. You will set in motion my instructions. Dismissed.'

'Heil Hitler.' Ulrich left the office.

'May I ask what is going on?' Wassermann inquired. 'When will Janitz be executed?'

'Janitz is not going to be executed, not at this time anyway. She is going to be used as the bait of a trap which will complete the destruction of your friend Tito. Is that not what you wish to happen?'

Wassermann snorted. 'You are going to attempt to exchange her for our officers held by the Partisans?'

'I do not think that the word "attempt" comes into it. I have no doubt at all that Tito will want one of his most famous people back.'

'And you are going to try another trap? With respect, Anton, Tito is not a fool.'

'I am sure he is not. But then, neither am I.'

Wassermann gazed at him for several seconds. He supposed that self-delusion was the greatest weakness a man could have. 'Then what is your plan?'

'It is not necessary for you to know that, Fritz. You will be informed at an appropriate time.'

'But Ulrich, my subordinate, knows of it.'

'Ulrich is setting it up. And he is not your subordinate, Fritz. He is mine. At the present time you are holding a field command.'

'One brigade?'

'I intend to increase your responsibilities. But that depends on what develops. Now why don't you go and see Angela. I am sure she has missed you terribly this last month.'

'And Frau Geisner?'

'Is she that important to you?'

'Yes, she is.'

Blintoft regarded him for several moments. 'More important than Angela?'

'Angela is my wife. Mathilde . . .'

'Is your mistress. I do not wish to pry, or be indelicate, but . . .'

'She does things for me. Things that Angela would never contemplate. She understands me, and is sympathetic.'

'And I presume that Angela does not know of her existence?'

'I have not told her.'

'Well, I suppose you are entitled to obtain satisfaction where and how you can. Just keep her out of sight, and make sure that she does not again interfere with my plans.'

'I have been humiliated,' Mathilde complained.

'And I have been humiliated – by your action,' Wassermann told her. 'All of us, even I, have to subordinate our private wishes to the good of the Reich. Why did you not tell me what you were going to do?'

'I thought you would forbid me.'

'As I would have done. You must have patience. We are going to beat these thugs. You will have her back again.'

'Then, as you say, I will be patient.'

'And you will stay here with me?'

'I have nowhere else I wish to be.'

Tito stood with Tony, Sandrine, and several other of his officers to watch the group of men approaching them through the trees. The visitors were surrounded by a company of Partisan women, but they were not anticipating trouble; they had had the newcomers under surveillance for several days. Now Tony went forward. 'Pete! Welcome back.'

Colonel Peter Johnstone clasped his hand. The two were old friends, having served together in the British embassy in Belgrade before the invasion, and Johnstone having already acted as a liaison officer with Tito's men since then. 'I'd like you to meet Brigadier Wharton.'

Tony saluted. 'Welcome to Yugoslavia, sir.'

Wharton, a heavy-set man who wore a moustache, returned the salute and then shook hands. 'I was told we hold the same rank.'

Tony smiled. 'In this army. I don't think it has been gazetted by Whitehall yet.'

'If everything I have heard is true, it should have been. And as we happen to be in this army, I'd like you to call me Hugh. Is that the man himself?'

'Indeed it is.'

Tony led the British party across to the waiting Yugoslavs, while Wharton looked around himself at the towering mountains to either side. 'I would not describe this as good campaigning country.'

'That's why we're here. At the moment, we are not in good campaigning shape ourselves. General Tito, I would like to present Brigadier Wharton.'

Tito shook hands. 'Have you had a good journey?'

Wharton replied in passable Serbo-Croat. 'Until we reached Yugoslavia.'

'You were not seasick, eh?'

'We spent most of the time under the sea, not on it. But this country makes a man wish he was a bit more fit.'

Tito grinned. 'We will make you fit. My officers.'

Wharton shook hands with each in turn, pausing appreciatively in front of Sandrine. 'The famous Mademoiselle Fouquet.'

'The famous *Colonel* Fouquet,' she countered.

'Touché,' He turned to Tito. 'Is your headquarters far?'

'My headquarters are right there.' Tito pointed to the black opening of a cave in the hillside, and grinned at the brigadier's obvious consternation. 'It has the all mod cons, as you would say, Brigadier. Running water, shelter from the weather . . . and it cannot be bombed.'

All the British party, save for Johnstone, were taken aback by the primitiveness of their surroundings, and even more to discover that the soldiers guarding the cave were all women. But they had to admit that the cave provided safety. It covered a large network of passageways and isolated chambers, and enabled a considerable force to take shelter; as Tito had promised, it was even serviced by a rushing underground stream.

Meanwhile the Partisans were impressed in turn with the sophistication of the radio equipment their guests had brought with them. 'It is possible to do almost anything with radio nowadays,' Johnstone explained.

Wharton wished to get down to business that very night. 'First of all,' he said, 'I have tremendous news. Yesterday morning the Allies landed in Sicily.'

'Sicily?' The Partisan officers spoke together.

'Italy is the soft underbelly of the Axis,' Wharton explained. 'The occupation of Sicily is the stepping stone to the invasion of the mainland.' He looked round their faces. 'I had supposed you would be pleased.'

'We had supposed that Yugoslavia, and Greece and Albania, populated by violently anti-Fascist groups, are the true soft underbelly,' Tony said.

'Well, I can tell you that your point of view has considerable support, even that of the PM himself. Unfortunately, we are no longer our own masters. This war has become an American show, and we must dance to their tune.'

'Does this mean that we are to be left out in the cold yet again?' Tito asked, his face grim.

'No. There is now a considerable Axis force concentrated in Yugoslavia, and we want them to stay there. Or here. That is, we wish your people to keep the beast occupied.'

'To do that we need supply, on a regular basis.'

'Of course. It is my business to tell London your requirements. But there are some questions I need answered.'

'They will be.'

'How many men do you have under arms?'

'There are about twelve thousand men and women hidden in these hills. I'm afraid that, since our disaster at the Neretva, we suffered sizeable desertions. But they will come back.'

'I was speaking of effectives.'

'I have told you, twelve thousand.'

'But you included your womenfolk in that figure.'

'I included my female effectives.'

Wharton looked at Tony. 'In these mountains I would back my women against the Brigade of Guards,' Tony said.

'Hm. Well, I'm sure you're right. But I think it would be a good idea not to inform London of that.'

'But do you not have women soldiers in the British army?' Tito asked.

'Yes, we do. They drive cars and carry out secretarial work. The idea of any of them ever coming under fire would drive the Ministry of Defence wild. As for the possibility of one of them getting hit . . . Have any of your women ever been hit?' Tony looked at Sandrine, who burst out laughing. 'Have I said something silly?' Wharton asked.

'I suppose you have,' Sandrine said. 'With respect, sir. Since the invasion my women have suffered over a thousand casualties. I am speaking of the dead, not the wounded. Nor have I included those taken prisoner and shot in cold blood by the Nazis.'

'My God!' Wharton commented. 'Well . . .'

'As you say, we will keep that dark until the war is over,' Tito said. 'Then they will all be heroines.'

'Yes. Well . . . You must give me a list of your priority requirements.'

'Anti-aircraft guns. Anti-tank guns – I understand that these can sometimes be alternated. Heavy artillery. Mortars. Tanks. And of course, rifles and ammunition. Modern rifles.'

Wharton nodded. 'I'll get on to London tomorrow.'

'Now tell me, Brigadier, are you going to visit Mihailovic when you leave here?'

'It is not my intention to leave here for a while. With your permission, of course. London would like me to observe your activities at first hand. Again, with your permission.'

'You are welcome, although I cannot promise you a very comfortable existence. But Mihailovic?'

'A mission is being sent to General Mihailovic, yes.'

'He is a traitor, who very recently was in arms against us.'

Wharton nodded. 'I would like you to put that in writing. I may tell you that London is, shall I say, disappointed in General Mihailovic's recent record. But we come back to the Americans again. They regard Mihailovic as still being the legitimate leader of the Yugoslav resistance, as he remains, of course, the representative of the government-in-exile. They are also suspicious of your, ah, political affiliations.'

'I thought we were on the same side at the moment.'

'At the moment, certainly. But . . . things change.'

'And they do not want a Communist Yugoslavia, eh? It will happen.'

'After the war, perhaps. Let's get there first. Don't mis-understand me, General. I am here to help you. I intend to do that in every way that I can.'

'Even if I tell you that if I ever lay hands on Mihailovic, I intend to hang him?'

'After a trial, I hope. I will also hope that you do not lay hands on him until the war is over. But yes, you can count on my support.' He looked round as a woman orderly entered the chamber in which they were seated.

'Yes?' Tito asked.

'Belgrade is calling us, sir. Again.'

'You're in contact with Belgrade?' Wharton was again surprised.

'We listen,' Tito said. 'But we do not engage them in conversation. They have nothing to say to us, save to call for our surrender. And if we reply, for long enough, they will endeavour to trace our signal and discover where we are. So what are they saying now?' he asked the operator.

'It is the same as before. They say it is a most important message. But this time they are being more explicit. They say the message has to do with Sasha Janitz.'

'What?' Sandrine started to her feet.

'Sasha is dead,' Tony said. 'She was killed at Bihac.'

'They say she is alive,' the woman said. 'And in their hands.'

'Sasha!' Sandrine cried. 'My God, what will they have done to her?'

Wharton was looking utterly bewildered. 'Major Janitz is one of the heroines of the resistance,' Johnstone told him in a low voice.

'Belgrade says she is unharmed. They wish to exchange her for Brigadier-General Marwitz and the other German prisoners.'

Wharton looked more amazed yet. 'You are holding German prisoners?'

'It does happen,' Tony said.

'We supposed you did not take prisoners.'

'It does happen,' Tony said again. 'We took these men several months ago and held them, just in case they ever came in handy for an exchange. Up till now, the Germans have had nothing to offer us. Now . . .' He looked at Tito.

'They are also offering to exchange the woman Malic,' the operator said.

'Do you mean she survived as well?' Sandrine asked.

'It is a trap,' one of the Partisan staff officers said. 'You remember the last time, when they tried to ambush us.'

Tito stroked his chin, and looked at Tony. 'What do you think?'

'That it probably is a trap. But if Sasha is alive, and there is a possibility of getting her back . . .'

'They wish to discover your whereabouts, sir,' the staff officer persisted.

'I am sure you are right,' Tito said. 'Tony?'

'We'll make sure they don't,' Tony said. 'We'll set up the exchange at least twenty miles from here, and you will have nothing to do with it.'

'Neither will you,' Tito said. 'Or Sandrine.'

'But, sir—'

'I do not propose to lose either of you in an attempt to get Sasha back. You will send one of your subordinate commanders, with a strong escort. They will make the exchange, and then return here. If they are shadowed by enemy aircraft, they will take shelter until the aircraft are gone.' He turned to the operator. 'Reply to that signal, but be very brief. Say that we will accept the exchange, and will inform them of the location later. Warn them that if there is any attempt at treachery, their officers will immediately be executed.' The woman saluted and hurried off. 'Now, gentlemen,' Tito said, 'let us have dinner.'

'Come in, gentlemen. Come in,' Anton von Blintoft said genially.

Ulrich and Halbstadt filed into the office, Halbstadt looking both bemused and apprehensive.

'I wish you to meet Colonel Stadtler, of the Parachute Brigade,' Blintoft said. 'Colonel Stadtler has been seconded to my command for a single operation. This will be called Case Ratcatcher. Major Klostermann you already know. Sit down, sit down.' He seated himself behind his desk, and the four officers arranged themselves in front of it. 'Now, gentlemen, this meeting is top secret. Not a word said here today is to be divulged to anyone until Ratcatcher is successfully completed.' The general tapped the sheet of paper on his desk. 'Is this genuine, in your opinion, Ulrich?'

'I would say it is genuine, Herr General.'

'Very good. This place . . .' He peered at the map. 'Pisnic. Do you suppose that is where Tito has his headquarters?'

'I would say definitely not. I would anticipate that his headquarters are a considerable distance away.'

Blintoft nodded. 'I am sure you are right. Now, Captain Halbstadt, you will command the exchange party. You will proceed to Pisnic, and you will hand over Janitz and Malic to the Partisans, receiving General Marwitz and his officers in return. You will behave at all times with complete integrity, and once you have obtained the release of our people you will return here.'

'Yes, sir. Suppose I am attacked by the Partisans?'

Blintoft looked at Ulrich. 'I believe they will act honourably, Herr General. I am certain that they are very anxious to have Janitz back.'

'Well, we must hope that you are right. Have you spoken with Malic?'

'Yes, sir.'

'And she is willing to play her part?'

'I would not say she is willing, sir. She feels certain that if she is returned to the Partisans they will execute her. But I have pointed out that if she does not play her part *we* will execute her, and her parents as well, but that if she assists us to this success we will grant her a free pardon and immunity from arrest at any time in the future.'

'And she knows how to activate the beacon?'

'She has been carefully instructed, sir.'

'Very good. Colonel Stadtler?'

'I will maintain a reconnaissance aircraft over the area, high enough to be unobserved from the ground. The moment the homing device is activated and its position established, I will take in my planes.'

'You are going to attempt a ground assault? In those mountains?' Halbstadt was horrified.

'We are going to *carry out* a ground assault, Captain, just because of those mountains. The chances of a bombing raid being fully effective are almost nil. By sending in paratroops we will have the advantage of complete surprise. Now, Major Klostermann?'

'I am to accompany the paratroops in order to identify the Partisan commanders, specifically Tito, Davis and Fouquet.'

'And if all goes well, we will have Janitz back as well. Very good, gentlemen. Major Ulrich, you will resume contact with the Partisans and tell them that we accept their conditions. Well, gentlemen, I will wish you good fortune, and good hunting. No, no. I mean good ratcatching, eh?'

Halbstadt followed Ulrich down the steps to the lower floor, and watched Angela get up from her chair in the garden. 'If you go near that woman, you need your head examined,' Ulrich remarked.

'But she is beckoning me.'

'Well, do not say that you weren't warned.' Ulrich touched the peak of his cap to Angela, and hurried on.

Halbstadt slowly went towards her. As always, she had a

table at her elbow, containing a bottle of schnapps and a glass. 'Erich! You have been avoiding me.'

'I have been very busy, Frau Wassermann.'

'Frau Wassermann?'

'Well . . . Angela.'

'Have a drink.'

'There is only one glass.'

'I am sure we can share it.' Halbstadt cast an anxious glance at the palace windows. 'Oh, Fritz is not here. He is out with his toy soldiers. Listen. He will be gone for three days.'

'I could not come here.'

'I know, it is a nuisance. But I can come to you. This afternoon, at four. I shall go for a walk. Be in your quarters.'

'That is crazy. You would be seen.'

'I shall be discreet. And I *will* go crazy if I do not feel a man's arms about me.'

'I cannot be there.'

Angela's expression changed to one of cold disdain. 'You are rejecting me?'

'No, no! Never. But I am leaving this evening, on a special mission.'

'Tell me.'

'I cannot. It is top secret.'

'Do you suppose I cannot keep a secret?'

'If it ever came out, I would be cashiered.'

She gazed at him for several seconds. 'Then tell me this: is my husband involved?'

'No. He does not know of it.'

'Well, well,' she said. 'Go and carry out your secret mission. But I want you when you return.'

Tony and Sandrine waited in the trees, watching the people coming towards them. They were obviously very tired, but they were triumphant as well: Martina gave them the thumbs-up sign when she saw them. Then Sasha saw them as well, and ran forward. She threw both arms round Sandrine to hug her, reaching past her to squeeze Tony's hand.

'Are you all right?' Sandrine asked.

'I am all right now. I have a sore ass. But I will make that bitch pay for it, one day.'

'And her?'

Rosa Malic had not run forward, but continued to trudge towards them, a satchel hanging from her shoulder. 'She is a traitorous scumbag,' Sasha declared. 'We should hang her.'

'Did she not fight with you at Bihac?'

'If you can call it fighting. As soon as we were overrun, she threw away her weapon and began screaming that she worked for Wassermann.'

'Rosa?' Sandrine asked.

'I was trying to save my life,' Rosa said. 'And I did work for Wassermann. You know this.'

Sandrine looked at Tony. 'But he locked you up anyway?' Tony asked.

'He sent me to be shot. He knew I had betrayed his plans to you.'

'But you hadn't, had you? You told us there would be no Italians waiting for us.'

'She must be hanged,' Sasha growled.

'I told you what I had heard,' Rosa insisted. 'I do not know what happened after that. Wassermann sent me to be shot.'

'But you weren't shot.'

'Halbstadt saved me.'

'Halbstadt?'

'Captain Halbstadt. He was in command of the SS detachment responsible for shooting the prisoners.'

'Then why did he not shoot you?'

'Because . . .' She looked embarrassed. 'I had been his mistress in Belgrade.'

'It's a small world.'

'That's why I have been exchanged instead of being

hanged. He told General Blintoft that I was very valuable to you.' She glanced at Sasha. 'As valuable as her. So I was made part of the exchange.'

Sasha snorted, while Tony considered. It made no sense for the Germans to have offered her in exchange if she really had been working for them – unless she had been sent to assassinate Tito. From what he had seen of this extremely nervous young woman, he found that difficult to believe. But he couldn't take any risks. 'Has she been searched?' he asked Martina.

'Oh, yes. She has no weapons.'

'And in the satchel?'

'I have a loaf of bread. Here.'

Rosa opened the satchel, showed him the large loaf. He remembered that the first time he had searched her she had had bits of food in this satchel; she obviously had no intention of ever starving to death. And she had clearly had it for some time: it was stale and in places was turning green. 'I think you should get rid of that.'

Rosa buckled the satchel and hugged it to her chest. 'It is mine.'

'If you eat any of it, you will be ill.'

'It is mine,' she said again.

'It's your stomach. The general is waiting.' He walked beside Martina. 'Was there any trouble?'

'None. They seemed frightened. They wanted only to make the exchange and get away.'

'Well, congratulations.'

'Sasha.' Tito embraced her. 'I thought you were dead.'

'No Nazi is going to kill me,' Sasha declared, and regarded Johnstone. 'Well, Colonel, do you remember me?'

'I do indeed. At Bihac.'

'Bihac,' she said. 'It is not a good memory now.'

'Was it very bad?' Sandrine asked.

'It was the worst.'

'But you did your duty.'

'Ha. Who is this man?'

'This is Brigadier Wharton,' Tony explained.

Wharton shook hands. 'I have heard a lot about you, Major Janitz.'

'Have you come to kill Germans with us?'

'Ah . . . yes. I have.'

'Then you can call me Sasha.'

'There is some plum brandy,' Tito said. 'Let us have some plum brandy.'

'What are we celebrating?' Sasha asked.

'Why, your return. And the news. You know that the Allies have conquered Sicily?'

'When are they coming here?'

'Soon. So tonight we celebrate.'

'What happened to Rosa?' Tony asked Sandrine.

'She went off to find a bivouac.'

'You don't suppose those girls will beat her up?'

'You don't suppose she deserves it?'

'I don't know what to make of that young woman. She is either very brave—'

'She trembles all the time. Did you notice that?'

'Yes. I was saying, if she is not very brave, then she is following some agenda of her own, and it is a very dangerous one.'

'Perhaps we should do as Sasha wants, and hang her.'

'I hope you don't mean that.'

'No I don't. But her very presence makes my skin crawl.'

Tony nodded. 'I think I'll just take a stroll, see what she's at.'

'Would you like me to come with you?'

He squeezed her hand. 'I won't be long. You stay here and get quietly drunk. Don't worry. She's not my type.'

He went outside, inhaled the fresh air. At this altitude, even in high summer the breeze was cool, but not cold. There was

164

no moon, but the sky was clear and the stars twinkled. It was difficult to realize that there was a war on, convulsing the entire globe.

He walked down the hillside to where he could see the glow of a campfire. The women mostly preferred to sleep in the open when the weather was fine, and they knew there were no German soldiers within a hundred miles of them; Tito maintained constant patrols.

One of the women left the group round the fire and came towards him. 'General?'

'Judith! I did not mean to interrupt your dinner. Is Malic with you?'

Judith shook her head. 'We invited her to eat with us. We wanted her to tell us about Bihac, but she said she didn't want to talk about it. She wanted to be alone.'

'Alone where?'

'I think she went up the mountain above the cave.'

'Thanks. I'll just go and have a word.'

'Would you like me to come with you?'

'No. You finish your meal.' He walked back up the slope, past the entrance to the cave. He could hear a good deal of conviviality coming from within; some of them were singing, amongst them Sandrine. It gave him a great sense of relief that she had overcome her grief at losing Charles so well. Of course he knew she hadn't, but she was at least capable of disguising it when with other people.

He passed the cave and continued his climb, now somewhat out of breath. He went up another fifty feet, and reached a small plateau overlooking the camp. Here he paused, getting his breathing under control, and suddenly became aware of a noise, a low hum. Frowning, he looked left and right in the darkness, but it took him several minutes to locate the source. He went towards the faint glint of metal, and saw scattered pieces of bread. His brain snapped with alarm, and he dropped to his knees to peer at a small metal box, from which there protruded a short folding aerial, and which was humming quite loudly. 'Shit!' he muttered. 'Shit, shit, shit.' The night exploded around him.

'That was very nice,' Tito declared. 'You have a very sweet voice, Sandrine. You should sing more often. Now Tony . . . Where is Tony?'

'He went outside to look for Malic. He said he would be back in a moment.' She looked at her watch. 'But that was half an hour ago.'

Tito guffawed. 'You mean he found what he was looking for.'

Sandrine scratched her ear. It was totally unlike Tony to behave like that. And with Rosa Malic? She got to her feet, somewhat unsteadily. 'I will go and find him.'

'What you need is a rolling pin,' Martina said.

'I'll come with you,' Johnstone offered.

'It is not necessary.'

He grinned. 'It may be, to protect Tony.'

'Ha.' She went outside, took deep breaths.

Johnstone joined her. 'Where, do you suppose?'

'There.' Sandrine led him down the slope to the campfire.

'Sandrine?' Judith looked up.

'Have you seen Tony?'

'Oh, yes. He was here, a few minutes ago. He was looking for Malic.'

'And where did he take her?'

'I do not know. She wasn't here.'

'Then where is he?'

'I don't know that either. He went up the hill.'

'Sandrine . . .' Johnstone said uneasily. Like Tony, he had known her in Belgrade before the invasion, and remembered that her apparent composure could hide some very deep feelings.

'I am not going to shoot him,' Sandrine said quietly. 'Or even her.' She stepped away from the fire, and then raised her head as there came a wailing sound from above them.

166

'Malic!' Judith said, scrambling to her feet.

Rosa emerged from the gloom, running towards them. 'Help!' she shouted. 'The general is hurt!'

Sandrine ran at her, grasped her shoulders and shook her. 'What do you mean? What happened to him?'

'I don't know. He is lying there . . .'

'Where?'

'Up there. I will show you.'

'You were with him?'

'No, no. I had gone for a walk, higher up, and I was coming back when I saw his body.'

'His *body*?'

'He's alive. I am sure of it. I stooped over him, and he was moaning. But there was blood . . .'

'Show me.'

Rosa led the way. Sandrine followed, with Johnstone and Judith and several of the women. They climbed up to the plateau, and saw Tony, sitting up and rubbing his head.

'Tony!' Sandrine shouted, and knelt beside him. 'What happened?'

'Someone hit me on the head.'

'Someone? Who? My God!' She had seen the blood on his fingers. 'You're hurt.'

'I'll live. Shit. My head hurts. But listen: find the device.'

'What device?'

'There is a device, right here. I think it is some kind of homing signal. It was humming, and there was an aerial . . .'

Johnstone and Judith shone their flashlights on the ground to either side. 'There is nothing here,' Judith said. 'Only some bits of what looks like . . . bread?'

'That is my bread,' Rosa said. 'I was eating it as I came down the hill. I was hungry. But when I saw the general . . .'

'There was a device,' Tony insisted.

'We must get you into the cave and fix your head,' Sandrine said. 'Come on, girls, give us a hand.'

167

The women surrounded Tony and lifted him to his feet.

'I am all right,' he protested. 'We must find that device.'

'You are more important than any device,' Sandrine told him. 'Just shhh until we have fixed your head.'

The officers in the cave, none of them entirely sober, gathered round. 'That is a nasty cut,' Tito observed. 'How did you get it?'

'Someone hit me.'

'Shhh,' Sandrine insisted.

'It is a nasty cut,' said Dr Trifunovic, parting Tony's hair to dab at the wound with a piece of cloth.

'Is that sterilized?' Wharton asked.

'There is no time for that. He will recover.'

'Who hit you?' Tito asked.

'I don't know. There was that device . . .'

Tito looked at Sandrine. 'I think he is concussed,' Sandrine said. 'There was no device.'

'There was, I tell you. I heard it humming.'

'Well, we will find it in the morning. Can you not give him a sedative, Doctor?'

'In a moment.' Trifunovic finished dressing the wound, then delved into his bag for the sedative. 'This will make you sleep for some hours. That is best. When you wake up, your head will be clear. It will still hurt, but I can relieve that.'

'I don't want to sleep,' Tony protested. 'That device . . .'

But a few moments later he was asleep. They carried him to his sleeping chamber, covered him with a blanket.

'What do you think really happened?' Tito asked.

'I have no idea. Rosa found him.'

Everyone looked at her. 'I have told you, I was walking, by myself, and I came upon him, lying there.'

'Did you see this device he spoke of?'

'I didn't see anything. I was terrified. I ran down the hill for help.'

'You were not with him earlier?' Sandrine asked.

'Earlier? How could I have been with him earlier? I was by myself.'

'You swear this?'

'Yes, I swear this.'

'Give her to me,' Sasha said.

'No!' Rosa shrieked. 'I did not see the general before. I swear it on my mother's grave.'

'Very good, Rosa,' Tito said. 'You are dismissed. Sandrine, you will double the sentries, just in case there is some madman wandering about bent on mischief.'

'And this device?' Johnstone asked.

'We will mount a serious search for it in the morning. If it exists. But I am afraid the most likely thing is that Tony had too much to drink, saw something shining in the darkness, bent over to see what it was, and fell over and hit his head.'

'What about the hum?'

'That was probably in his own head. I have a hum in my head, I can tell you. That plum brandy is stronger than you think. To bed, gentlemen. And ladies.'

Sandrine gave her orders, posting additional sentries.

'Is that what you think happened?' Sasha asked.

'No.'

'Then what is your opinion?'

'I don't know. But Tony did not have enough to drink to make him fall over.'

'Do you want me to have a go at Malic? I will not let her make a noise.'

Sandrine shook her head. 'Leave it until tomorrow, when we can mount a proper search.'

'Okay,' Sasha said, and kissed her. 'It is so good to be home. Now we have shared the same experience, of being in a Gestapo cell.'

'It is not something I wish to remember.'

'I do,' Sasha said. 'I want to remember every moment of it, until I catch up with that bitch Geisner again, and those wardresses.'

Sandrine lay down beside Tony. The cave was already filled with snores, and Tony himself was snoring gently. She adjusted his blanket and held his hand. Her emotions were still seething, but she was certain he had not betrayed their love – she was sure Rosa had been telling the truth. As for what had actually happened, well, Tony would probably remember quite clearly in the morning.

She awoke from a nightmare. There was a faint light drifting into the cave, and she realized it was morning. Tony was still sleeping peacefully. And now *she* had a buzzing in her head. Too much plum brandy. She sat up, and realized that the buzzing was even louder, and that it came from outside.

In the same moment she heard shouts of alarm from down the hill, and then several shots. She scrambled up, ran through the outer cave, where the men were sleepily stirring, and reached the entrance, to see grey-clad figures moving towards her. While others continued to float down from the planes that were immediately overhead.

PART THREE

THE KILLING GROUND

The martial brood accustomed to fight:
Then honour was the meed of victory.
And yet the vanquished had no despite.
                              Edmund Spencer

Eight

The Coup

S andrine saw that her girls, including the sentries, had been taken entirely by surprise, and were about to be destroyed . . . and there was nothing she could do to help them. She gave a scream of angry despair, and dashed back into the cavern. 'Alarm!' she shouted. 'Stand to! The enemy are here.'

Men stumbled to their feet, reaching for their weapons. Sandrine dashed past them to secure her own tommy gun, and then raced back to the entrance. Sasha was already there, with Martina and several of the men, spraying the slope with bullets and driving the advancing paratroopers to the ground for shelter.

'What the hell happened?' Wharton asked, reloading his revolver.

'We have been betrayed,' Tito said. 'There was a device after all. We should have listened to Tony.'

Tony now appeared at the back of the entrance. 'Get down!' Sandrine shouted.

He dropped to his knees beside her. 'Rosa! It had to be Rosa.'

'That bitch!' Sasha said. 'You should have let me have her.'

'Where is she?' Johnstone asked.

'I will find her,' Sasha promised.

'You realize we are trapped?' Wharton said.

173

Tito surveyed the slope. The firing had ceased. 'I do not think they will try a frontal assault, now that they know we are awake.'

'Well, they know we aren't going anywhere. Is there any hope of relief by your people?'

'In time,' Sandrine said. 'My women have been scattered. They will rally, and they will send for help. But it will take a day or two.'

'And the Germans aren't planning to wait,' Johnstone said. 'Look there.'

More aircraft had arrived overhead, these even bigger than the troop carriers, and they were already unloading their cargoes. 'Shit!' Wharton commented as they watched each field gun, swaying beneath its multiple-parachute canopy, slowly dropping to the earth. 'They mean to seal us in.'

All heads turned to look at Tito. Who gave one of his disarming smiles. 'Then we had better make our preparations to leave.'

'You mean to charge those people? That would be to commit suicide.'

'That is not my style, General. But every house should have a back door. Why do you think I chose this cave?'

'There is a way out?'

'Indeed. We must follow the stream. It will not be easy, and it will be very wet, but it comes out several hundred feet down the reverse side of the mountain. Now, Brigadier, will you start with your people. Martina will show you. It is necessary to drop through a hole in the floor of one of the chambers. From there you will be in the stream. It is only a few feet deep. Then it is just a matter of following the water.'

Johnstone gulped. 'Dark, airless places were never my strongest point.'

Sandrine squeezed his hand. 'It will be better than the sewers of Belgrade. I have tried them both.'

'You will have to carry your equipment,' Tito went on.

'And Tony,' Sandrine said.

'Forget that,' Tony said. 'I can still shoot.'

'Now wait just one moment,' Wharton said. 'What are you intending to do?'

'Follow you, in due course,' Tito said.

'Would you explain that?'

'We cannot simply abandon this entrance, otherwise the Germans will not use their artillery but will simply come in after us. We must hold our position until they are convinced either that we have been destroyed or the entrance is sealed.'

'That sounds a highly hazardous operation.'

'There will be some risk, yes.'

'Then may I respectfully suggest that you leave this defence to your subordinates and come out with us? You are the commanding general. You cannot afford to die in the breach, as it were.'

Tito grinned. 'I am the commanding general of what, at this moment, Brigadier? Two dozen devoted men, and women, to be sure. I do not intend to abandon them. Besides . . .' He winked. 'It is time for me to be a hero. How else am I to get people to follow me, after this second disaster?'

Wharton gazed at him for several seconds, then nodded. 'You know, that is very sound reasoning. Colonel Johnstone, you will lead our people out, taking our radio equipment with you. We will rendezvous later.'

'But, sir, what are you going to do?'

'I came here to see the Partisans in action, Colonel. This is my first, and it may well be my last, opportunity to do so. I would regard it as a grave dereliction of duty were I to pass it up.'

Reluctantly the British party withdrew. The remaining defenders sheltered behind the outcroppings of rock within the cave. The Germans had now opened a fairly steady fire. Obviously they couldn't see into the cave, so they were directing their fire into the entrance, and the bullets ricocheted from rock face to rock face.

'Damnation,' Wharton exclaimed. 'I'm hit!'

'Let's have a look.' Dr Trifunovic crawled up to him with his first-aid box. 'Nasty little nick,' he commented. 'This will hurt.' Wharton did some swearing under his breath.

'They're having a go,' Sasha said. Needless to say, her position was nearest the entrance.

'Return fire,' Tito said. 'We must remind them that we are still here.'

The grey-clad figures were running up the slope. The Partisans commenced firing with both rifles and tommy guns. Several men went down, and the rest hastily retreated to shelter.

'Now for the big stuff,' Tony muttered.

'You should not be here at all,' Sandrine grumbled. 'You should have gone with the Britishers.'

'I have to keep an eye on my unborn child,' he whispered. Only he knew that she had missed her last period.

The first gun fired from behind the hiding soldiers. The shell smashed into the rock above the entrance, and there was a shower of stones and small boulders. The explosion was immediately followed by fresh volleys of small arms fire, and Trifunovic was kept busy as several more people were nicked by flying rock splinters. Then the gun boomed again, this time more accurately, the shell bursting immediately on top of the entrance and bringing down a small avalanche. 'Sasha?' Tito called.

'I am all right.'

'That was too close. Come back inside.'

'That is what they expect us to do. They will come again. Now!'

Tony and Sandrine and the rest of the tiny garrison ran forward to pour bullets into another wave of attackers, and again send them tumbling back down the slope. 'Back into the cave.' Tito commanded, just in time, for as they withdrew there was another rumbling crash. The gun now had the range, and this shell actually penetrated the entrance before exploding with an ear-shattering crash, bringing down the cave ceiling and entirely shutting out the daylight. 'No flashlights,' Tito said. 'They must not see the gleam. Withdraw one by one to the inner chamber.'

'Will you lead, sir?' a staff officer asked.

'I will come last.'

Sandrine peered at him in the darkness. 'You are hit.'

'It is nothing I cannot stand. Now go.'

Three of the defenders were dead, and had to be abandoned. Almost everyone else had at least a minor wound. The exception, amazingly, was Sasha, even if she was covered in dust.

They crawled back through the cave to the inner chambers to listen. They could hear sounds from outside, but there was no indication that the Germans were trying to get in. A few minutes later the Partisans were dropping, one by one, through the escape hole to follow the stream to safety.

'May I say, General Tito,' Wharton remarked, 'that you live far too adventurous a life for a commanding general. My advice is that you should find somewhere safe to make your headquarters.'

'Where would you suggest?'

'Why do you not make use of the islands off the coast?'

'Most of them are occupied by the Germans.'

'But not all. And we will be able to reach you more easily. And, incidently, take you in or out whenever you wish it.'

'Why should I wish it? My place is here.'

'But you also need to organize your resistance to the Germans on a much bigger scale than at present. Besides, I happen to know that there is someone who wishes to meet you, as soon as it can be arranged.'

'I love islands,' Sandrine said.

*   *   *

'You are sure of this?' Blintoft asked the parachute colonel.

'Absolutely.'

'But you did not go into the cave to make certain,' Wassermann remarked. He was still furious that the apparently successful coup had been carried out without his knowledge, much less his participation.

'I suspected that it would be booby-trapped, quite apart from the likelihood that any survivors would fight like rats in a trap. Besides, I was informed by the prisoners we took from the women outside the cave that the inside is, or was, a perfect rabbit warren of passageways and chambers. To search them all would take weeks. I am sure that you remember, Herr General' – he addressed Blintoft – 'that my unit was seconded to your command for one short, sharp operation. My men are required in Italy.'

Blintoft nodded. 'Of course. You have done a splendid job. You must not blame us for still being anxious. We have been so close to destroying these vermin on so many previous occasions, and they have always managed to wriggle off the hook.'

'They will not do that this time, sir.'

'How can you be so sure?' Wassermann asked. 'Any survivors may be able to dig their way through the blocked entrance.'

'No, sir, they will not. Not without mechanical digging equipment. When we were certain all resistance had ceased, my men planted explosive charges, both above and below the blocked entrance. We brought down half that mountain. I can assure you that if there are any survivors in there, they are entombed for the rest of eternity.'

'But that is brilliant,' Blintoft said. 'Brilliant.'

Ulrich cleared his throat, and all heads turned to look at him. 'There is one thing,' he said. 'How do we know for certain that Tito was in the cave when you attacked?'

'Again, I have the evidence of the prisoners we took. One of them was a colonel in the Partisan army. She told us that not only was Tito in there, but also the members of a high-level English mission.'

'And who else?'

'Oh, several of Tito's main officers as well, including the woman Janitz who we had just exchanged. There was also an English renegade, a man named Davis, and a French person named Fouquet. Are these names familiar to you?'

'Oh, indeed,' Blintoft said. 'They are familiar to us. Let me congratulate you again, Colonel. In my report I intend to give you the highest commendation.'

'Thank you, Herr General.'

'These prisoners you took,' Ulrich ventured. 'Where are they?'

'Once we had obtained the information we wanted, I had them shot. This is in accordance with the Führer's general orders regarding guerillas captured in arms against the Reich.'

'Oh, quite,' Blintoft agreed. 'Absolutely.'

'And Malic?' Ulrich persisted.

'Oh, yes, our agent. We found her cowering in a ditch, and brought her back to Belgrade. I'm afraid I had to put her into hospital. She appeared to be on the edge of a nervous breakdown.'

'I would say that is entirely likely, after what she did. Thank you, Colonel. I will wish you good fortune.'

'Heil Hitler!' Stadtler left the room.

'Well,' Blintoft said. 'The end of a chapter, eh? One could almost say, the end of the war here in Yugoslavia.'

'My congratulations, sir,' Ulrich said.

'Thank you, Ulrich.' Blintoft looked at his son-in-law.

'Oh, congratulations,' Wassermann acknowledged. 'What will happen now?'

'That depends on Berlin. However, I am detaining you here for a while, with your Waffen people. There are still the Cetniks to be dealt with.'

'They are a spent force.'

179

'Nonetheless, they are still there, bearing arms. We shall have to work out a strategy for dealing with them.'

'And Malic?' Ulrich asked.

'Oh, give her back her job in the Gestapo canteen. I really think she has done very well.'

Wassermann snorted.

'So there it is.' Wassermann sat on Mathilde's bed, shoulders hunched. 'I have been outmanoeuvred. To think that brainless oaf is going to get the credit for all the hard work I have put in . . .'

Mathilde reclined; she wore a negligée, and her bare feet rested against Wassermann's thigh. 'If he really is a brainless oaf, then he will betray himself sooner or later, and be sacked, and you will be the man to replace him.'

'If I could think that . . .' He raised his head. 'But you must be very pleased.'

'I would have preferred to have seen her dead body. Or better yet, to have her back in her cell. '

'Still, both your scar and your husband have been avenged. Will you now go back to Germany?'

'You keep asking me that. Don't you wish me to stay?'

'Of course I wish you to stay. But . . . will you?'

'I would marry you, if you asked me.'

'You? Marry me? You are not pretending to have fallen in love with me?'

'No,' she said. 'It would be difficult to fall in love with you, Fritz. You are not a loveable man. But I have become used to you. And you are a general, and a powerful man. I have always wanted to be married to a general. My first husband would have been a general, had he lived. Now . . .' She touched her scar.

'I have told you, that makes no difference to me.'

'I know. That is why I am staying.'

His shoulders hunched again. 'Unfortunately, I am married.'

180

'Can't you get a divorce?'

'Angela would never agree to it. She also likes to be married to a general. And her father is my commanding officer. I would have to have a very good reason.'

'Well, then,' Mathilde said. 'Let us find one.'

Tony and Sandrine, with Sasha, Martina and Judith – who had survived the German attack and indeed brought out most of her women – stood on the little dock jutting into the Adriatic Sea from the tiny island of Vis, and watched the cutter nose its way alongside. The destroyer was at anchor, no more than a shadow in the darkness.

'Time,' Tony said, and Judith called her women to attention.

The boat came alongside, and Tito stepped over the gunwale. Behind him came the destroyer captain, while the British sailors started unloading various pieces of luggage and equipment. 'Tony! Sandrine! Sasha! Martina! Judith!' He embraced them in turn. 'It is good to be back.'

'Success?' Tony asked.

'Promises of success. This is Captain Dawkins.'

'Actually, lieutenant-commander,' the officer said, shaking hands. 'My great pleasure, sir. And madams. You understand, Marshal, that I must take my ship out of here within the hour.'

'You have time for a drink.'

'Marshal?' Tony asked as they walked up the dock past the guard of honour.

'It is the prime minister's idea. He felt it would be a more appropriate title.'

'Marshal,' Sandrine said. 'We have marshals in France. Or we did. Now there is only that bastard Petain. Is there news of Brigadier Wharton?'

'He is recovering well, and will be returning to us shortly. And – wait for this – we are to be joined by a Russian mission as well.'

'Is he bringing guns with him?'

'It is all promised. You know that the Russians have smashed the German armour at Kursk? It seems that there is nothing but victory. Churchill expects them to be in Poland before the end of the year.'

'You mean the end is in sight?' Tony opened the door of the small house they were using as a command centre.

'He seems sure of it.'

'And us?'

'Oh, we are to be supplied with everything we need.'

'Starting when?'

'As soon as we tell them where to drop. It cannot be here. Then we would have to ferry it across to the mainland. So we must return there ourselves, as quickly as possible, and start recruiting.'

'Well, then,' Tony said, pouring glasses of schnapps, 'I think we should all drink a toast. To victory, however long it may take. Commander?'

'Oh, indeed, sir. And it may be closer than you think. I received a signal while we were at sea, but I was instructed not to release the contents until I had put you ashore, Marshal.'

'And what was this so secret signal?' Tito inquired.

'It said to inform you that a treaty has been signed, and tomorrow Italy will announce its surrender.'

'Mussolini has agreed to surrender?'

'Mussolini, sir, is under arrest. By his own people.'

'Bastards,' Tito remarked as they watched the destroyer fade into the night. 'They still do not trust me.'

'If Dawkins only received the signal yesterday . . .'

'Oh, come now, Tony. You know as well as I that the surrender of an entire nation is not agreed overnight. The negotiations will have been going on for weeks. And if it is going to be announced tomorrow, it will have been agreed several days ago. That is, while I was staying in the same Egyptian villa as Churchill, meeting him several times a day, discussing grand strategy with him – and he said not a word of any impending Italian surrender.'

'Well, it has to be good news from our point of view, however belated, if it means we do not have to keep looking over our shoulders at Albania.'

'And what do you suppose is going to happen *in* Albania? And with the considerable Italian forces in Yugoslavia?'

'Well . . . shit! I hadn't thought of that. They have no one to surrender to.'

'Except the Germans.'

'Poor buggers.'

'It is not the fate of the men that concerns us, Tony. Even if they are no longer our immediate enemies, they have still spent the last three years murdering our people. But we *are* talking about at least six divisions, over a hundred thousand men, every man armed with a rifle, and ammunition, every company equipped with at least one heavy machine gun, with ammunition. Each division has at lest one battery of artillery, with ammunition, and each division has at least one squadron of tanks. The Italians do not concentrate their armour into panzers like the Germans; they use them as infantry support.'

'None of their tanks is equal to a Tiger,' Sasha pointed out.

'They are still better than nothing. And there are also quite a few Italian aircraft up for grabs. We must have them. And we would have them – if I had been told in time of the surrender. Still, we must do the best we can.'

'There is the small point that none of our people know how to fly an aircraft. Or how to drive a tank.'

'They will have to learn, and the British will have to send in instructors. I know what their game is. They do not wish us to become too powerrful, too independent of them. Well, whether they like it or not, we are going to have those weapons. Because when we do, people will flock to our support. We will have a real army, not just a

183

couple of divisions. And then' – he drew a deep breath – 'I intend to announce that I have taken over the government of Yugoslavia.'

They stared at him. 'Can you do that?' Tony asked.

'Who is going to stop me?'

'What I meant was, there already is a Yugoslav government, in London.'

'They support Mihailovic, who is a traitor. By definition that makes them traitors also.'

'But they are still recognized by the British. And the Americans. Should you not inform London of your intention, and get their agreement?'

'Why do I need their agreement? Do they ask for my agreement before holding an election in England?'

'With respect, Josip, you are not planning to hold an election, but to make a unilateral declaration.'

'That is because we are at war. Do you have any doubt that the majority of the people in the federation would support me?'

'I'm sure you're right. Outside of Serbia, anyway. But still, a unilateral declaration will be sure to offend London.'

'What can they do about it?'

'Well, they might decide to withhold, or at least delay, those arms shipments they have promised.'

'But once we have the Italian arms we do not need them, at least not so urgently. And besides, do we not have this Russian mission on its way? But do you know, Tony, I do not think the British will refuse to supply us. Churchill has decided to back us in preference to the Cetniks, no matter what, or despite what the Americans may think. Our meeting is to be publicized in the British press. He cannot turn his back on me after that. But we must act with all possible speed. The Italian weapons come first. Tony, Sasha, Sandrine, Martina, Judith, prepare to leave for the mainland at once. Contact must be made with Doedjic and Gronic and all our surviving commanders. We must act before the Germans can.'

*   *   *

184

'I would like Sandrine to remain here,' Tony told Tito when they were alone.

Tito raised his eyebrows. 'She commands the women.'

'She also happens to be pregnant.'

'Good God. Does she know?'

'Of course she knows, Josip. She herself will never let it interfere with her duty, but if she were to lose this babe I am not sure what effect it would have on her mind. She is three months gone. This is the most dangerous period. But in any event it will soon be impossible for her to risk any heavy physical labour. You must order her to remain here on Vis.'

'Do you think she will accept such an order?'

'Yes, if you leave her in command, tell her that it is vital for you to have someone on whom you can totally rely to maintain the sea link with the Allies.'

Tito considered for a few moments, then nodded. 'Of course. We will leave her in command with a regiment of her people as a garrison. Martina can stay with her. But if you don't mind, I will leave it to you to tell her.'

'That is absurd,' Sandrine declared. 'It will be another three months before I am showing. I am perfectly capable of campaigning for that time.'

'No one doubts that for a moment,' Tony said soothingly. 'But it is absolutely necessary to have someone reliable here. Vis is our lifeline, and will become even more important after the surrender. Believe me, we are not trying to sideline you. We are trusting you with a great responsibility.'

'And you are a liar. And a bad one.'

'Don't you want to have this baby?'

'Of course I do.'

'Then please, please, obey orders.'

'And when I am told you are killed? This is *our* baby, Tony. I do not wish to be a widowed mother.'

185

'I am not going to be killed. This campaign is to be simply a matter of rounding up the Italians and relieving them of their weapons. We shall be in radio contact with you on a daily basis. Then we will recruit an army to drive the Germans out of Yugoslavia. That will take several months; you will be back with us in time for that.'

She clung to his hands. 'Is that the truth, Tony?'

'That is the absolute truth,' he told her.

'Well?' Wassermann demanded, standing before his father-in-law's desk. He had come straight from his headquarters south of Belgrade, where he had spent the previous week exercising his men; he still carried his steel helmet.

'It is shocking,' Blintoft agreed. 'Those bastards. When I think of the effort we made to maintain them in North Africa, and now they will not even help us defend their own fatherland. They are scum.'

'That is history, Anton. What matters is the here and now. There are six Italian divisions in the south of this country and Albania.'

'Well, I suppose we can no longer count on them for any assistance, if they are laying down their arms.'

'It is who is going to pick up their arms that matters.' Blintoft frowned. 'Six fully equipped divisions, Anton. That is not just an army corps. It is an army. If those weapons fall into the wrong hands . . .'

'My God!' Blintoft said. 'But the Partisans are defeated. We have heard nothing of them for three months. And without Tito they are finished.'

'There are other guerilla bands roaming about. Most of them are just bandits. But if they became fully armed . . .'

Blintoft snapped his fingers. 'The Cetniks!'

'I do not think they are any longer a threat.'

'But you have just said that they could become one, if they obtain those arms. Have them rounded up and destroyed.'

'I will do so, if you will give me the men.'

186

'Use your own people.'

'Anton, I have one brigade.'

'Do you not claim that the Waffen SS are the best troops in the world?'

'I would claim that. But there are still only twenty-five hundred of them, and a quarter of that number are on the sick list. There are something like twenty thousand Cetniks. You have an army corps sitting on its ass in Croatia and north-west Bosnia. Now, the Hungarians and the Bulgarians are certainly not the best troops in the world, but they will fight if well led. I proved that at Bihac. They will do the job – if I am placed in command.'

Blintoft sighed. 'Both the Hungarian and the Bulgarian divisions have been withdrawn.'

'To go where?'

'Back to Hungary and Bulgaria.'

'That is madness. They are needed here.'

'I'm afraid Berlin does not agree with you. There have been some severe reverses on the Russian front. It is anticipated that they will make a move through Romania and Bulgaria rather than attempt a frontal assault on the Reich through Poland.'

Wassermann slowly sank into the chair before the desk. 'Then what have we got to defend Yugoslavia against an Allied assault?'

'Not a great deal at the moment. But OKH do not think an Allied invasion is likely. They consider that the enemy will concentrate on capturing Italy, and we have powerful forces there, and powerful defences: a series of fortified mountains. I am assured that should that estimation be proved wrong, sufficient forces will be returned to my command to deal with the situation.'

'And you believe that?'

'Of course I do. Berlin has never let me down. Now, let us deal with practicalities. I suppose you are right, and it would be best to leave the Cetniks alone for the time being. But

187

they must be watched, most carefully. Who knows which way they will turn when the news of this Italian debacle filters through. But they certainly must not get their hands on any Italian equipment. You will take your people down to Montenegro immediately, and demand the surrender of all vehicles, arms and ammunition.'

'And if they refuse?'

'They will not dare.'

'I have one brigade. They have six divisions.'

'I do not think they will resist you. Their government has surrendered to the Allies, because they have managed to get rid of Mussolini. But to the ordinary Italian, and even more, the ordinary Italian soldier, he is still Il Duce, the leader, *their* leader. Their loyalty will remain with him, and his allies, rather than with what they are being told to do by a bunch of traitors in Rome.'

'I hope you are right. I will leave tomorrow.' Wassermann stood up. 'Has it occurred to you, Anton, that the war is not going well?'

'Every war has its ups and downs.'

'For us, this war has been going down for over a year. Ever since Stalingrad, in fact.'

'Really, Fritz, I never expected to hear an officer of your rank and experience expressing such a view. It comes close to treason.'

'I would have said it comes close to reality.'

Blintoft wagged his pen at him. 'That is because you do not know the true facts.'

'Tell me about these facts.'

'There are only two worth considering. The first is that although we have been let down time and again by our so-called allies – and I am not speaking only of the Italians – Fortress Europe is still unbreached, and will remain so.'

'So we hold the line of the Channel, the Alps and Poland for the rest of the century.'

'We hold the line for another year. Two at the most.

Then the tide will turn. As soon as our secret weapons are deployed . . .'

'Oh, come now, Anton.'

'They are being developed, Fritz. They are there. I have been to the test firing range.'

Wassermann frowned. 'Firing what?'

'Rockets, Fritz. The biggest and most powerful rockets ever seen. Half a dozen of them will reduce London to rubble. And they cannot be stopped, by either aircraft or gunfire: they fly too fast. Once they are fully deployed against England, they will have no choice but to make peace, or be destroyed.'

'Are you serious? Is this true?'

'I told you, I have been to the test range on the Baltic coast. So as I say, it is merely a matter of holding fast for a few more months.'

'Then I apologize for expressing any doubts. I will leave for the south tomorrow.'

'Don't forget to look in on Angela before you do. She has been having one of her moods recently. I put it down to the fact that she sees so little of you. Even when a man has a mistress, he must pay proper attention to his wife.'

Silly old fool, Wassermann thought. But in fact, never had he felt so relieved as at what his father-in-law had told him. He knew that over the past few months he had slipped into a mood of profound depression. Professionally, all his hopes of an outstanding success against the Partisans had dwindled. True, everyone seemed to accept that he had gained a great victory at the Neretva River, but he had doubts whether that opinion was shared by Himmler, otherwise surely he would have been given a more responsible position than merely policing Yugoslavia, as he had done two years previously when he had been only a major.

But even his relationshp with Mathilde was a cause of frustrated worry. The frustration had always been there, of course: it was there with any woman. But it had been controllable when *he* had been in control. Recently she had taken over his life. She still submitted to him without demur, but he knew she was working to a plan. She had spelled it out for him: she wanted to be a general's wife; love, or even affection, did not come into it. She was a woman with a purpose, to rise above the position of inferiority inflicted upon her by the scar on her cheek, which, she believed, prohibited any prospect of remarriage save to someone as scarred and repulsive as herself. And since his failure to attempt to divorce Angela she had from time to time become quite difficult. She did not seem to understand that to attempt to divorce Angela, without absolute proof of her vicious character, could well damage his career, at least as long as Blintoft remained his commanding officer. The poor old sod actually continued to suppose that Angela was a loving and devoted wife, tormented when unable to be with her husband!

His problem was that without concrete proof that she was not fit to be the wife of a German officer, much less a general, much less a general in the SS, to challenge her would be highly dangerous, and not just professionally. He had willingly participated in her perversions before his wound, and he knew of her wild orgies recently in Berlin. He also knew that they had been shared with the daughters, sisters, and even the wives of some of the Nazi party's leading men, and to involve any of them as witnesses to his own marital disorder would be to take the shortest route to a bullet in the nape of his neck. And although he was also certain that she had had an affair with Halbstadt, he had no proof. The information had been given to him by his erstwhile housekeeper, Madame Bestic, and she was now dead, murdered by Angela to keep her guilt a secret.

But he supposed he would have to visit her, or she might mention his neglect to her father. He went to the apartment they had been given in the palace, and found Angela's new maid, a woman named Olga, pottering about. 'Where is Frau Wassermann?'

'She has gone out, Herr General.'

Wassermann looked at his watch. 'At two o'clock on a Saturday afternoon? Where does she go at this time?'

'I do not know, Herr General. She goes out every Saturday afternoon.'

Spending my money, Wassermann thought, although not many shops were open on a Saturday. Well, he had tried to see her. He went down to his command car and was driven to Gestapo headquarters. Ulrich was there; Wassermann wondered if he ever left the office.

'I assume you have heard the news?'

Ulrich nodded. 'It creates a very grave situation.'

'Not really. It is merely a nuisance. I am taking my people south tomorrow to collect the Italians' equipment before it falls into the wrong hands.'

'But have you not just returned to Belgrade?'

'So now I am leaving again. We happen to be fighting a war. I will need your people as well. All you can spare.'

'You wish me to come with you?'

'No. You stay here. I will take Halbstadt. Where is he?'

'He is off duty.'

'I see. Well . . .'

'Shall I call him?' Ulrich reached for the telephone.

Wassermann grinned. 'What does he do with his afternoons off?'

'Well . . .'

'You mean he is in bed with some woman. Rosa, is it?'

'I do not know, Herr General.'

'I think I will get him up myself. It should be amusing. Heil Hitler!'

'Oh,' Angela said. 'Oh. Don't come. Not yet.'

Her kneeling body surged to and fro, carrying his with it.

'I cannot . . .' he gasped. 'I must . . .' He gave a gasp and a convulsive jerk as he ejaculated.

Angela's elbows gave way, and her face sank into the pillow. Slowly her knees followed, her legs sliding down the bed. 'You are a useless shit,' she remarked. 'Well, you will have to finish me off.' Halbstadt rolled off her back and lay beside her, and she turned to face him. 'Well?'

He was panting. 'Give me a moment. I am exhausted.'

'From one fuck? You are even more useless than I supposed.' She was not even breathing heavily. 'Well, I suppose beggars can't be choosers.' He gave a sigh, which became a strangled exclamation when the phone rang. 'What the shit . . .?'

'I must answer it.' Halbstadt got up and went to the desk on the far side of the room while Angela watched him with brooding eyes. 'Halbstadt.'

'Ulrich. I think you should know that General Wassermann is on his way to see you now.'

Halbstadt grinned. 'It is your little joke, Herr Major. Wassermann is with his men.'

'He is crossing the courtyard to your quarters at this moment,' Ulrich said. 'I can see him from my window. Good day to you.'

Angela was sitting up. 'Fritz is back?' She scrambled out of bed. 'I must go.'

'You cannot go. He is outside now.'

'Outside where?'

'Outside this building. Inside this building. Listen.' The tap of his stick was clearly audible as Wassermann came up the stairs.

'Well, then,' she said. 'We will just have to face it out.'

'Are you crazy? He is entitled to shoot us both. He *will* shoot us both. You must hide. In here.' He opened his wardrobe door. 'Hurry.'

Angela stared at him, then turned her head when there was a rap on the door. 'Halbstadt?' Halbstadt grabbed her arm and bundled her into the wardrobe, then scooped her clothes from the chair where she had thrown them and hurled them in after her. Her shoes remained, and these he kicked under the bed. 'Halbstadt?' Wassermann asked. 'Open this door.'

Halbstadt dragged on a pair of underpants, and unlocked the door. Wassermann looked him up and down, then looked past him at the tousled bed. 'I was asleep, Herr General.'

'Alone? You amaze me. Well, prepare to leave tomorrow morning.'

'Where am I going, Herr General?'

'You are coming with me down to Montenegro, to disarm the Italians. I assume you know they have surrendered?'

'I heard a rumour . . .'

'The rumour happens to be fact. We leave at dawn. Good day to you.'

'At dawn. I will be ready. Heil Hitler!'

'Heil.' Wassermann went to the door, and checked, frowning. Then he turned back. 'That scent . . .'

'What scent, Herr General?'

Wassermann gazed at him; the young officer was barely suppressing a shiver. Wassermann came into the room. 'That is my wife's scent.'

'Ah . . .'

'You have had my wife in this room! You miserable little bastard.'

'I . . .'

'Oh, what is the use,' Angela said, opening the wardrobe door and stepping out. 'So he has been fucking me. Well, someone has to do it.' Wassermann's hand dropped to his pistol holster. 'That would be very stupid of you,' Angela pointed out. 'I am Angela von Blintoft.'

'You are *in flagrante delicto.*'

'So beat me.' She scooped her clothes out of the wardrobe and pulled on her knickers.

Wassermann could not believe his eyes. His hand still rested on his holster, and Halbstadt knew their lives were still in danger; he was shivering uncontrollably now. The phone rang. And again. 'Oh, pick it up,' Wassermann snapped.

Halbstadt took the phone off the hook. 'Halbstadt.'

'Are you all right?' Ulrich asked.

'Ah . . .' Halbstadt stared at Wassermann. 'At the moment, Herr Major.'

'Is General Wassermann there?'

'Yes, Herr Major.'

'Let me speak with him. It is urgent.'

Halbstadt held out the receiver. 'Major Ulrich, Herr General. It is an urgent matter.'

Wassermann took both phone and receiver. 'Yes?'

'A report has just come in from one of our agents in the south, Herr General. He says the Italians are evacuating both Montenegro and Albania and being shipped back to Italy.'

'Damnation. Taking their equipment, I presume.'

'No, sir. Well, only a small part of it.'

'What have they done with the rest?'

'Well, sir, our agent says they have handed it over to the Partisans.'

'What? The Partisans no longer exist.'

'My own opinion, Herr General. However, the agent says there can be no doubt of it. He saw some of the handover himself. He says there were many thousands of the guerillas. And he says – you will not believe this, sir – that they were commanded by Tito.'

'*Tito*?' Wassermann shouted.

'That is what he says, sir.'

'That is impossible. Tito is dead, buried beneath that mountain.'

'Yes, sir. However, our man swears that it is him. He says he is now calling himself Marshal Tito. And he says that he also saw the Englishman Davis, standing beside the . . . ah . . . marshal.'

Wassermann stared at the phone, his hand clutching the receiver so tightly he seemed to be trying to crush it.

'There is more,' Ulrich said.

'What more?' Wassermann asked, his voice quiet. What more can there be? he thought.

'Tito has declared himself head of state of the government of Yugoslavia.'

Nine

The Assault

'Dead!' Wassermann shouted. 'Buried under a mountain. Davis at his side! Do you know who else has been identified? Janitz!'

'And Fouquet?' Blintoft asked wearily.

'She has not been mentioned. But you can be sure she is around somewhere. The whole unholy crew, still alive, and now armed and equipped on a scale they have never known before. And now calling themselves the government of Yugoslavia. Do you realize the propaganda value of that? If we let them get away with it, the entire country will rally behind them. All because I was not allowed to finish the job.'

'Stadtler was so sure . . .'

'Stadtler is a Wehrmacht officer. The Wehrmacht are always sure – just as they are always out of touch with reality.'

Blintoft squared his shoulders and sat straight. 'I think you should remember, Fritz, that *I* am a Wehrmacht officer. Looking over one's shoulder is a waste of time, except where reflection and experience can be used to correct previous mistakes. Now, I fully accept that we are faced with a serious situation. The first thing you need to do is make contact with Mihailovic.'

'What good will that do? After this coup he will not be strong enough to take on the Partisans.' That is, he thought, if he will ever be prepared to fight for me again.

'Perhaps not, at this moment,' Blintoft said. 'But he has his own position to consider. Tito has stolen a propaganda advantage. If Mihailovic does not get it back, he will find himself outlawed by his own people. But he must still retain a good deal of support, certainly in Serbia, and no one can have any doubt that this self-proclaimed government of Tito's will be Communist in character, and therefore will be unacceptable to a good many people, whether they are Serbs or not. Mihailovic must proclaim his own government. Tell him that we will support him. Once he declares himself head of state with the avowed intention of returning King Michael to the throne the moment hostilities cease, he will cut Tito's support by more than half.'

'Hm,' Wassermann said. 'There is a problem.'

'Tell me.'

'Well . . . Mihailovic and I quarrelled at the conclusion of the Bihac campaign.'

'What was the reason?'

'I felt that he had not supported me as vigorously as he should have done, and told him so. He was very angry.'

'One day you will just have to learn to be diplomatic. But in this case, as it is his neck on the line, I think he will be willing to cooperate. You can confess to him that you spoke hastily.'

So I am now required to crawl to that slimy little bastard, Wassermann thought.

Blintoft went on. 'At the same time, we must take immediate steps to destroy Tito.'

Wassermann snorted. 'I had him destroyed back in the spring, and was not allowed to finish the job.'

'I said, looking over one's shoulder is a waste of time. You now have the opportunity to destroy him again.'

'With one brigade, when he has an army.'

'There must be some way of striking at him.'

'Indeed. Persuade OKH to give me eight divisions of motorized infantry, with artillery, two panzer divisions, and ten squadrons of heavy bombers.'

'You are being absurd. That is quite impossible.'

'As you say. So, will you inform me how it is to be done?'

Blintoft leaned back in his chair. 'There has to be a way. What other information did your agent discover? Think of everything he reported.'

'I have told you everything that he reported,' Wassermann said wearily. 'Tito apparently escaped from the caves by means of a secret exit, and took refuge on the island of Vis, which he has made his headquarters. From there he is in constant touch with the British in Italy, and it was they who tipped him off that the Italians were about to surrender. So—'

'Stop. This island, Vis, where is it?'

'One of the islands off the Dalmatian coast.'

'I was under the impression that we had occupied those islands to forestall an Allied invasion.'

'We occupied some of them. But we could not possibly garrison them all; there are hundreds of them. And since the Allied invasion of Italy, most of them have been abandoned. We simply do not have the men.'

'So Tito has been sitting right there in our midst for the last six months.'

'You could put it that way. You could also say that he has been sitting right here in our midst in Yugoslavia for the past two and a half years.'

'But now we can pinpoint him. We can occupy Vis, wipe out his headquarters, and hopefully him as well, but in any event deal a severe blow not only to his communications but also to his reputation and the morale of his people.'

'May I ask how we are to do that? With what? As I said, almost all the island garrisons have been withdrawn for Italy.'

'But you have your brigade.'

'Ye – es. Tito has over fifty thouand troops.'

'But they cannot all be on Vis, can they? How big is it?'

'Only a few square kilometres.'

'Exactly. It is a nerve centre, not an enemy concentration. You will not need more than a single battalion. We hold Dubrovnik. If you were to descend on Dubrovnik, in the strictest secrecy, commandeer every boat or small ship that is in the harbour and attack Vis before the enemy knows what you are about, you would achieve a great victory. Perhaps a decisive one.'

Wassermann considered. 'You wish me to lead this attack personally?'

'I think it is important enough to require your personal command, yes.'

'I am not fit enough for combat.'

'Fritz, I do not expect you to lead the assault, sword in hand. You can command from the bridge of a ship, and not go ashore at all. But I want you there, to control events, to make sure nothing goes wrong. And I wish you to bring back any ranking officers you find there, alive. Tito, certainly, and also people like Davis, Janitz, Fouquet, Doedjic, Gronic. It is essential for us to regain the initiative in the propaganda war. We will put those people on trial in public, and we will have them confess to being murdering bandits before newsreel cameras, and then we will hang them in public, to leave no one in any doubt that we still control Yugoslavia.' He pointed. 'I am particularly thinking of Davis and Fouquet. I want them standing there, in front of me, to answer for the death of my wife.'

'This will take time to set up.'

'Just make sure that it is not too much time. And when the operation is completed, I wish you to evacuate Dubrovnik. The Partisans will undoubtedly react, and I do not wish you to become sucked into a battle against superior forces.'

'What about Mihailovic?'

'I will deal with Mihailovic. Have Ulrich set up a meeting. You concentrate on the capture of Vis.'

*   *   *

'Well?' Angela demanded.

'Well what?' Wassermann inquired. His brain was teeming. If that old fool could be right, for once in his life, it could entirely restore both his reputation and his prestige. Why hadn't *he* thought of such a simple solution to their problems?

'You have just spent an hour with my father,' Angela pointed out, coldly. 'I assume you were discussing me?'

'Your name was not mentioned. Right now there are more important matters to be dealt with.'

'More important?'

'I don't suppose you have even taken in what has been happening in the war.'

'I do not give a fuck what is happening in the war.'

'Well, some of us have to fight it. I shall be leaving in a week or two to carry out a campaign. A campaign which will result in a decisive victory for the Reich. I will consider our situation when I come back.'

'And Erich?'

'Ah. Of course, Erich. I think he will be campaigning with me. We can consider his future also when we come back. If he comes back.'

'You bastard! You mean to murder him.'

'I mean to make him earn his pay – on his feet, for once in his life.'

He left the bedroom, and Angela threw herself on to the bed.

'Isn't that a pretty sight?' Tito asked as he stood with his staff watching the parachutes drifting downwards from the circling aircraft on to the gentle slopes of a Bosnian hillside. Winter was close, and the weather was threatening, but his men and women wore relatively new uniforms, and carried bright new weapons. Behind him there were several thousand more, equally well armed, and equipped with tanks and artillery. He had his army. 'You are sure these are dual purpose guns?' he asked Peter Johnstone.

'Absolutely. We learned that trick from Rommel in North Africa. Their eighty-eights fire armour-piercing shells, designed to bring down aircraft, but when used on the flat, at much shorter ranges, they proved quite devastating against our tanks. These guns will even stop a Tiger.'

'Then let us see them.' The first crate had struck the ground. Tito led his staff forward, and orderlies commenced tearing at the wood to expose the gun. But instead of a gun, they uncovered several small boxes.

'This must be the ammo,' Johnstone said.

'Open them,' Tito commanded. The lid of the first box was removed, and they gazed at layer after layer of thin steel utensils with a flattened head about four inches square. Tito looked at Johnstone, who was staring into the crate with an expression of incredulous horror.

'Those are fly swatters,' Tony said.

'Oh, my God!' Johnstone said.

'Do we use them when the enemy aircraft come low enough?' Tito asked sarcastically. 'Or merely wave them to and fro to drive them away?'

'I don't know what to say,' Johnstone said. 'I can only apologize, sir. There has been an administrative cock-up. I will get on the radio right away.' He hurried off.

'I suppose accidents will happen,' Tony remarked.

'Undoubtedly,' Tito agreed. 'I wonder what the Russians will bring with them?'

The Soviet mission arrived the following day. It consisted of four large aircraft, and far from dropping their cargoes, these landed at an abandoned Italian airstrip. Tito had his officers looking their best, and Judith commanded a guard of honour; there was even a band. 'We must make a good impression,' he told them.

But none of them were prepared for the man who emerged from the first aircraft. He was extremely fat, and the entire left side of his green tunic, from the shoulder to his waist belt, was smothered in medal ribbons. He beamed, genially, at the waiting Partisans, and stood to attention as the band struck up the Soviet anthem. Then he came down the steps, followed by his staff, who were only slightly less decorated.

'I am Korneyev,' he announced.

Tito saluted. 'Tito.'

'Our hero!' General Korneyev embraced him.

'My officers.' Tito introduced them in turn, and Korneyev embraced them also.

When he came to Tony, he gazed at him for several seconds. 'I have heard of you,' he said. 'You are famous. But where is the Frenchwoman? The so beautiful Frenchwoman? I wish to meet her.'

'Colonel Fouquet commands our base in Vis, sir,' Tony explained.

'But I will meet her soon, eh?'

'As soon as is possible, sir.' Tony wondered what he would say if he were to meet Sandrine *too* soon: she was now seven months pregnant.

'I will look forward to that.' He walked towards the guard of honour. 'And these are your famous women warriors, eh? We have women soldiers in Russia also. They are famous too. But we cut off their hair. These women have hair.'

'We prefer them this way. Allow me to introduce Colonel Hanisch.'

Judith saluted, and was embraced in a bear hug, giving a little shriek as Korneyev's hands slipped down her back to squeeze her buttocks. She gazed at Tony with outraged eyes, but kept still until the general released her to inspect the guard, spending some time with each good-looking woman or well-filled blouse. Tony could only be grateful that Sasha was commanding a forward observation post.

Tito had been watching, and now he came across. 'I think we should get him away as soon as possible,' he muttered. 'Judith, your people are relieved of guard duty until further orders. You will be replaced by men.'

'Yes, sir. Thank you, sir.'

Korneyev came back to them. 'A fine body of women,' he declared. 'I look forward to seeing more of them.'

'Unfortunately,' Tito said, 'they are about to leave for training camp. Now, shall we get back to HQ?'

'As soon as my gear is unloaded,' Korneyev said. 'I always attend to this personally.' He led the way back to the aircraft, from which box after box was being removed and placed on the ground. 'We will need some transport.'

'We have trucks,' Tito said. 'What is all this?'

'Let us say it is ammunition.'

'You travel with your own ammunition?'

'Of course.' He tore open the lid of one of the boxes, and took out a bottle of sparkling wine. 'Champagne, eh? Soviet champagne. There is none better. I begin every day with a bottle of champagne. This makes everything brighter, eh? Be careful with that,' he shouted, and hurried off to the next plane.

Tito looked at Johnstone. 'I would say that it is now I who owe you an apology, Colonel.'

Sandrine always took the radio calls herself, because they were usually made by Tony. Now she laughed. 'The man is a cretin. There is no such thing as Russian champagne. The only genuine champagne comes from Champagne.'

'You will have to give him a lecture when you meet him.'

'When will that be?'

'Hopefully not for a while yet. How are things?'

'I am bored. Martina is bored. We are all bored.'

'I meant, with you.'

'I seem to grow bigger by the day. I never knew it was such a tiresome business.'

'How long, do you reckon?'

'Trifunovic says two months. Will you be here?'

'Hopefully.'

'You are not starting a campaign? Without me?'

'No campaigning until the spring. You'll be around.'

'And then?'

'Well, it all looks pretty good. Korneyev assures us that the Russians will be into Romania by then, and then they intend to move on Bulgaria, and then—'

'Bulgaria is right next door.'

'That's it. Our offensive is to be timed to coincide with theirs.'

'Oh, Tony! I cannot believe it. What about in the west?'

'Bit of a stalemate, I'm afraid. Our people are still held up south of Rome. And while there is some talk of a landing in France, nobody knows where or when or if it's really practical. I think our best bet is to concentrate on our own little business.'

'Just remember to start nothing without me. I love you. And so does baby. Over and out.'

She handed the mike to the operator, and went outside, buttoning her coat. The winter wind coming down the Adriatic was freezing, the sea constantly turbulent. Martina was standing on the dock gazing at the open water between Vis and the next island. 'Is all well?'

'Oh, yes. They seem to have accumulated a Russian general who is either amusing or irritating them all of the time. Apparently he drinks like a fish and complains about the latrines. Well, I suppose if he drinks that much he needs to spend a lot of time in them.'

'And the war?'

'Is going well. Don't worry. There will be no campaign before the spring, and we will be involved. What are you watching?'

'A fishing boat.'

'In this weather? They must have strong stomachs.'

'That is what is interesting. I don't think he is fishing. He is just drifting to and fro. I think he is watching us.' Sandrine took the binoculars and levelled them.

'Do you think the Germans have discovered us?' Martina asked.

'The Germans discovered us long ago. They simply have not been able to do anything about it.'

'Then what—'

'Shit!' Sandrine said. 'There is another one. And another. Call out the guard, and warn Trifunovic to prepare for casualties.' She herself hurried as fast as she could back to the radio shack, panting, heart pounding. 'Send a message to General Tito's headquarters,' she said. 'Tell them we are under attack.'

'Attack?' the woman's voice rose an octave.

'Just send it, and wait for a reply.' But what reply could there be? No help could possibly reach them for several days, even if there was a Partisan group near the coast, and she did not know if there was. She went outside and gasped when she saw that the sea was now covered with boats and small ships; she estimated that there were at least fifty of them. And on more than one of the steamers there was mounted a gun. As she watched she saw the flashes of light, and a moment later there was an explosion amidst the houses of the little village the Partisans had created, accompanied by screams of dismay and shrieks of pain.

She hurried towards them and saw that Martina had assembled her command and was deploying them in front of the houses to cover the beach and the dock. Machine guns were being mounted; their four mortars were already in place, although the range was as yet too great for them to be used. 'How many, do you reckon?' Martina asked as she came up.

'Maybe fifty ships, maybe twenty-five men in each, more in the steamers . . . Over two thousand, anyway.'

'And we have seven hundred effectives. Can we do it?'

'If they are Cetniks or Ustase, yes. If they are Wehrmacht . . . We must do the best we can.'

'You must take shelter.'

'I am in command.'

'What about your baby?'

'He will have to get used to the sound of gunfire.'

'Well, at least keep your head down.'

'I must know who they are and what they are intending.' She went forward again, moving from tree to tree. The guns were still firing, but as the only target the enemy had was the houses, they were aiming their fire at those. The village was being systematically destroyed, but as it had been evacuated by the women, the only casualties they had so far suffered were those taken by surprise in the initial bombardment. Fortunately, Trifunovic's small hospital was situated at the very rear.

But the ships were coming steadily forward, now in a V-like formation, headed by the largest of the steamers. Sandrine refocussed the glasses, and her heart gave a curious little leap. The men gathered on the decks of the steamer wore steel helmets and black uniforms. 'Shit,' she muttered. 'Oh, shit.'

The radio operator panted up to her. 'Headquarters wishes to know the strength and composition of the attacking force.'

'Tell them that it is a brigade of the Waffen SS, and that they have artillery.' The woman gulped, and ran off. Sandrine returned to the perimeter. 'Germans,' she said to Martina. 'The SS. Brigade strength.'

'My God!' Martina said. 'What are we to do?'

'I think,' Sandrine said, 'that we are going to have to die.' Because there could be no question of surrendering to the SS, who would simply shoot them anyway. It was far better to die with weapons in their hands, taking as many of the enemy with them as they could.

Sandrine was aware principally of anger. The war was so close to being over, at least in Yugoslavia. The Germans were beaten, and the best thing they could do was get out and go home. Instead of which they were intent on killing, and being killed, up to the very last moment. And for her, far away from

Tony, and with the child they both wanted so badly already stirring in her womb, it was so utterly pointless. Yet it was going to happen, and if it was going to happen . . .

She watched the steamer nose its way alongside the dock, the black-clad men leaping ashore. 'Open fire!' she told Martina.

'A brigade of the SS,' Tony said savagely. 'And we thought they were done. I must get down there, Josep.'

'Can you do it in time?'

'If they can hold out for a few days . . .'

'It will take you at least a week, over those roads, in this weather.'

'We must go, sir,' Sasha insisted. 'If there is a chance . . . And we are doing nothing here.'

Tito sighed, then nodded. 'Take your brigade. I wish you success. But I wish you back here a month from today. And under no circumstances must you allow yourselves to be drawn into a pursuit which may suck you into superior forces and lead to your destruction.'

'Permission to accompany them, sir,' Peter Johnstone said.

'Will there be anyone left? Very good, Colonel. Bring them back safely. And Sandrine.'

The first wave of attackers went down before the concentrated fire of the Partisans. But they were quickly supported by more and more men as the rest of the ships came into the dockside, mooring three and four abreast while their occupants scrambled from gunwale to gunwale. And now they were supported by heavy machine-gun fire from the decks of the steamers, aiming over their heads, and these had a target as they had pinpointed the Partisan positions. Women fell left and right, but the survivors kept on shooting.

Martina crawled to where Sandrine crouched, firing her tommy gun. 'Listen,' she said. 'We are about to be overrun.

You must get away. Go into the trees and hide there. They will not know you were here. They will not waste the time to look for you. They must know that we have summoned help. As soon as they have destroyed us, they will go away again.'

'This is my command,' Sandrine said. 'How can I abandon it?'

Martina kissed her, and crawled away again. But the end was very near. The Germans had been creeping forward under the cover of the chattering machine guns, and now they were close enough to hurl their grenades. The women threw their own, but now there were too few. The firing slackened, and the black-uniformed figures rose and dashed at them, bayonets gleaming. Sandrine's tommy gun clicked empty, and she reached into her haversack for another drum, and found nothing: she had used all of her spares. She wondered what it was going to feel like as the steel rod entered her body, whether she would cry out – whether her baby would cry out. She looked up at the man standing above her, bayonet thrust forward; she tried to push herself backwards, and saw his expression change from one of ferocious determination to one of confusion. 'Hey, Sergeant!' he shouted. 'This one's pregnant.'

Men surrounded her, dragging her to her feet. 'They are bitches from the pit of hell,' someone said.

Sandrine could not stop herself from looking from face to face, and the sergeant frowned. 'She understands what we are saying. Do you speak German, woman?'

'Yes,' Sandrine said. 'I speak German.'

'Then tell us who is in command here.'

'I am in command.'

'You? A pregnant woman? Do you take me for a fool?'

'I am in command,' Sandrine repeated. 'I am Sandrine Fouquet.'

'Well,' Wassermann said. 'What a happy surprise. I had hoped for more, mind you. But you will do for now. You will make an excellent Christmas present.' He sat in the captain's cabin of the steamer; he had not been ashore. With him were Mathilde and Halbstadt. Mathilde had not been ashore either, but Halbstadt was flushed with the excitement of battle, the euphoria of victory. Sandrine stood in front of them, between two guards.

'You have met this woman before?' Mathilde asked.

'Oh indeed, we have met before,' Wassermann said. 'Haven't we, Sandrine?'

Sandrine did not reply. She counted herself already dead; that she was standing was merely an accident of time.

'And what did you do with her the last time?' Mathilde asked. 'Apart from allowing her to get away?'

'*I* did not allow her to get away. That fool Blintoft did that. As for what I did to her—'

Sandrine could not stop herself. 'He tried to rape me, and he could not. And he was not even wounded then.'

Wassermann glared at her, but she would not lower her eyes. 'Well,' Mathilde said, 'think of what you can do to her now. We could deliver her baby for her, Caesarean section.'

'Shut up,' Wassermann said. 'Keep her under close guard,' he told Halbstadt. 'Do not be taken in by either her looks or the fact that she is pregnant. Believe me, she is far more dangerous than Janitz.'

Halbstadt clicked his heels, and gestured Sandrine to the door. 'What about my people?' she asked.

'You have no people,' Wassermann said.

'There were seven hundred of us. You cannot have killed them all.'

'No, we did not. The survivors are being killed now. One prisoner is sufficient – when her name is Sandrine Fouquet.'

Sandrine strained at the hands grasping her arms as if she would have attacked him, then she was dragged from the cabin. 'You are not going to do *anything* to her?' Mathilde asked.

'Sadly, not at this moment. Blintoft wants her first. But I am sure she will be returned to us in due course.'

Tony and Sasha actually reached Dubrovnik in four days, driving recklessly over the icy roads, the brigade strung out behind them. 'This is the only way to campaign,' Sasha said. 'Why have we spent all of these years walking?'

'Driving makes you fat and lazy,' Tony said. He was experiencing a strange mixture of despair and exhilaration. He knew there was no possibility of reaching Vis in time, but if perhaps the SS were still in the seaport, with their prisoners . . . Only the SS did not take prisoners. Yet he refused to believe that Sandrine could be dead, after having survived so much, even as he recognized that was not logical thinking. But until he saw her dead body . . .

They halted outside the town and made a careful reconnaissance. But there was not a German soldier to be seen. They entered the port in skirmishing order, and were vociferously greeted by the inhabitants, who crowded round to hug them and kiss them and shower them with food and drink. 'The Germans evacuated the town two days ago, General,' the mayor said.

'Two days?' Sasha cried. 'Then we can catch them up.'

'The marshal said, no pursuit,' Tony said. 'What happened on the island?' he asked the mayor.

'It was very bad, I think. They were triumphant. They said they had wiped out the entire garrison.'

'There were no prisoners at all?'

'There was one. The commanding officer, Colonel Fouquet. You will have heard of her.'

'Yes,' Tony said. 'I have heard of her. What did they do with her?'

'They took her with them. They were very pleased.'

'Was she ill-treated?' Sasha asked.

'No, no. She was pregnant. They seemed to find this amusing.'

'Get us a boat,' Tony said. 'We wish to visit the island.' The mayor bustled off.

'They have Sandrine,' Sasha said. 'And they are only two days ahead of us. We can catch them, Tony. We can rescue her.'

'We cannot,' he said. 'Whatever their reason for taking her alive, Wassermann will certainly kill her if he is in danger of losing her yet again. Besides, Tito gave us definite orders. If we were to lose this brigade in a vain attempt to rescue one person we would deserve to be shot. We probably would be shot.'

'One person? This is Sandrine.'

'Don't you think I know that?' he asked savagely. 'At least we know she's alive.'

'At this moment. And even if she is alive, what do you think they will do to her when they get her back to Belgrade?'

'I do not believe they will do anything to her for a while. She has nothing to tell them, because they already know all about our new strength and our intentions as soon as the summer comes.'

'And you think that will stop Wassermann from torturing her?'

'Yes, because Wassermann is no longer in command. Blintoft is still looking for vengeance for the murder of his wife, and he knows that Sandrine and I were involved in that. I believe he still means to have us put on trial, condemned, and executed.'

'But then—'

'It will take time. We must hope we can get to Belgrade first. As an army.' Did he really believe that? In his heart he knew he did not. But he had to make himself believe it, because it was the only hope to which he could cling. Besides, he reminded himself, he had thought her dead twice before, and each time she had turned up again. Sandrine was indestructible. He had to believe that.

'You do not have a heart in there,' Sasha said. 'It is a lump

211

of rock. So what are we going to do now? Rejoin the army and celebrate Christmas?'

'Yes,' Tony said. 'But first we are going to bury our dead. Martina is somewhere over there.'

'Sandrine Fouquet.' Anton von Blintoft got up from his desk, and walked round it. Sandrine stood between two guards, as usual. Wassermann, Halbstadt and Ulrich were behind her, Wassermann beaming. Blintoft stood in front of her. 'Do you know you are every bit as attractive as in your pictures, Fräulein?'

'I am not a fräulein,' Sandrine said. 'I am a mademoiselle.'

'And every bit as arrogant. So, General Wassermann, your campaign was a success.'

'A regiment of the Partisans has been wiped out, Herr General.'

'And this woman taken prisoner. But no Tito, no Davis, and no Janitz.'

'They were not there.'

'So the success can only be regarded as partial. However . . .' He addressed Sandrine. 'When do you expect your baby, Fräulein? I beg your pardon, Mademoiselle?'

'I am seven months pregnant.'

'Ah. Then we must be patient.' He returned behind his desk and sat down. 'However, we should not waste our time. You are guilty of my wife's murder.'

'I did not shoot your wife.'

'I accept that. But you were a member of the assassination squad.'

'Our target was you, Herr General. That your wife was hit was an unfortunate accident.'

'I accept that also. However, you were bent on assassination. You will hang for it.'

'Even if I did not shoot anybody?'

'On that occasion. But will you deny that you have shot quite a few people since?'

'Not enough.'

'I hope you will die with such defiance. Now, I do not wish to ill-treat you. I dislike ill-treating women under any circumstances, and I believe that pregnant women should be treated with the greatest respect. However, I also believe that the guilty should suffer the appropriate penalty for their crimes. I am going to lock you up until you are delivered. For that period you will suffer no more discomfort than is necessary. I will, however, require you to be photographed, both as a criminal record and for propaganda purposes. Once you are delivered, your trial will commence. It will be in public, and you will confess to the murder of my wife. Your confession will include incriminating your paramour, Davis, and your master, Tito, who you will denounce as the man who specifically ordered the assassination of my wife, not of me. I think you should spend the next two months composing your confession. As soon as you are ready, I will have one of my secretaries take it down.'

'And if I refuse to lie for your satisfaction?'

'That would be very unwise of you. I have said that I would be very reluctant to ill-treat you, but if I am forced into it, I will hand you over to General Wassermann, in order that you may be, shall I say, persuaded to cooperate. You should also bear in mind the fate of your baby.'

'You call yourself a gentleman,' Sandrine said. 'You are nothing more than scum, like all your people.'

Blintoft regarded her for a few moments, then he said, 'I would reflect very carefully on everything I have said, Fräulein. Ulrich, this prisoner is in your personal care. Dismissed.'

'Do you not wish her punished, at least by a whipping, for her defiance of you?' Wassermann asked.

'No, I do not wish her whipped, or punished in any way. I wish her to reflect. Thank you, gentlemen.'

'That man is such a fool,' Wassermann declared. 'He lives in a world of his own. With the war coming up to a climactic situation, all he can think of is bringing his wife's murderers to justice.'

'Presumably there will be some propaganda value in a show trial of a famous Partisan commander,' Mathilde suggested.

'There may have been once, two years ago. Then, depicting Tito and his people as common murderers of women might have had some effect on neutral opinion. Now, there is no such thing as neutral opinion. The world has polarized, and no one on the Allied side is going to believe anything bad about Tito, just as no one on our side will believe anything good.'

'All those people, hating us. Does that thought not frighten you, Fritz? It frightens me.'

'They cannot harm you. Not while the Reich is dominant.'

'But is the Reich still dominant? Our frontiers are steadily shrinking. If we were to lose this war . . .'

'We cannot lose the war. We are too powerful.'

'Words.'

'They happen to be fact. I know things you do not.'

'Do you, Fritz? Do you? Is that the truth, honest to God?'

'That is the truth.'

She held his hand. 'Then when can we be married?'

'Ah. Yes. I must—' He stared at the door as it opened without a knock. Angela stood there.

Wassermann stood up. Mathilde drew up her legs; she was wearing only a dressing gown. Angela looked from one to the other. 'Who is this person?' she demanded.

'Frau Geisner is my secretary.'

'And you find it necessary to visit her in her bedroom?'

'As you find it necessary to visit Halbstadt in his bedroom.'

Angela threw back her head and gave a peal of laughter. 'And what do you do to her, Fritz? What do you give her? What *can* you give her, you poor broken creature?'

'It is what I give to him, Frau Wassermann,' Mathilde said in a low voice.

Angela stared at her, then turned back to her husband. 'I think Papa would be very amused to learn how you employ your spare time. Now, I wish something of you. Is it true that you have captured Fouquet?'

'It is true.'

'I wish to see her. Write me out an order.'

'And do you think that "Papa" would like to know that his daughter prefers girls to boys, and once fell madly in love with a Partisan commander? Or are you perhaps still in love with her?'

'I wish that permission,' Angela said.

'And I cannot give it to you. She is confined under your father's orders, in the specific care of Ulrich. I have nothing more to do with her. If you wish that permission so desperately, go to "Papa".' Angela gave him another long stare, then turned to the door. 'You wouldn't enjoy her, anyway,' Wassermann said. 'She is seven months pregnant.' Angela slammed the door behind herself.

'Can she make trouble?' Mathilde asked.

'Not for us.'

'But if she goes tattling to her father . . .'

'Blintoft already knows about us.' Mathilde's mouth made an O. 'I told him,' Wassermann explained. 'He quite accepts the situation.'

'But he will not let you divorce his daughter.'

'He does not know I wish to do that, yet. But Angela is on the way to destroying herself, my dear. All we have to do is give her enough time.'

Ulrich started in apprehension and rose to his feet as his secretary showed Angela into his office. 'Frau Wassermann.'

'Oh, for God's sake, Hermann.' Angela sank into the chair before his desk. 'My name is Angela.'

'Angela. Is there something wrong?'

'Yes. You have been playing tricks on me again.'

'Me?'

215

'And you are the world's worst liar. Why did you not tell me you have Fouquet in your cells?'

'Ah . . . I did not think you would be interested.'

'Are you really as stupid as you look?' She unfolded the newspaper. 'Did you take that photograph?'

'My people took it.'

'She is every bit as beautiful now as she was two years ago. Is she really seven months pregnant?'

'More, I would say.'

'I wish to see her.'

'No one can see her. Those are your father's orders.'

'Do you not see her?'

'I am required to visit her once a day.'

'And who feeds her?'

'Karin, the head wardress.'

'So she is being given the same VIP treatment as the last time. Why?'

'Because your father intends to place her on trial for the murder of your mother. As soon as she is delivered.'

'I wish to see her.'

'It is impossible. Only General von Blintoft can give you the necessary permission.'

'Hermann, you are going to make me very cross. I am not going to harm her. I just wish to see her, again, one more time.'

'See her . . .' Ulrich said thoughtfully.

'Well, it would be nice to speak with her. Just a few words.'

'It would be a direct disobedience of orders. Your father's orders.'

'Pooh. Daddy won't mind my talking with her. But I won't mention it to him, if it bothers you.'

'Well . . .'

Angela fluttered her eyelashes. 'I should be ever so grateful.'

*   *   *

Sandrine lay on her back on the camp cot, staring at the ceiling. Life was a business of emptying her mind of thought, of memory as much as of anticipation or apprehension.

In the beginning, when she had realized the catastrophe that was overtaking her women and herself, all her thoughts had concentrated on her baby, on its survival, and perhaps, even more, on its survival without any permanent injury. That single thought had dominated her mind on the journey back to Belgrade, shutting out every other terrible consideration. She had had sundry aches and pains, and, not ever having been pregnant before, she could not help but relate all of them to a possible miscarriage. Her actions, her words, her defiance of her captors, had been more instinctive than calculated.

But she had been examined by a doctor, and he had said both that she was fit and well and that the baby was unharmed. And she had Blintoft's word that she would not be put on trial until after the birth. So, for almost another two months there was nothing to think about. Anticipation was both dangerous and a waste of time. Two months! In two months' time it would be spring. The armies would be on the move, even if the Germans seemed blissfully unaware of it, or at least blissfully confident that they could deal with anything that could be thrown at them. To allow herself to feel otherwise, to feel that somehow Tito, with his new arms and equipment, his vast accretion of strength in men and munitions, would come storming into Belgrade, that her cell door would burst open and Tony be standing there, would be to hover on the edge of madness. Just as to anticipate that she would not be rescued, but have to give up her baby and submit to torture, and then to mount a scaffold before a crowd of people and have a rope placed round her neck, and then know only a moment of flashing light before eternal oblivion, would be to tumble over the edge. So, no anticipation.

But no remembering either. To attempt to recall her experiences with Tony, firstly when they had been fleeing Belgrade with Elena and dear old Ivkov the bathhouse-keeper, the horror of their capture by the Ustase and the glory of their escape, accomplished by her own courage and gallantry, the night she had first earned her reputation, the month she and Tony had survived alone together, slowly getting to know one another, then the battles they had fought together under Tito's command, the victories they had gained, was also to recall the death of Elena, her previous incarceration in this cell, the death of little Charles, and most recently and possibly most traumatically of all, the way her women had been cut down, the death of Martina . . . That way left only misery. Better just to exist, counting aimlessly to a hundred.

She heard movement at her door, and sat up. She had been fed and bathed earlier; there should be no more interruptions until tomorrow. Her muscles tensed as the door swung in. If Blintoft had somehow been removed from command, and she was back at the mercy of Wassermann . . .

It was Karin. Karin was unfailingly good-humoured, always smiling. Sandrine supposed that when she escorted a prisoner to the torture chamber and set about her victim with a whip, she would be smiling even more broadly. She was smiling now. 'You have a visitor, Fräulein.'

Sandrine looked past her at Angela. This cannot be happening, she thought. Because here was a memory which could not be resisted; it was present in the flesh.

'Leave us,' Angela said.

'I have been told this woman is very dangerous,' Karin pointed out.

'How can she be dangerous, with that belly?'

'Well . . .' Karin considered. 'I will be right outside if you need me.'

Angela waited for the door to close. Then she said, 'How the wheel does turn.'

'But you will be hoping that it has stopped turning now,' Sandrine suggested.

'Has it not? I am not leaving Belgrade to be captured by your friends. There is going to be no exchange this time.'

'But my friends will still avenge me.'

'Do you really think so? Even if they do, you will not be here to enjoy it.'

Sandrine lay down again. 'If you have something worthwhile to say, why don't you say it.'

Angela advanced to stand beside the bed. 'I loved you. I would love you still.'

'There is no accounting for tastes.'

'But you had no feeling for me at all. You used my feelings to escape me.'

'I'm a cold fish,' Sandrine agreed.

'Sometimes I feel like strangling you.'

'I don't think your daddy would approve.'

'He'll forgive me.'

Sandrine turned her head. 'Then why don't you?'

'Wouldn't you prefer me to help you? I know that you hate everything I stand for, but that is no reason to hate *me*. Listen, I could persuade Papa not to place you on trial, not to hang you. He will do anything I ask him to. I am all he has left in the world.'

'And the price?'

'Well . . .' Angela flushed, and sat on the bed. 'We could go back to Germany, together. We'd take your baby, and we'd set up house together, just the three of us. I'd see no harm ever came to you, or the child. I could make you very happy, Sandrine.'

'That is not a price I am prepared to pay.'

'But why?'

'Because you represent everything that is evil in the world.'

'Evil,' Angela said contemptuously. 'Good. Words, invented by people who had never had the courage to *live*. Don't you understand that if you refuse me you are going to die?'

'It's a little late,' Sandrine said, 'for me to be afraid of death.'

Ten

The Victory

The wind coming down from the mountains was almost balmy. Tony stood in front of Tito's desk in the new Partisan headquarters of Skopje. 'Well?' he inquired.

'I am waiting for instructions.'

'*You* are waiting for instructions? From whom?'

'In this instance, Moscow.'

'You have never accepted instructions from Moscow before.'

'It has never been necessary before. This offensive has got to be conclusive, Tony. It will not commence until the Russians are ready to assault Yugoslavia from the other side. Then we will crush the Germans between us.'

'Don't you suppose the Germans are aware of this?'

'I have no doubt of it. Which is why we must oppose them with overwhelming force.'

'So we sit, and wait, while Sandrine is executed.'

Tito indicated the newspaper on his desk. 'Don't you believe this?'

'I don't believe anything put out by the Germans.'

'Well, I do, in this instance. They have made a big thing about their capture of Sandrine, about how, as soon as she is delivered of her child, she will be placed on trial for her murder of Frau von Blintoft. They are working to a very definite, and very subtle plan here, Tony. This wish to show the world, or at least the Yugoslav world, firstly, that the

220

process of Nazi justice is inexorable, and secondly that it is also merciful, in that they will do nothing to impair the birth of her child. They are hoping this will earn them support to withstand any attack by Communist forces, whether from within or without.'

'Can they seriously suppose that any Yugoslav will support them now, after three years of subjugation?'

'I think they can. And they may very well be right.' He indicated the paper again. 'There is another item of news which you may find of interest. Mihailovic has announced that he has set up an interim government of Yugoslavia, with German support.'

'He is cutting his own throat.'

'I think he understands that his throat is going to be cut if he just sits and waits for the war to end. Even the Americans have withdrawn support for him. He is attempting to establish himself as a national leader, and from what I hear he is obtaining a good deal of support. There are a lot of people in this country who do not like the colour red. You are not that fond of it yourself.'

'You know that my opinions are personal. I would never let them interfere with my determination to bring down Nazi Germany.'

'I do know that, Tony. Unfortunately, not everyone is as single-minded as yourself.'

'But you do realize that even supposing Blintoft sticks to his word, Sandrine will be delivered at any moment now?'

Tito sighed. 'I do know that. But show trials take some time to be staged. We must put our faith in that.'

'He is a bastard,' Sasha said. 'All generals are bastards. With the exception of you.'

'I am quite sure I would be a bastard,' Tony said, 'if I was charged with delineating the future.'

'So we wait?'

'We obey orders.'
'While Sandrine . . . ?'
'She will wait too – for us to come to her.'

'Well?' Wassermann asked his father-in-law. 'Is the report true?'
'That the Russians have overrun Romania? I am afraid it is true.'
'It will be Bulgaria next. And then—'
'Us. I do not think there can be any doubt of that.'
'So?'
'My orders are quite clear. We must hold them for as long as possible. I have told you why. Our new weapons are on the verge of completion. Once that is done, the war is won, no matter where the Russians may be. We shall simply blow them out of existence. So we hold, to the last man, for the future of the fatherland.'
'Do you not suppose those same orders were given to our commanders in Romania and Bulgaria?'
'I have no doubt of it. We were failed in Romania. We must hope that Bulgaria does better.'
'And if they do not?'
'Then we will have to do better.'
'With what?'
'We have garrison troops amounting to two divisions. And we have your brigade. We also have the Cetniks, worth another division at least.' Wassermann snorted. 'Oh, they will fight,' Blintoft insisted. 'They have no choice now. If we are invaded, we will concentrate our strength here, to defend Belgrade.'
'I do not regard Belgrade as defensible. There are no natural defences.'
'There are the three rivers. Rivers are always defensible. In any event, we must do the best we can. Our orders are explicit. There can be no withdrawal.'
'I see. So what are you intending to do about Fouquet?'

'Exactly what I have said we will do. No one except us knows the true situation. No one must know. There must be no panic. Thus the trial of Fouquet will take place as I have said it will. When is she due?'

'I believe any day now.'

'Then we do not have very long to wait.'

'And Angela?'

'Our orders only apply to military pesonnel. I will make arrangements for her to be returned to Germany.'

'I was speaking of her flagrant disregard of orders in visiting Fouquet.'

'I quite understand her motives. They have known each other in the past. I imagine she was sorry for her.'

'Sorry for her? Do you really believe that?'

Blintoft frowned at him. 'What are you trying to say?'

Wassermann opened his mouth and then closed it again. For all his contempt, and indeed, hatred, for both his wife and her father, with the military situation becoming critical, his training as an officer warned him that now was not the time to provoke a domestic crisis as well. 'It is simply that I cannot believe Angela could possibly feel any sympathy for a woman like Fouquet.'

'You judge her too harshly. She is a very sympathetic person.'

Wassermann suppressed a snort.

'Well?' Mathilde asked.

'Well, what?'

'Is the matter settled? You said she had at last betrayed herself.'

'I did not discuss the matter.'

She gazed at him. 'You do not intend to do it.'

'My darling, of course I do. It is simply that now is not the time. The military situation is serious. Anyway, she is being sent back to Germany.'

'Why?'

'There is a chance that we may have to withstand a Soviet attack. It will be very dangerous here.'

'So she is being sent away to safety.'

'Yes. You can go with her, if you wish.'

'Do you want me to do that?'

'Of course I do not.'

'Can we beat the Russians?'

'Oh, yes.'

'Then I will stay and watch you do it.'

But she was resolved that that bitch was not going to survive.

The next day she summoned the canteen mangeress; Mathilde now had her own office. 'You have someone working for you named Rosa Malic.'

'Oh, yes, Frau Geisner.'

'I wish to speak with her. Send her to me, please.'

She waited, sitting back in her chair. Rosa sidled, as she always did. 'Sit down,' Mathilde invited. 'Do you remember me?'

Rosa perched on a chair. 'Yes, Frau Geisner.'

'Then you understand that I am General Wassermann's closest aide.'

'Oh, yes, Frau Geisner.'

'Then you will appreciate that the general has no secrets from me.'

Rosa licked her lips.

'So, the general has determined to put certain matters right. He has deputed the task to me, because he does not wish to be personally involved. It is to do with his wife.'

Rosa gulped.

'You perjured yourself to save her from a murder charge, did you not?'

'I did what General Wassermann wished.'

'Of course. Now he wishes you to write a statement stating

exactly what you did, but without mentioning that you were told to do so by the general. You will say that you were suborned by his wife.'

'But if I do that . . .'

'You will be convicting yourself? Nothing can happen to you, Rosa. Do you not have a document absolving you from any blame or guilt for anything that you may have had to do prior to the assault on Tito's cave, as a reward for your services on that occasion?'

Rosa nodded, slowly.

'So, you see, you have nothing to worry about. You will write that statement, and deliver it to me. You will tell no one of this.'

Rosa nodded, again slowly.

'But there is something else you must do. You spent several months as Frau Wassermann's personal maid. You must know all her secrets.'

Rosa sucked her upper lip between her teeth.

'You know about her affair with Captain Halbstadt. Did he approach her, or did she seduce him?'

'Oh, she seduced him.'

'Excellent. And who else did she seduce?'

Rosa rolled her eyes.

'Come along,' Mathilde said.

'There was no one else.'

'I do not believe you. Do not make me angry.'

'I meant, there was no other man.'

Mathilde frowned, while her hearbeat quickened. She had not hoped for so much. 'Go on. You mean there was a woman?'

'There was Jelena Brolic. She was a Partisan spy. And before her, there was Colonel Fouquet.'

Mathilde could not believe her ears. 'The woman who is in our cells now?'

'Oh, yes. I think Frau Wassermann allowed herself to be captured by the Partisans so that she could be exchanged for

Colonel Fouquet, and thus save her from execution. She was not pregnant then,' Rosa added ingenuously.

'Rosa, you are a treasure. You will write that all down, and you will swear to its truth.'

'But if Frau Wassermann were ever to find out . . .'

'Frau Wassermann will never be able to harm you, Rosa, once you have written that letter. I will swear to that.'

Sandrine gasped, and pushed, as she had been ordered. She was in the prison hospital, and the nurses were being very kind. It was far easier than she had dared hope. And then she held him in her arms.

'What will you call him?' Sister asked.

'Tony.'

'That is not a name. It is a diminutive. He must be called Anthony.'

'I will call him Tony.'

Sister raised her eyes to heaven, and then looked past the bed to the door, and hastily stood to attention. 'Herr General.'

Blintoft came into the room and stood by the bed. Sandrine hugged the babe to her breast. 'You must be very pleased,' the general said.

Sandrine did not reply.

'I had expected to hear from you before now,' Blintoft said. 'Concerning your confession.'

'I have nothing to confess, save what I have already told you. I came to Belgrade with three comrades, to assassinate you, General von Blintoft. When your wife stepped in front of you, inadvertently, General Davis, who was in command, refused to fire in case she was hit. Another one of our party lost his head and fired anyway, and Frau von Blintoft was killed. That man is now dead. So is the fourth member of the squad.'

'But Davis is still alive.'

'Yes, General, Davis is still alive. For which I thank God.'

'Is he the father of your child?'

'Yes.' Still she held the baby close, as if she could protect him.

'You are a very courageous woman,' Blintoft said. 'And I believe that you are telling the truth. However, it is necessary for you to lie in court. Your movement must be condemned by world opinion.'

'Do you suppose that world opinion matters now?'

'Yes. I will send my secretary to you.'

'And I will say nothing except what I have just told you.'

'That would be very stupid of you. Colonel Fouquet, Sandrine, you are an exceptionally beautiful woman, as well as a courageous one. I believe, in different circumstances, I would like you very much. But I have said what will happen. And I will make it happen. Listen to me. Sign that confession, and I will see that you are not executed. I will have you sentenced to life imprisonment. You will be able to keep your baby. But if you continue to defy me, I will hand you over to Wassermann, and your child will be taken away.'

Sandrine looked down on the wizened face. Women have honour too, she had once told Tony. 'I will not sign a lie. And whatever happens to me, he will still be my son.'

Blintoft gazed at her for several seconds. Then he said, 'I will allow you one week to reflect, and change your mind. One week in which you may keep your child. If at the end of that time you are still determined to defy me, then may God have mercy on you. I know Wassermann will have none.'

The radio operator stood to attention, with difficulty; he was trembling with excitement. 'Message from Moscow, sir.'

'Yes?'

'The Bulgarian army has laid down its arms, and is cooperating in every way.'

'Very good.' As always, there was no emotion in Tito's voice, but his eyes were dancing. 'Reply that the message has been received and understood.' The operator hurried off. Tito

227

stood up, and looked around his officers. 'Well, gentlemen. Let us move on Belgrade.'

'Oh, hurrah,' Sasha cried. 'Hurrah, hurrah and hurrah. Will we be in time?'

'Let us believe that. But there is not a moment to be lost.'

'So there it is,' Anton von Blintoft said. 'We may expect Soviet forces to cross the border within a week. General Wassermann?'

'I have called in our outlying garrisons and deployed them on the east side of the city, sir. I am holding my brigade as a mobile reserve. I have also concentrated all of our anti-aicraft batteries in and around the city.'

'Very good. General Mihailovic?'

'As instructed, I have concentrated my people to the south-west of the city. However, I must express my opinion, Herr General, that Belgrade is indefensible. It would make more sense for us to operate as guerillas in the hills, and harass the Soviets, rather than sit in one place and await their attack.'

'We have not the resources for that,' Blintoft pointed out. 'Our troops are garrison soldiers, men over thirty, incapable of rapid or sustained movement. They will do better behind defences. In any event, our orders are to hold Belgrade to the last man. Now you will excuse me. Fritz.'

Wassermann followed him out of the office and along the hall to the drawing room. 'Do you still think he will fight?'

'I still believe he has no alternative. Kurt.'

Hartmann looked embarrassed. 'This really goes against the grain.'

'Why should it? This has now become a purely military matter. You no longer have a country to govern.'

'I still feel that I am running away.'

'You are doing your duty, as am I. Are the ladies ready?'

Hartmann nodded. His butler opened the inner door to the

small parlour in which Frau Hartmann and Angela were waiting. Each had a single suitcase, while a third waited for Hartmann himself.

'Anton!' Frau Hartmann embraced him. 'Fritz!' She embraced Wassermann in turn. 'We will wait for you downstairs,' she told Angela.

Angela waited for the door to close, then hugged her father. 'I wish you could come with me.'

'But you know that is impossible. I am serving the Reich. There can be no greater glory. And you will remember me.'

'Oh, Papa! You are speaking as if you are going to die.'

Blintoft kissed her. 'This is the culmination of my career. And who knows, perhaps I will win. I will wait for you outside, Fritz.'

He too left the room.

'Well,' Angela said. 'Are you also going to die?'

'Would that please you?'

She shrugged. 'I have become used to having you around. Is your "secretary" also being evacuated?'

'I offered her the opportunity, but she prefers to stay.'

'And die at your side? The woman must be demented.'

'Or she is genuinely in love with me.'

'As I said, the woman must be demented. Well, no doubt I shall see you in hell.'

'Aren't you going to kiss me goodbye?'

She considered. 'I don't think so. I might catch something.'

Wassermann stood at Blintoft's shoulder to watch the car, escorted by four motorcycle outriders, leave the grounds.

'We should have gone to the station,' Blintoft said. 'But that station has too many bad memories for me. This would have been one more. Will they make it?'

'Of course. We must put Angela out of our minds, Anton, and concentrate on matters here. Beginning with Fouquet.'

'Fouquet,' Blintoft muttered. 'Always Fouquet. What about her now?'

'She must be hanged, now. In the circumstances, I do not think a trial is necessary.'

'Her death, now, would be meaningless. Who are we going to impress, if we are wiped out in a week's time?'

'It would give me a great deal of satisfaction.'

'I suggest that, instead of murdering a single defenceless woman, you devote your energies to killing Russians. She is not to be harmed. That is an order. If it is disobeyed, I will have you shot.'

'She just left,' Erich Halbstadt said, slumped in his chair before Ulrich's desk. 'Just like that. Without even a word of farewell. Not even a wave.'

'Do you honestly suppose that she was ever interested in anything more than a single part of your anatomy?' Ulrich asked.

'She is a bitch.'

'It has taken you a very long time to find that out.'

'It is so unfair. She has gone off to security and prosperity. While I—'

'Are being given the opportunity to fight for the Führer. Do you not wish to do that?'

Halbstadt raised his head. 'Are you not afraid?'

Ulrich considered. 'I wish it could be different. I wish I could be home in Hamburg with my wife. But as that is impossible . . .' He opened the drawer and took out a Luger pistol. 'Do you know that I have never fired this gun in anger? Well, there is a first time for everything.'

'You're not going to—'

'No, no. Not now. There are nine bullets in this magazine. Eight are for the enemy. Now go away and pull yourself together.'

'So all the rats have deserted the sinking ship,' Mathilde said.

'Did you send my letter with them?'

'It went in the official bag,' Wassermann said wearily. 'What was so important about it anyway?'

'I felt I should write my sister and tell her that I might not be seeing her for a while. Do you not think that was the correct thing to do?'

Wassermann shrugged. 'I would say so.'

'So tell me, what are we going to do with Fouquet?'

'Nothing.'

'Nothing?'

'It would appear that our esteemed commanding general has fallen in love with her.' He snorted. 'Everyone who comes into contact with that woman falls in love with her.'

'Including you?'

'Oh, yes. Once.'

'But not now. Will you be in command were Blintoft to be killed?'

He raised his head to look at her.

'Just considering,' she said.

Crowds lined the streets as the Partisans swept through the towns and villages. People cheered hysterically, and at every stop they were plied with food and drink, while everyone wanted to hug and kiss them. 'Why isn't war always like this?' Sasha asked.

'Because this isn't war,' Tony told her. 'This is victory.'

But he was uneasy. 'Where is the enemy?' he asked Tito.

'Pulled out, it seems.'

'Out of Yugoslavia?'

'I do not think they have done that.'

'They are in Belgrade,' General Korneyev announced that night at dinner, having been on the radio. 'Our probes have encountered considerable resistance east of the city. They have thus ceased their advance until your people are in position, Marshal Tito. When will you be ready?'

Tito looked at the map. 'We will be in Uzice in three days' time.'

'Then we will plan the final assault for the fourth day from now.'

'The fifth,' Tito said. 'After such a fast advance, we need twenty-four hours to rest and concentrate.'

Tony knew he was right, but every day, every hour, every second seemed an eternity as he thought of Sandrine dangling at the end of a rope. But on the third day the army was in Uzice. What memories it brought back. It had all really started here, the scene of the Partisans' first victory – and also, to be sure, their first substantial defeat. It was here that Sandrine had first been captured by the Germans, that they had first heard the name of Wassermann. And it was from here that he and Sasha had led the women's regiment, as it had then been, over the mountain into Bosnia. And it was only twenty miles from Belgrade.

'Do you think she is still alive?' Sasha asked as they gazed across the plain on the fourth evening.

'Yes,' Tony said. 'I have to believe that she is alive, until I see her dead body.'

'And do you think Wassermann is still here?'

'I hope he is.'

'So do I,' Sasha said. 'And that bitch girlfriend of his.'

'Report?' Wassermann said.

'The Partisans are in Uzice,' the patrol captain said.

'You are certain of this?'

'Our people penetrated to the town's outskirts, and were then fired upon. They say there is no doubt that there is a large body of troops in the town.'

'And the Russians?'

'There is no evidence that they have advanced for the past two days. They are twenty miles away.'

'Roughly the same distance as Uzice to the west. They intend to come in together. Very good. Have your men get some sleep.'

He went outside, looked at the night. The city had been bombed several times, and there were several fires burning. It hummed with restlessness, but the sound was generally muted. Belgrade was preparing to die. Or to be reborn.

He summoned his command car and drove to the palace, slowly, because of the blackout and the several craters in the roads. The palace itself had been turned into a mini-fortress, with machine-gun emplacements dug into the lawns, and even a few field pieces mounted, while the building itself was filled with soldiers.

Anton von Blintoft stood at the top of the stairs. 'Report?'

Wassermann jerked his head and went into the office. Blintoft followed. 'They are in Uzice. They will attack tomorrow, I would say. The Russians also.'

Blintoft sat behind his desk. 'Well, then, that is it.'

'Is there no hope?'

'None.'

'Have you been on to Berlin?'

'Yes, I have. The orders are the same. Belgrade must be held to the last bullet and the last man.'

'Hitler has been giving those same orders to all our people since December 1941.'

'The Führer,' Blintoft said stiffly, 'sees the overall picture, which we, on the ground, cannot. Every hour that we can hold out helps preserve the Reich, helps ensure our eventual victory.'

'If you still believe that, Anton, you are a bigger fool than I thought you were.' Wasserman walked out of the office, back to his car. Mathilde was waiting for him. She was his last refuge.

The officers' council was called for two in the morning. 'As far as we have been able to ascertain,' Tito told them, 'there are two bodies of German troops here, and here.' He prodded the map. 'That is the east side of the city, and we must assume that they will be attacked by the Russians. They have not yet

233

told us their plan of battle. However, they are not anticipating great resistance. They have checked our estimates, and reckon the Germans are in some strength, perhaps forty thousand men. But they agree that these have mostly been drawn from the abandoned garrison towns, and there is no evidence of any divisional organization. They have a limited number of guns, fewer tanks, and no aircraft. The Russians have double that number, with some Allied elements, and they have a large force of tanks as well as complete air superiority. However, I have requested them to cease bombing at noon tomorrow. The Russian general has agreed that our forces will liberate the city, although of course they will support us the moment the Germans are dispersed.

'Our field of operation is the west and south, here, held by the Cetniks. They are our preliminary target, and I am sure that our people will be happy about that. However, we know that there is also a brigade of the Waffen SS in the city, and our scouts have not been able to identify their position. Neither have the Russians. It is my estimation that these troops, which are the best they have, and, incidentally, the most fanatical of Nazis, are not on the perimeter at all, but are being held inside the city, to keep order amongst the civilian population, to guard vital installations, and perhaps to carry out strategic demolitions. I therefore regard their destruction as our province also. I am sure you agree with me, Major-General Davis.'

'I do, sir.'

'And I'm sure that you, and your division, remember that it was the SS who wiped out the garrison at Vis.'

'We have that in mind, sir.'

'Very well, then. Now, the advance commences in one hour's time. We should make contact with the enemy at noon. General Gronic, you have the left wing. Your division will commence the assault at thirteen hundred, probing towards the confluence of the Danube and the Sava. Hopefully this will draw out Mihailovic.'

'He will be able to observe our dispositions,' Gronic pointed out.

'That is inevitable, and irrelevant. You will continue with your advance until you enter the city, or until you encounter substantial resistance, at which time you will maintain your position. General Doedjic, you have the right. You will commence your advance at fourteen hundred, with the same orders. Again, Mihailovic should move forces to meet you. Should he not, you continue. I will command the centre, and my attack will commence at three. If the enemy centre has been weakened, we will smash through it. If it is not, we will fix it, and your two divisions will swing in to envelop him. Understood?'

Both generals nodded.

'Major-General Davis, your women's division will be in reserve. As soon as a gap has been forced in the Cetnik position, or their army disintegrates, you will advance at your best speed into the city to seize the Gestapo headquarters and the royal palace as well as the military HQ.'

'Yes, *sir*,' Tony said.

'Sandrine,' Sasha said. 'Here we come!'

Sandrine watched the door of her cell open. With it ajar, the noise of the firing was much louder. Three wardresses came in, headed by Karin. Sandrine hugged little Tony tighter to her breast, but they merely placed her food and her ration of wine on the table, then Karin waved her hand, and they withdrew. Karin remained.

'Have I not been kind to you?' she asked.

'I have no complaints,' Sandrine said.

'It could have been very different.'

'I know. What is happening out there?'

'The bombing ceased an hour ago, and we are under attack from both sides. I do not think we can hold them.'

'Ah.'

'When they break into the city, it is possible that there

are those who may wish to execute you before you can be rescued.'

'I understand that.'

'If you wish, I can remain with you, and protect you until your people can come for you.'

'Why would you do that?'

'I will save the life of you and your baby in return for my own. I have been the head wardress here for over a year. This is well known. People know what I do, what I have done. I cannot surrender. I would be lynched. But if I was your prisoner . . .'

'I cannot guarantee your life.'

'But if you will promise to try . . .'

'I will try,' Sandrine said.

Shells screamed overhead, rifles cracked, buildings burst into flames as Tony and Sasha led their people into Belgrade. Tony had divided the division, several thousand strong, into three columns, each with a separate objective. Sasha he directed to the palace, the second column to various important installations, from the railway station to the central electricity generating plant; he retained personal command of the brigade making for the military headquarters.

As Tito had predicted, the Cetniks had broken under the three-pronged assault; thus they had encountered little resistance in the city itself. But suddenly, as they approached the headquarters, they came under very heavy fire from a roadblock. Several women went down, and Tony waved the others to shelter. 'Colonel Martinovic, take your regiment down that street and get behind them,' he said. 'Judith, you will command here. As soon as Martinovic attacks, move forward.'

'And you?'

'I will wait for your breakthrough, and then assault the headquarters.'

She nodded, and gave her orders.

'Colonel Obrenovic,' Tony said. 'Your battalion will accompany me.'

'Yes, sir. Where are we going?'

'Down that street over there. It leads to Gestapo head-quarters.'

Sasha led her people at a run. They were totally surrounded by gunfire and explosions and burning, collapsing buildings, but this street was quiet. 'One more block,' she told her adjutant.

'People!' someone shouted as they reached a corner.

Sasha swung round, gazed up the adjoining street, at the far end of which there was a group of men. 'Take cover!' she shouted. 'Prepare to open fire.'

'Wait there!' a man shouted. 'We are your allies.'

Sasha peered at him. Alhough it was still early afternoon, the smoke from the burning buildings was obliterating the sunlight, and behind the houses the street was gloomy. But she frowned as the man came closer. 'I know you,' she said.

'As I know you, Colonel Janitz.'

'You are the Bulgarian bastard who arrested me in Bihac. Your men raped me. Well, now you will pay for it.' She levelled her tommy gun.

'Wait!' he shouted again. 'We are on your side now. We are fighting the Fascists.'

Sasha stared at him, and he came closer. 'I am sorry for what happened at Bihac,' he said. 'Then we were ordered to fight for the Fascists. Now we take our orders from the Soviets. As do you.'

Sasha snorted. But she believed him, without forgiving him. 'Well, then,' she said, 'if you are now fighting with us, you can do your share of dying with us. Follow me.' She waved her women forward.

Halbstadt panted. He had lost his cap. 'They are in the city.'

'Then what are you doing here?' Ulrich asked.

'I came to report. Colonel Dreiser has organized a block, but there are so many streets. They are moving round us.'

'Then you had better get out there and rally your men.'

'But the city is lost. We are lost.'

'Then try to die like a man,' Ulrich suggested.

Halbstadt hesitated – he looked close to tears – then turned and ran from the office. Ulrich followed him outside. 'Doerner!' he shouted. 'Have all those files burned. Quickly, now.'

Mathilde came out of her office. 'Where is General Wassermann?'

'I hope he is where he should be, Frau Geisner: at the head of his troops.'

'That firing is very close.'

'The enemy are in the city.'

'My God! That was quick. What are you going to do?'

'My duty.'

'Well, what am *I* to do? Wassermann should be here.'

'Do you ever pray, Frau Geisner?'

'Sometimes.'

'Then now is a good time to get on your knees.' He ran down the stairs.

Mathilde hesitated for a moment, then followed. But while Ulrich went into the yard to supervise the burning of the files, she went on down the steps to the cell block. She panted, knowing she was soon to die, but was still consumed with hatred of the people who had ruined her life. And there was only one she could reach – Blintoft's orders meant nothing now.

'Frau Geisner!' The sergeant in the tram hurried out. 'What is happening? We have had no orders . . .'

'Remain at your post. You will receive orders soon enough.' She hurried past the cells. There was a great deal of noise now from behind the closed doors, banging and shouting, but no one was making any effort to shut the prisoners up. In fact, she did not see a guard before she arrived at the door of Sandrine's cell. Wassermann had given her a pistol, and she levelled this to shoot out the lock when, to her surprise, it opened. 'Karin? What are you doing here?'

'I would say the same as you, Frau Geisner. Seeking shelter.'

'And you think you will find any? There is only vengeance left. Where is the prisoner?'

'She is here.'

Mathilde pushed her aside and stepped into the cell. Sandrine sat on her cot, baby Tony beside her. 'Well,' Mathilde said, 'so you have triumphed after all.'

'I never doubted it,' Sandrine said.

'But you won't enjoy it. The babe first, I think.'

She raised the pistol, and Sandrine gave a gasp. 'Karin!'

'Just stop there, Frau Geisner,' Karin said. She had drawn her truncheon.

Mathilde turned towards her. 'What did you say?'

'This woman is not to be harmed,' Karin said. 'That is the order of General von Blintoft, which I intend to enforce.'

'You?' Mathilde sneered. 'You are an insolent pig.' She squeezed the trigger.

Karin gave a shriek and fell backwards, her arms thrown up, the truncheon flying through the air. She lay on her back, gasping, her white shirt-front turning red. But she was still alive. Mathilde stood above her, and fired again, into her head. Then she turned back for Sandrine, and was struck a tremendous blow across the face; Sandrine had caught the truncheon. Mathilde screamed and staggered backwards. She squeezed the trigger, but the shot smashed into the ceiling, while Sandrine hit her, again and again, smashing the truncheon into her face, breaking her nose and shattering her teeth. Mathilde fell to her knees and then to the floor. Sandrine stooped, and took the pistol from her fingers.

Ulrich watched the smoke rising from the burning documents

and files. A funeral pyre, he thought. For all of us. He agreed wih Halbstadt: it seemed so unfair that he should suffer the same fate as Wassermann when he had never willingly committed a crime in his life.

'Herr Major! Herr Major!' Lieutenant Doerner ran out of the back door. 'The Partisans are at the gate. What are we to do?'

'Fight them,' Ulrich said, and led the way into the building. 'Hold the doors,' he commanded. 'Every door.'

'Herr Major!' The canteen staff were running in search of shelter. Rosa threw both arms round him. 'Oh, Herr Major, save me.'

'I cannot perform miracles.'

'If they catch me, they will hang me. They will torture me to death.'

Ulrich freed himself, and she slid down his body, both arms round his knees. There was a crash and the front doors were thrown wide. His staff fired a despairing volley and then fled in every direction. Ulrich levelled his pistol and fired, several times, counting. Three of the Partisans went down. But their leader had not been hit, and Ulrich recognized him as Davis. He had one shot left. But that was for himself. Or . . .? He looked down at Rosa, clinging to his legs, screaming in terror. He lowered the pistol and shot her through the head, at the same moment feeling a tremendous jar in his own body.

'Rosa,' Tony said, standing above the dead couple.

'The bitch who tried to kill you, kill us all,' Elsa Martinovic said. 'She had it coming. Is this man important?'

'He was chief of the Gestapo.'

'Then he also deserved to die.' Elsa had fired the fatal shot.

'I wonder,' Tony said. 'Take command.'

He ran down the steps to the cell block. The door of the tram was open, and several people stood there, blinking at him. None of them wore uniform. 'You are free,' he told them. 'Get out.'

He ran along the corridor. People screamed and shouted at him, even if they could not see him. But they had to wait. He reached an open door and paused, almost afraid to pull it back. He drew a deep breath, levelled his tommy gun, jerked the door wide – and stared at the two bodies on the floor, and then at Sandrine, sitting on her cot, her baby in her arms. Beside her there lay a pistol and a truncheon.

He looked again at the two women. 'They are both dead,' Sandrine said. 'One was my gaoler. She wanted to save my life. The other is the woman we spoke with at the ambush in March last year. She was Wassermann's mistress. She tried to kill baby Tony, so I shot her.'

Tony sat on the bed beside her, and took her and the baby into his arms.

Manfred drove the command car through the centre of Belgrade, swinging wildly from side to side to avoid shell craters and collapsing buildings, and the occasional fleeing soldier. He raced into the palace gardens and screeched to a halt. Wassermann got out of the back.

'What do you wish me to do, Herr General?' Manfred asked.

'Anything you wish.' Wassermann strode into the building, past the waiting SS soliders crouching behind their barricades.

'Are they coming, Herr General?' a captain asked.

'They are here. Where is General von Blintoft?'

'I have not seen him recently. I think he must be upstairs.'

Wassermann climbed the steps, as quickly as he could, and went into the office. Anton von Blintoft was seated behind his desk, looking at a photograph of his wife and daughter, both wearing summer frocks and smiling at the camera.

'The city is lost,' Wassermann said. 'We must surrender.'

Blintoft raised his head. '*You* wish to surrender? To the Partisans?'

'We can surrender to the Russians.'

'Would that be an improvement? Anyway, we cannot surrender. The Führer has forbidden it.'

'The Führer is not *here*,' Wassermann shouted. He flung out his arm. 'Listen. *They* are here.'

The firing was coming from the garden.

'Then I suggest you go and shoot back,' Blintoft said. 'Kindly leave the room.'

Wassermann hesitated.

'Get out!' Blintoft shouted. 'And close the door.'

Wassermann obeyed, slamming the door behind him. He was halfway down the corridor when he heard the shot. He checked, then went on down the stairs. His men were firing at the figures in the garden, but the figures continued to advance. 'Cease firing!' he shouted. 'Cease firing.' He went on to the gallery, hands raised above his head. 'We surrender,' he shouted. 'We claim the right to be treated as prisoners of war under the Geneva Convention.'

He watched Sasha Janitz coming towards him, her tommy gun in her hands. 'You!' he gasped. 'I claim—'

'You have no rights,' Sasha told him, and squeezed the trigger.

Angela sat in her Berlin apartment, listening to the radio. 'After an heroic resistance,' the newsreader said, 'Belgrade has fallen to the combined forces of the Soviets and local Yugoslav guerillas. Our men fought gallantly to the last bullet, in accordance with the finest traditions of the German army.'

Angela switched off the set. They're all dead, she thought. All of them. Fritz, Ulrich, Halbstadt. And surely the women as well, that bitch Geisner and that other bitch Rosa. All dead. All the people who knew her secrets, and could possibly harm her. Papa as well, of course, but even he represented a potential threat, with his rigid ideas on right and wrong. Now, as the widow of a dead hero, she would be the toast of Berlin. Now she could really begin to live.

The doorbell rang. She got up, reflecting that the first thing she needed to do was get herself a maid. She opened the door, and gazed at the three men who stood there. They wore plain clothes, but she knew immediately that they were policemen.

'Frau Wassermann? Gestapo. May we come in?'

'Of course.' She stepped back. Perhaps Fritz was to get a posthumous medal.

The three men entered the hall, and carefully closed the door. The first man took a folded piece of stiff paper from his pocket. 'I have a warrant for your arrest.'

'For . . .' She gazed at him in consternation. '*My* arrest? I am the wife of the late General Wassermann. How can I possibly be arrested? What is the charge?'

'There are two charges. One is perverting the course of justice. The other is collaborating with the enemy. That is, treason.'

'Perverting . . . treason . . . That is nonsense. How can you say such a thing?'

'We are in possession of a confession made by a woman named Rosa Malic. Do you know the name?'

'Rosa? That bitch!'

'I see you do know her. In her confession she states that the evidence she gave at your trial for murder was perjured. That she was forced to give it because you threatened that she would be arrested and executed by your late husband if she did not.'

Angela's knees gave way, and she sank into a chair.

'The second, more serious charge is that you deliberately allowed yourself to be captured by the Partisans in November 1941 in order that you might be exchanged for a notorious terrorist, the Frenchwoman Sandrine Fouquet, with whom you had formed a lesbian relationship.'

'How can you believe that?' Angela muttered. 'Rosa hates me. She made it all up.'

'Fräulein Malic is dead, Frau Wassermann. Her submission

243

has the validity of a deathbed confession. Do you wish to deny the charges? Can you?'

'I . . . They can all be explained.'

'I see. Well, you will have an opportunity to do that in court. Perhaps.'

Angela's head jerked. 'I wish to see Reichsführer Himmler.'

'The Reichsführer has issued specific instructions that you are not to be allowed into his presence.'

'Why has he done that?'

'Because he believes you are guilty.'

Because he knows the truth, she thought. That Fritz had organized the whole thing with his knowledge. But were that to come out, it would bring disgrace to the SS.

'What am I to do?' she whispered.

'Your best course would be to plead guilty. If you stand trial, and are convicted, as you will be, you will be executed by decapitation.'

Angela clasped both hands to her neck.

'If you plead guilty, it is possible that you will not be executed, but sentenced to imprisonment.'

'Where?'

'In view of the gravity of the charges, I would say it would be the women's concentration camp at Ravensbrück.'

Fritz had said that Ravensbrück was worse than having your head cut off because it lasted longer.

'General Mihailovic is outside, sir,' the staff officer said. 'He wishes an interview.'

'I have nothing to say to him,' Tito said. From outside the open window there came the sound of marching men, the rumbles of too-damaged buildings being pulled down, the grinding of bulldozers: the business of returning Belgrade to prosperity had already begun.

'He is in a highly nervous state.'

'Well, tell him that he has nothing to worry about at the moment. As soon as we have a government and a judiciary in place, he will be tried, and given every opportunity to defend his actions over the past three years. It will all be done properly and publicly. But he will have to remain in custody until then.'

The officer saluted and withdrew.

Tito looked at Tony. 'I meant what I said.'

'But it will be your government, and your judiciary.'

'Is that not my right?'

'Oh, absolutely.'

'Well, then, let us forget about Mihailovic; he has troubled us for the last time. Tell me about you. You know that you are welcome to stay with us.'

'Thank you. But I am required to return to duty.'

'As a general in the British army?'

'Ah . . . no. I am still a captain in the British army. But the brigadier says he will see to it that I am immediately promoted. At least to major.'

'But you will go back to war? In France?'

'Sadly, no. In view of my wounds I am to be given a staff job, in England.'

'Sadly?' Sandrine demanded. 'Ha! You have done enough fighting to last a lifetime. It is time you put your feet up.'

'And you, Sandrine?' Tito asked.

'I am also finished with fighting, and killing. I am going to be a wife and mother. And put my feet up as well, next to his.'

'Do you really think you can walk away from all this? What is the word you use – switch off?'

'No, I don't think we can just walk away from it, Josep. But we can try.'

'Because you think I will become a tyrant. I have a country to unite and rule. Some of the decisions I will have to take will be hard. I regret this. But I will not lose my way.'

'I do not expect you to,' Tony said. 'You never did in the past. But . . . May I say something?'

'You are going to suggest I cease being a Communist?'

'I would not be so presumptuous. I was going to suggest that you deal warily with the Soviets.'

'Your masters,' Sadrine said softly.

Tito grinned. 'My *allies*. Never my masters.' He got up and embraced them both. 'You are always welcome. Remember this.'

'Now, see?' Sasha said. 'I am going to cry.'

'You?' Sandrine asked.

'I can cry. I can cry for all those brave comrades we lost in battle. But I can also cry for all the good times we have had together.'

'Yes,' Sandrine said. 'I can cry for those too.'

Sasha kissed her, and then baby Tony, and then looked at Tony.

He held her close. 'Take care.'

'Will I ever see you again?'

He kissed her. 'Who knows, Sasha. Who knows.'